A NOVEL BY

Lucia Miller

ALL CHARACTERS AND EVENTS DEPICTED IN THIS
NOVEL ARE ENTIRELY FICTITIOUS. ANY SIMILARITY
TO ACTUAL EVENTS OR PERSONS, LIVING OR DEAD, IS
PURELY COINCIDENTAL.

This book is dedicated to my dear Dad, Dusty, who gave me the Love of laughter and words.

To dearest Rose, who encouraged me to write and spread sunshine and smiles all over the world.

CHAPTER ONE

BANG!
Suzy yanked the door handle as hard as she could, slamming the apartment door shut, almost tearing it from its hinges, as the walls shook. Suddenly the door flew open again. BANG!

POWWWW!!!

The noise reverberated, echoing through the darkened hallway as if a bomb had gone off in the building. Even Suzy flinched, shocked at the impact until she remembered she didn't care. She was finally getting out. She turned on her heels and marched toward the elevator.

"*DIOS MIIOO* – Ay Caramba, Miss Suzy!" Jose, the perpetually sweaty, gold-toothed, mustachioed Puerto Rican porter shuddered, recoiling in horror. He wiped the beads of sweat from his brow and genuflected, his big brown eyes widening, almost popping out of his head like a cartoon, his open mouth inviting flies, as he covered his ears like a scared little girl. Suzy kept walking while Jose struggled to keep up.

"Mr. Kane! Dios Miooo!" he wheezed in disbelief. "Maybe he die of fright! You wake the whole building!" He hurriedly trundled along the hallway trying to keep up with her, pushing the luggage rack loaded with

Suzy's bags. He glanced around the rack and saw Suzy's nose pointed high in the air, her profile like granite, as her high heels clicked in rapid succession against the dimly lit marble corridor like pistons in a Formula One racing car. At the elevator, afraid to make eye contact, Jose nervously pressed the button repeatedly.

I hope he does die! That'll teach the bastard. Who knows? Who cares? With those damn ears of his he can probably hear what I'm thinking right now, she thought to herself, icily laughing inwardly as she tossed her long blonde hair over her shoulders and breathed heavily through her pursed lips. She was emotionally and physically exhausted, drained. Tired of fighting, disillusioned, despondent. It had been a long night. She couldn't sleep for fear she might oversleep and miss her flight. Then what? The thought was too awful to even contemplate. *Maybe I'd have to hitch a ride all the way to Miami to get away from that son of a bitch!* Her thoughts were spinning, a tornado roaring around in her mind. Blonde hitchhiker found dead along I-95. Autopsy reveals she wasn't really blonde. Details at eleven. She grinned despite herself.

"No Jose, I doubt he's dead. I'm rarely that lucky," she smirked. "But feel free to go check on him after I've left."

The porter glanced nervously in her direction as they entered the elevator.

Dios Mio, don't let her go ape shit crazy on me, please, he prayed silently. Suzy just stared stonily into the distance, her eyes flashing every now and then like a light bulb about to blow. As the elevator hummed to a stop, Jose breathed a sigh of relief and Suzy stepped out into the lobby. Sean, the tall, good-looking Irish doorman, stood by and, eyeing the suitcases, tipped his cap, and wished her well.

"I hope you enjoy your trip, Miss Grant. When will you be back?" he cheerily asked as he held the door for her.

"Never!" she snapped.

She felt sorry for an instant; he was such a nice fellow, always pleasant, always obliging. She really hated to hurt his feelings, but her anger was spewing out like a belching volcano.

Wow lady, who pissed in your coffee? Sean wanted to say, but instead he went for the upbeat, "Have a safe trip, Ma'am!" God, he hated rich people; they thought they were so entitled.

Jose loaded Suzy's suitcases into the trunk of the cab, and she handed him a tip as he opened the door for her. She fell into the backseat, exhausted.

"The airport - JFK, please, driver." Sunk back into the seat, she glanced at her watch: 7:45 a.m. Sunday. Wearily closing her eyes she thought, *And not a moment too soon... God, I can't wait to smell the ocean breeze and see palm trees again!* Suzy gave Second Avenue one last peek as the cabbie headed toward the tunnel. The East River was still and calm that morning, not a soul in sight. The dark, dismal gray morning matched her mood. Her muffler was really dragging, totally sapped of energy.

It's a funny thing. Everybody is either trying to get into a relationship, or trying to get out of one. Or both. She smiled.

Suzy was attractive, mercurial, and impulsive, with an underlying fiery streak. "Suzy is a bit of a challenge" was how a friend once laughingly described her.

Suzy was a brunette. Well … maybe a brunette this week, maybe a redhead, or a blonde the week after; it all depended on her mood. She loved clothes, loved to get dressed up and go out on the town. Paul eyed her outfits admiringly when she walked into the room. She remembered when she walked into the apartment once wearing a fur coat she found at the thrift store down the street, how his eyes popped approvingly. "Gee, you look like a million dollars!" he exclaimed, his eyes dancing with delight. Suzy loved excitement. She lived for it. She loved to laugh. She had a great smile and men were drawn to her vivaciousness. She needed a strong man to keep her in line. A strong man would have her melting like putty in his hands.

But where were all these strong men? That was the problem. Paul certainly wasn't one. Maybe, if things were different, they would have been able to work it out. No, who was she kidding? Life did not have to be this difficult, but what was the point now? They were done ... el fin, the end. She caught her reflection in the taxi window, somber, worn out. Not the happy-go-lucky girl she was when she arrived.

Closing her eyes, Suzy leaned her head against the seat and sighed, "Thank God for palm trees." Fort Lauderdale was less than a three-hour flight. Soon she'd be where the skies were sapphire blue, balmy tropical breezes blew, and palm trees waved their fronds at passersby. She opened her eyes then closed them again, imagining the sound of gently lapping foam-topped waves chasing each other to the shoreline, and she took a deep breath. "No wonder they call it God's country."

"Ladies and gentlemen, welcome to Fort Lauderdale," the deep masculine voice of the captain announced over the intercom. "The temperature is 75 degrees and sunny. We'll be landing in about five minutes. Local time is 11:35 AM." And with that, they were coming in to land. Suzy heard the wheels lower, the flaps in place and the slight rocking, lowering the aircraft and landing gently on the tarmac. "Ooh. Smooth landing, good pilot!" She was impressed. The pilot pulled back on the throttle and taxied down the runway, slowly turning toward the gate where the ramp agents were waiting patiently with their equipment to unload the luggage.

Suzy smiled, hardly containing her excitement. "Yes. Thank God!" She looked at the passengers around her, craning her neck to look out the small window beside her, and stretching to get a glimpse across the aisle to the window opposite her, excitedly watching the many airplanes slowly taxi on the tarmac to their subsequent gates ahead. "Home, sweet home." She was tempted to kiss the ground she was so thrilled to be back home. It felt like it had been ages, like she'd gone off to fight a war of words and come back tired but stronger. Everything seemed normal again, like she finally made it to her happy place.

Carrying her suitcases to the curb, Suzy felt the soft warmth of the sun bathing her shoulders, head and back, as a slight breeze tousled her hair. Stepping into the cab, she slumped back, took a deep breath, and sighed with relief as calmness swept over her. Suzy looked up, noticing the rows and rows of majestic swaying Royal Palm trees and shrubbery lining the road out of the airport, the bluest of blue skies up above, not even a wisp of a cloud in the sky. The stillness and tranquility overcame her except for the cars dashing toward downtown Fort Lauderdale with the high-rise buildings hugging the shoreline in the distance.

"Is this Heaven, or what?" Her heart skipped a beat. She couldn't help but grin from ear to ear.

Fumbling with the locks, Suzy realized she had been away so long that she had forgotten which key fit each lock. It had been too damn long, she thought. Long enough to lose herself. The door creaked as she opened it. "I gotta WD-40 that," she muttered, dragging her luggage into the living room. Walking into the bedroom, she stood for a moment and exhaled, taking it all in, so happy to be back in her own home. Gazing at the dresser, Suzy noticed everything was just the way she left it. Her perfume bottles lined up on the mirrored tray, her carved wooden jewelry box where she kept her favorite pieces, especially the pair of diamond and pearl earrings. They made her think of the Prince song *Diamonds and Pearls*. She peeked inside the box, and there they were. Her dear friend Emily had given them to her one night as she was getting ready to go out with Paul. "Here Suzy, try these; they'll go perfectly with your dress," she offered.

To the side of the dresser, in its place of honor, stood Emily's smiling picture, surrounded by a gold carved frame. Suzy tenderly picked it up, "Dear, sweet Emily…" She thought of Emily's soft, throaty voice and all the good times and yes, even the bad times they had been through together.

Suzy was an only child, and her parents had died some years ago so now she was all alone.

Emily was like a second mother to Suzy and in many ways treated her better than her real mother. Emily had so much love to give, and Suzy loved her in return. She still had that childlike quality to be thrilled over little things. That was so endearing to Suzy. She used to watch Emily, and eventually concluded that finding happiness in small things was the essence of staying young. Suzy would take Emily for an ice cream cone in Coconut Grove; buy her detergent or soap on sale or skeins of wool since she liked to crochet. Emily's eyes would widen and she would giggle with joy, as if you had bought her a diamond necklace. Suzy smiled while thinking of dear Emily.

Some people come into your life for the better, and Emily certainly had, Suzy reflected, as she recalled those days when they didn't have much but love in that modest little home—that, and the smell of good home cooking as one entered the front door. She missed those days.

Emily had worked hard all her life, had a family, but never had the love of her husband. It was one of those arranged marriages, to meet your intended husband from your country and be his bride here in the States.

"You know, I never had a diamond ring, he never gave me anything. Just this wedding band," she confided to Suzy as they sat watching TV one evening. Her daughters had married and each husband had given them fine jewelry set with multiple diamonds. She felt cheated and resentful. Emily was a good woman, a very loving mother, and a dutiful wife in a loveless marriage.

Suzy, feeling badly for her, had gone into her room, and after going through her jewelry, selected a cluster diamond ring that looked like a big sprouting flower formed by diamonds. It was so pretty.

"Okay Emily, close your eyes," She took Emily's little hand in hers and slipped the flowering diamonds on the ring finger of her right hand.

"Okay, open your eyes!" Suzy whispered, as she kissed her cheek, "Just for you, Emily," she said softly as they both burst into tears of joy. Dear Emily deserved so much more for her goodness and kindness to those she met in her life. Her door was always open, always ready to help all those who came by. Nobody could ever say a bad word about her. At the least, she truly deserved the Hope diamond.

Suzy always confided in Emily, no matter what the problem was, and Emily always somehow understood. It amazed her how Emily came up with solutions to her problems. She was the wise old owl who knew Suzy better than Suzy knew herself. Emily was her ballast in the sea of life. Both ladies were gigglers and they both loved blue eyes, each intrigued by movie stars with blue eyes: Paul Newman, Robert Redford, and Elizabeth Taylor's were Emily's favorites.

"Suzy, look, look," she remembered Emily excitedly saying. "Look! Just look at those beautiful blue eyes. Oh my word!" she'd swoon when Paul Newman came on the screen, cupping her hands to her cheeks, looking heavenward to the ceiling. Even though she was a great-grandmother, Emily found him irresistible.

Suzy smiled at Emily's laughing face in the picture, noticing that in that split second, as she threw her head back and laughed that soft, throaty, rippling giggle, the photographer unwittingly caught her soul. She smiled at the laughing face. "God bless her cotton socks. Dear, sweet Emily, no one else like her…"

Looking over at her queen size bed, Suzy found herself taking a flying leap and flinging herself down, stretching out and burying her head in the pillows while twisting and writhing from side to side, laughing uncontrollably. Who would have thought a good sturdy mattress was such a luxury? No more sofa bed metal bars sticking into her back. *Not sure I know how to act now,* she thought while laughing as she twisted, turned, and rolled around like a pig in a mud bath.

"Free at last. Free at last. Thank God Almighty, I'm free at last!" Martin Luther King Junior's voice echoed in her head. How wonderful it was to be back home.

She snuggled into her pillow and a feeling of warmth and peace swept over her. Suzy closed her eyes and took a deep breath. In the quiet stillness, she could hear the birds singing and chirping their songs in the distance. This was her corner of the world. Hers, and hers alone. "Aaaahh, life is good," she smiled. As she once again writhed and stretched, contentment and joy overwhelmed her whole being. She lay still, savoring the moment, closing her eyes once more. Suddenly, Suzy was jolted by the shrill tone of the phone by her bedside.

"Welcome to Fort Lauderdale!" It was her good friend Karen. Karen's voice always reminded her of thick, creamy chocolate. It was deep and luscious. "Did you say goodbye to the Weasel?" she asked.

Suzy giggled, then burst into laughter. That was Karen's pet name for Paul … the Weasel. She never used his real name. It was always the Weasel.

"Oh yes," she said, laughing. "And I'm sure he won't forget me in a hurry."

CHAPTER TWO

On a humid June evening in the early 90s, in Coconut Grove, Florida at a city commission fundraiser event, Suzy Grant hoped to meet a rich GQ lawyer type who would sweep her off her feet, make her laugh, and be the start of a new, happily-ever-after life. Instead she met Paul Kane.

The waiters were solicitously carrying trays of champagne, making their rounds through the crowds. Over to one side was the buffet with the usual hot, drying roast beef, turkey, seafood and chicken, behind which the chefs were standing in their tall white hats and white jackets, ready to serve. The room was getting packed.

Where the hell is Elizabeth? Suzy looked at her watch. It was already seven thirty, and Elizabeth was again late. Suzy frowned. Damn her. As the waiter approached, she reached for another glass of champagne. She sipped it slowly. It was very dry, but well chilled. Looking around the room, she recognized a few of the town's key people. There was the Mayor talking with a prominent attorney from the Gables and his blonde wife, who was always immaculately coiffed. This woman's sole ambition in life was to be seen wearing her latest designer outfit and being read about in the local society gossip column. She was about as deep as a Petrie dish. Now the

Stepford wife was turning around restlessly as if she was about to blow a fuse, her browbeaten husband trying to talk to her, as she kept looking off into the distance. "Must-find-Miami-Herald-photographer," was no doubt playing on an endless loop inside her computerized head. She was waiting to strike her pose, Suzy thought as she again realized she could not stand phony, plastic people. It always struck her as amusing when she saw these people in person, how insipid they appeared and how much shorter they were in real life. Seldom did they ever appear impressive - except for the Washington Senator that she met one time at the Biltmore hotel years ago. He was tall and handsome, impeccably dressed. He had a certain masculine stance that she thought was very attractive.

Suzy nervously looked at her watch. It was now a quarter to eight, and no Elizabeth. She wasn't coming. Typical, selfish Elizabeth. Suzy was ready to leave. It was time to go home. When the chance came she was going to give Elizabeth a piece of her mind. They had been friends off and on over the years, and when Elizabeth was between husbands, she would make plans with Suzy, but if Elizabeth ever had a date then she would drop Suzy like a hot potato. Tonight she was doing it again. Suzy took the last sip of her champagne, turned and in one fluid movement, placed her flute on the waiter's silver tray as he walked by.

"Hi. Great turn out, don't you think?" a male voice by her side resonated. He was looking at her, smiling. Suzy noticed his eyes. Big, twinkling blue eyes. The whole picture was average looking, maybe in his late fifties, maybe early sixties, with a wide smile, and a pencil-thin mustache. He looked into her almond-shaped blue eyes and then his gaze swept over her face, her brown seductively wavy hair, bright red lipstick, porcelain skin, and high cheekbones. She was petite, wearing a black lace cocktail dress and jacket trimmed with satin. Her neckline plunged ever so slightly, exposing her ample bosom, draped with several different lengths of pearls. He noticed her patent leather high-heeled stiletto pumps complementing soft-shaded black stockings. Very conservative, yet very feminine. *My,* she thought, observing him, *he does take everything in...* She always first appeared to come across as demure, a little shy, and perhaps a little passive. It drew men to her. It was a tough gig, but she was up to the challenge. Suzy's eyes and features bore an air of sultriness, a hint of mystery and genteelness, but hidden just under the surface was a surprisingly aggressive, boiling fiery volcano and a will of steel.

Suddenly she remembered his question, "Ah, yes, it is," Suzy smiled. At the least she had someone to talk to now. Another waiter walked in their direction with a tray of champagne. "How about another?" asked Paul as he grabbed a glass and handed it to her. "Oh, by the way, I'm Paul."

"Of course you are. Cheers! I'm Suzy," she smiled brightly. They toasted each other and sipped. They went inside and sat together on a sofa by the piano. A sexy blonde vocalist began singing a Frank Sinatra tune, accompanied by a pianist in his black tux. Drums, guitar, and bass completed the quartet. "Fly me to the moon and let me play among the stars," she sang with her sultry voice while snapping her fingers and sensuously swinging her hips to the beat of the music.

Turned out Paul loved politics and gave Suzy the scoop on some of the more controversial figures. She found his anecdotes of power-hungry politicians amusing and laughed as he tossed out insights concerning the marital problems of one particularly prominent Democrat in Congress. Suzy looked at Paul as he spoke and then it happened; she couldn't help it – the silent appraisal. Those big, blue watery eyes, like lakes she wouldn't mind taking a dip in. However, his hair looked a bit like a flattened steel wool scouring pad balanced on top of his head. She wondered what that was all about. *Note to self – never try to run my fingers through his oddly wooly hair.* But then again, Paul had an Old World charm about him that made up for that mess he called hair. Suzy also noticed that his brown suit and tie clashed.

Either he's color blind, a bachelor, or both, she thought. Nonetheless, he was intelligent and he amused her, and that was all Suzy really cared about.

"So, uh, why don't you give me your number? Perhaps we can get together?" he asked as he fumbled in his jacket pocket for his card. "Here, I'm Paul Kane, and my office is on Brickell. Oh, wait, that's not the right card. I must have left my business cards in the car; here, you can write on the back of this." Suzy wrote her number on the back of Paul's Wild Oats card. Funny, she thought, he didn't look like the type to patronize that kind of a store.

After turning the key to unlock the door, Suzy stepped into her apartment and turned on the light. Dropping her bag on the chair, she glanced at the blinking light on her answering machine, and then pressed the button.

"Suzy, Suzy!" It was Elizabeth. "I tried calling earlier but you had already left. Joe came into town and we had dinner at the Forge. Sorry I missed you, but we'll talk soon," she purred.

Like hell we will, Suzy thought, as she deleted the message, snapped off the light, turned, and headed toward the bedroom.

CHAPTER THREE

"I was wondering if you'd like to go to Tula's in the Grove next Saturday?" Paul was very prompt; he always was. This time he wore a tie that was more becoming and it went well with his beige Italian silk jacket. Maybe he wasn't colorblind after all, she mused. She wore an emerald green dress. Casual, but dressy at the same time. The waiter seated them by the window, and they proceeded to order drinks.

Suzy had discovered that Paul was quite witty. He'd discuss his legal cases, and the people with whom he associated in his prestigious firm, with the verbosity of a seasoned advocate. He would throw his head back and laugh at his own wit and audacity. Suzy couldn't help but smile inwardly. He reminded her of a mischievous little boy who would take his mother's car keys, hide in a closet while she tore up the house looking for them, and then suddenly leap out dangling the keys, eyes dancing with devilment, howling with laughter.

Paul enjoyed art and collected paintings and etchings during his frequent European travels. Originally from Pennsylvania, he had spent many years in New York and had collected numerous paintings, oils, and watercolors of New York scenes by the best local artists. His great love was France, where one could find "great food, great art and great wine, and all in one country." He had traveled to Paris and Provence many times and always came back rejuvenated, like a Catholic completing a pilgrimage to Rome to meet the Pope. It didn't even bother him that he didn't speak the language. The closest Paul got to speaking French was what Suzy called "Menu French": escargot, pomme frite, crème brulee, chateaubriand, avec le fruit et fromage, and champagne. Linguistically, that was pretty much it. But every time Paul returned from France he came back refreshed, and thrilled to have found an artifact of some sort, like a painting from an up-and-coming artist, a bowl, a plate, or some other treasure for his apartment.

In his younger days, Paul had tried his hand at sculpture and after several weeks he had created a mound of clay that appeared to be a crude Picasso-esque female form. He made Suzy laugh until tears were rolling down her cheeks as he recalled a former girlfriend who took one look at this aberration, cupped it in her hands, and held it up toward the light as she breathlessly exclaimed, holding this exquisite masterpiece before her, as if she was holding a rare Rodin appraised for millions, "Purely primitive. Just purely primitive!" Paul threw back his head and laughed. Suzy grinned.

CHAPTER FOUR

I t wasn't long before Suzy realized Paul loved to gamble. He loved the
horses, especially. "Why don't we go to Gulfstream on next Saturday?"
he had asked the night they were at Tula's in the Grove.

Gulfstream Park in Hallandale was the home of the Florida Derby.
Upon arrival, they hurriedly ran to the turnstile with the other bettors, and
then scrambled through to make their way to the clubhouse. Paul liked to
overlook the track. With his binoculars wrapped around his neck he almost
looked like an Asian tourist, except for the racing form in his hand. Suzy
noticed a determined set to his face, and a strangely unfocused look in
his eyes as they swept over the track spread out below them. *Something's
cookin'*, she surmised.

Suzy had been to the track before and enjoyed it. Her strategy was to put
a few dollars on the long shot, and that was about as crazy as she got. Post
time would be announced and the red-jacketed bugler would step out and
play the ritual *Call to Post* tune on his elongated trumpet in his red jacket
as the owners, sitting in their private boxes overlooking the racecourse,
silently prayed for a win. For Suzy, a day at the races was about enjoying
the outdoors, admiring the magnificent horses, seeing all from the stands

while watching the race, and then relishing the excitement of the winner coming home in the final stretch with the crowds cheering and then feverishly running to pick up their winnings. The losers sat or stood quietly. In the end, losing tickets became the tossed confetti of lost hopes strewn across the ground, as if after a parade.

To Suzy, horse racing was a lazy, lovely afternoon, but not to Paul. Oh God, no. Slowly, yet surely, she realized that there was another side to Paul, a side that was not the least bit attractive or charming. It was like a second personality that was an evil twin. Paul would throw his head back, unhinging his jaw to allow the alien Paul to rain hell upon Earth. Okay that might be a little over the top, but still. She never expected to see him so out of control. Paul was a hopeless gambler, but we all have our faults, right? He probably won the first time he went to the track, and immediately fell in love with the horses.

The way Paul prepared for a race you'd think he was the sole person appointed by the government to come up with a plan on how to survive a worldwide zombie apocalypse. She thought about how his preparations began the night before, and then progressed to a full-blown anxiety attack by the time they arrived at the track. First, Paul had to study the racing form. He would sit huddled up, pen in hand, pensively studying the minutiae of each race. Which horse was running? Who was the mare? Who was the sire? When did it last race? How well did it do? Did it like turf or mud? Who was the jockey? At what weight did it run? These were all questions considered and studied pedantically and frantically. And after hours of exhausting his grey matter, he'd fall into a fitful sleep, tossing and turning as though his brain was still seeking to divine the next day's events. This was an exercise in winning, and Suzy was totally impressed. She had visions of champagne, and pots of dollars being strewn to the wind, of laughing gaily as she flung another handful to the masses while the crowd roared for more.

"I KNEW I should have put Kiss My Ditty first, with Ride 'em Tiger second and Last Call for the trifecta. Damn, I would have won $550!" he wailed, grimacing as he shook his head from side to side while tearing up the tickets. Paul was not a gracious loser. Not by a long shot.

"But isn't that what you did?" Suzy exclaimed. She looked at the program to see what he had marked down.

"No, I changed my mind when I saw the horse over there before the race," he explained sheepishly. "It didn't seem as robust in person."

She stared at him in disbelief, but Paul was looking at the board. It was five minutes to post time. "Let's go over there and see how these other horses are doing. Julie Krone is riding this race." Paul grabbed her hand and tore off to the paddock as the jockeys mounted their horses.

"Oh, who is she?"

"Julie Krone? Only the first female jockey to be inducted into the Thoroughbreds Hall of Fame, that's who!" No bells rang for Suzy. "She's the greatest woman jockey of all time," he added, as he stared at the horses passing by. All of a sudden, names like Shane, Santos, Velasquez, Day and Bailey were bandied about. This was all new to her.

"Jeez, that one has a wild look in his eyes." Paul pointed to the gray horse walking by, "I'm not sure." Looking at the racing form, pen in his mouth, adjusting his cap, Paul mumbled, "It looks a little skittish to me..." The jockey was having a hard time controlling the horse. Paul eyed the horse and checked the form again.

"I don't care for the jockey, either. He hasn't won a thing in months. And Shane is running in this one, too." As he spoke, he made more circles and scratched out others as seriously as a brain surgeon about to operate on the President of the United States. After looking at the other horses and scribbling a few more notes, Paul grabbed her hand and, with binoculars flailing in the air, tore off to the crowded betting line. He was like a man possessed. His hand fumbled frantically around in his pockets, seeking the money, which he immediately threw on the counter, while grabbing the tickets.

"Come on," he yelled at Suzy as he tore off to the stands just as the race was beginning. By the time they got to their seats, Suzy was out of breath, panting like a fish on the freeway, and flopped down on the seat beside him as she watched him, totally engrossed. His eyes took on a strange gleam, as if he were possessed. She wondered if his head was going to start spinning and fly off but she lost that thought when in that instant, Suzy was startled as Paul, in one swift movement, suddenly leapt forward up onto the seat, where he stood while screaming at the top of his lungs, *"Come ON. Come ONNNN!! LET'S GOOOOOOOO!"* while peering through his binoculars. The word fanatic snuck its way into Suzy's mind. But Paul wasn't alone. At this point the entire crowd was now in a frenzy like some Pentecostal worship service where congregants danced around and spoke in tongues and waving snakes. The jockeys were frantically whipping the horses in the last stretch.

"LET'S GOOO! COME ONNNN!!" Paul was still screaming. *"COME ONNNNNN!!!!"* The noise was deafening and Suzy covered her ears. The crowd was cheering, louder and louder, as Paul began to whimper in pain. The color drained from his face and he looked like he might cry.

"Oh no, I can't believe it!" screeched Paul, shaking his head from side to side. Suzy looked over at him as Paul slowly stepped down from the bench, practically keeling over, his knees were so weak. Still shaking his head he scolded himself, "Damn, I knew I should have put $20 on Piece of Cake. That damn jockey hasn't won a thing since January, but he came in second three times, and the horse likes the turf. Damn it!" He spit the words out in self disgust. "Look," he pointed to the form, "I had him down to win." Suzy looked at him, looked down at the form, and then looked back at him.

"So why didn't you bet on him?" None of this made sense to her. It was like trying to predict the future with a boomerang.

"I don't know." He stared at the ground between his splayed feet. "He didn't look as good as King For A Night." He began slapping the program loudly. "But see here, I had it down to win with Santos." She looked straight at him. None of this was making sense; why hadn't Paul played what he had written down? After all that studying the night before, why would he change his bet at the last minute? She shook her head.

The horses were now waiting at the starting gate. "And they're off!" shouted the announcer, and with that, the horses attacked the track. Paul was excitedly watching through his binoculars, and once again, he had jumped up on the seat for a better view.

"Come on, Jerry, Come on, Jerry!" Paul turned to Suzy excitedly. "He flew in just for this race." The crowd was getting louder and louder. "*COME ON, COME ONNN, JERRY!*" screamed Paul at the top of his lungs. Suzy was surprised Paul hadn't blown out a vocal cord yet, as she winced and covered her ears. She couldn't even see what was going on because people in front of her were now standing on their seats, too. She patiently waited. Suzy had not placed a bet and the favorite was five to two, so there was no point in her getting worked up.

"*LET'S GOOOOO!!!!! YESSSSS!!!!!*" Paul was waving his hand in the air. "*LET'S GOOOO!*" he bellowed as he gleefully jumped down, grinning from ear to ear like a kid at Christmas. "Oh, thank God!" he could not contain his excitement as he dropped the binoculars down to the bottom of the strap and let them hang. "Jeez, for an awful moment I thought Simple Sam was going to win! He was the favorite, but I knew Jerry would pull ahead at the last minute!" he said excitedly, almost hysterically, his eyes shining as he cockily announced, "I just knew he was going to make it!" as if he had been told by God himself.

Suzy laughed at his brazenness and smiled. "Oh, Paul. You did it." She was happy for him. Amazed, but happy for him nevertheless.

"Yeah, now we can go celebrate!" He chuckled at his good fortune. "Yep, he just scraped by, by half a length - phewww!" He stuck out his tongue, surprised by his good luck. They flowed with the thinning crowds to the parking lot, retrieved their car and headed to their favorite bistro to celebrate.

CHAPTER FIVE

"W hy don't we go on the Discovery one night? It leaves about sevenish." Suzy knew that Paul was always available for poker and once the ship was in international waters they could gamble. Sure seemed, from a Paul perspective, that might be a less hysterical event than horse racing. Plus, she was curious to see Paul's poker face, especially if he was losing. Suzy and Paul met her friend Libby and her boyfriend Danny at the port. Danny was a professional man with quite a thriving dental practice in the Grove. He had never married. His mistress was four-legged because his addiction took him to the track every weekend at Gulfstream or Hialeah with Libby. She also was addicted. They were perfectly matched, in a dysfunctional way. Libby and Danny were always taking junkets either to Las Vegas or Biloxi, or sometimes they were comped in the Bahamas. And boy, oh boy, would they brag about their winnings. Losses, of course, were never mentioned.

Danny would bet on anything – raindrops on a window, ants in a hill, leaves on a tree, how many people would be at a party, or what the gender of the next person entering the restaurant would be. A classic compulsive.

They had lost thousands of dollars over the years and always were convinced the next time they'd hit it big.

Suzy met Libby through a mutual girlfriend, and they had gone to several single's parties together, always hoping for Mr. Right but, as luck would have it, there were many Mr. Wrongs instead.

Danny was a date, a longtime date. He didn't have anybody else at the moment and neither did Libby, so they just were buds hanging together. However, Libby was a lot of fun. She was tall and had long, billowing curly blonde hair that hugged her shoulders. Men found her very attractive. Danny was also tall; despite his deep, darting eyes, he was quiet and introspective—the kind of guy who after the police found dead bodies buried in his backyard, neighbors would say, "But he was always so quiet." Who knew what he thought - he had the personality of a cardboard cutout and only came alive when gambling was mentioned. Any other time he was a slack-jawed statue with a faraway gaze, and trying to have a conversation with him was like trying to reel in a rebellious shark.

For example, on one trip they took to the Caribbean, Danny bet Libby that the next person to walk into the room would be a man with a ten-gallon hat and laid odds at 10-1 for $200. "You're on," she gleefully laughed. They watched in silence, their eyes peeled in anticipation. Libby sat there and confidently rubbed her hands together, laughing inwardly while thinking how easy it would be to make $200.

Suddenly she sat bolt upright and to her amazement there was a tall, tanned Texan wearing a goddamn 10-gallon hat! Danny caught Libby's eye and followed her amazed stare to the entrance. He leaned forward, his lips curled around his mustache in a mischievous grin as he thrust out his upturned palm, his fingers bending slightly rhythmically, gesturing for her to pay up, as he winked, "Gotcha!"

She spun around, speechless and devastated; her mouth dropped open. Her mind was racing at the incredible odds of this happening. She looked into the distance, shaking her head slowly from side to side in disbelief and hoarsely whispered, "How could that happen?"

She slumped forward, dazed, staring into space. Snapping his fingers, Danny slowly rose, laughing, "Get it up now - I'm going to the blackjack table," then walked toward the door where the Texan was standing, winked at him and quickly slipped him a $20 bill, laughing, as he said, "Thanks Joe, I'll see you in the bar. I owe you one, buddy." He didn't burst out laughing until he went through the door.

As the two couples boarded the Discovery, they were ushered into the dining room and took their seats. The waiters began to serve them. "This chicken is delicious; how's yours?" Paul looked over at them.

Libby looked up for a second. "OK! I like the shrimp, too." She quickly gobbled another mouthful, glancing at Danny. "How's yours?" Danny was deep in thought, light-years away in another galaxy. Libby was outgoing and bubbly; where the hell did she find this dud? He had less personality than a limp noodle. He must have hidden talents, Suzy surmised.

He caught her eye. "It's good," he said vaguely, and proceeded to look down at the plate. Paul and Suzy looked at each other. All of a sudden, BOOM!! Libby and Danny flew out of their seats like the thoroughbreds out of the starting gates in Gulfstream, and ran off toward the door.

Suzy spun around to look. *Jeez, is the ship on fire? Where did they go?* She and Paul looked at each other in disbelief. They finished their desserts and proceeded to the casino, hoping to catch up with Libby and Danny. They could barely walk into the casino; it was so crowded that people pressed into each other. It was hot, and the bright lights shining on the one-armed bandits made it seem hotter. Squeezing through the casino's aisles from one side of the ship to the other, Suzy and Paul went searching for their friends. By now Paul was getting antsy. He was wasting precious time when he could be playing poker. And what was more irritating, he did not see a sign to the poker tables. "Look, Suzy, you go wherever you want. I'll meet you at 11:45 upstairs at the bar. Maybe you will run into them before that." He waved, then was gone.

Suzy finally found Libby with a big bucket by her side at the one dollar machines. She looked up and gave Suzy a quick, stony smile as if to say, "Get lost," as she fed more dollars into the machine and pulled the handle. "I just won the jackpot!" she explained, but she wanted to be alone. Suzy sensed this, and smiling, walked on by. *Now what the hell am I going to do for three hours?* she thought as she walked by the machines. It was quiet in this far corner of the casino, so she checked her purse for some quarters and decided to play.

Ding, ding, ding … the machine chimed. She stared at the three oranges in a row! And down came an avalanche of quarters. Her eyes widened; she grinned to herself. This time, an orange, a cherry, and a seven and out came more quarters. "Boy, this is fun!" she laughed and played on. Now she really was having fun. By now she had half a bucket full. Suddenly, out of the corner of her eye, she noticed Paul walking toward her with his dejected expression. Just when she started to have fun – figures. She really did not want to see him at that moment but there was no way around it.

"What's wrong?" she asked, without looking up, as she fed the machine more coins.

He leaned on the machine next to hers. "I'm bored," he replied as he looked around. "I can't find the poker table," he shrugged. He threw in a few quarters and lost.

He can't find the poker tables, so he comes over here to irritate the hell out of me! she thought. She stared hard at him. "Well, I think if you go in that direction, there may be one," she suggested. Anything to get rid of him. He followed her glance to the far side of the casino.

"Hmmm, yeah." He could see that she didn't want him around. "I'll probably be back in a little while," he muttered as he strode off in that direction.

"Damn it, I hope not," she muttered, as she fed more quarters.

Later, Libby and Suzy met at the bar and had a drink to celebrate their big night. "Well, how did you do?" Suzy asked as she sipped on the wine. They were both smiling.

"Oh wow," gushed Libby, "I could do no wrong! I won $300 and then when I left that machine, this girl came over and won another couple hundred! Then I went over to another machine and won the jackpot with the three sevens, and then I won with the triple bars. What a night!" Libby was ecstatic. Suzy looked at her and smiled. *What a liar,* she thought.

"Gee, Libby, you'll have to go home in a Brinks truck!" They clinked glasses at her good fortune.

"Have you seen Danny?" Libby asked as she swiveled around in her chair, bobbing up and down to see if she could spot him in the crowd, looking toward the door. "He's never been this late." But it was unsmiling Paul who came bobbing through the crowd. Danny was also making his way over to the bar.

Uh-oh, Suzy thought, *guess he didn't do too well.*

"We're over here," she called out, as she waved to him.

He looked tired as he hunched over the bar stool. "Give me a Scotch on the rocks," he hoarsely muttered, staring into space. His eyes were empty and lifeless. He must have lost his shirt once again.

CHAPTER SIX

A s they drove to the Gables, they rode in silence listening to the
symphony. Paul had a vast collection of classical music and every
now and then he would reach under his seat whenever he got bored with
one, and slip in another. As the music started playing, he would conduct
the orchestra as if he was Zubin Mehta at the Met. His eyes would close
for a second, enraptured, and as the music built into a crescendo, his hand
movements became more and more frantic. She noticed he had long, beautiful hands and fingers. She wondered if he was going to conduct the Flight
of the Bumblebee, smiling at the thought. He seemed to be in a world of
his own sometimes. She watched as his artistic fingers slowly moved to the
rhythm of the music.

Suzy had very eclectic tastes in music: rock, jazz, country, classical—it
didn't matter. Paul also loved swing. He reminisced about when he was a
young man in Philadelphia in the '40s and had dated a beautiful Italian girl
from South Street. Benny Goodman was his favorite and they jitterbugged
all night.

"I fell madly in love with her," he said, as his big, watery eyes filled up,
recalling the heartbreaking experience. His eyes looked like a dam ready

to burst its banks, Suzy thought. He spoke in hushed, reverent tones. After all these years, the pain was still intense. "I wanted to marry her! I loved her!" he blurted.

"So why didn't you?" She felt sorry for him.

"Because I wasn't Italian," he stammered. "Her father wouldn't let me!" He threw up his hands. "I would have given her anything. I even introduced her to my family. My mother adored her." He was almost in tears. "My life would have been totally different." He looked down to the floor, embarrassed at his sudden revelation.

Suzy felt bad for Paul. She could relate. She also had a lost love, her first love. Yes, it was just like The Godfather and "the thunderbolt." Love at first sight.—yes, it was true, there was such a thing. It was exhilarating, confusing and deliriously joyful. And frightening.

Hearing the soft voice in front of her, she slowly looked up into the most beautiful eyes and sweet smile and sun-kissed light brown hair. Their eyes connected, as if electrified, her heart pounded, and for a moment, she felt dizzy. It was real, so exciting, like electricity, and yet so sweet and tender. And so very special. "Come, come, please come visit me," he begged when he was leaving to go back home to a country so far away…His words echoed in her mind so many times…She was too young and so innocent in those days, and was afraid, and couldn't handle it; it was so emotionally consuming of her whole being....

She knew only too well the gnawing, aching emptiness, leaving one with a great sadness. The void was as deep as the ocean. The pain was excruciating, recalling the tender happy moments they shared. Many times, over the years, she would pick up the phone and just as she was ready to dial, hesitate, placing the phone back in its cradle. She wondered if her lost love would ever call her. But that was a million years ago, a million tears ago. *How foolish we are to ourselves,* she thought grimly, looking off into the distance, quickly wiping a tear from her eye.

CHAPTER SEVEN

P aul was a generous man; he loved the good life and wanted someone who appreciated the same things. Suzy fit the bill. But there was an odd facet to their relationship – Paul was never able to express his feelings toward Suzy and they never had an intimate relationship. Suzy assumed that Paul liked the arrangement of companionship and she wasn't really that interested in sex at the time, having recently left a relationship that had declined into nothing but a loveless athletic event, which really made her feel empty of any true emotion anymore. She was just enjoying the adventure. The few times Paul asked her at the end of a date, "So, um, why don't you come up and see my etchings?" She'd say, "I'm sorry - maybe next time," as she pecked him on the cheek. Suzy always had an excuse, and though he appeared disappointed, Paul still called her to spend more time together.

Paul had a knack for finding little out-of-the-way restaurants, movies, or art galleries that somehow nobody else knew about, gems of special charm or uniqueness, like the movie house tucked away in the back of a shopping plaza on Lincoln Road. It always intrigued her that he was able to find these places.

Once he took her there to see *Night on Earth* with Roberto Benigni.

"Who is that? Is the movie any good?" she asked.

"Well, it got good reviews. It's one of those artsy low budget films, you know," he tugged at her arm, "about taxi drivers in different cities."

"Taxi drivers?" *Who the hell wants to see a movie about taxi drivers?* She had her doubts. *Sounds like the perfect time to study the backs of my eyelids,* Suzy thought. After the feature, when the lights came on, as they shuffled slowly out of the theatre, Suzy couldn't help giggling, holding back, and giggling again, covering her mouth, trying not to embarrass herself. The man walking beside her caught her eye and shot her a huge grin. But Paul just kept walking, as if he was embarrassed. *Now that's a little odd,* she thought.

Early on a Saturday afternoon Paul called. "Hey, how about another movie? There's a place in the Gables that shows foreign films. I think you'll find this one interesting. It has Catherine Deneuve in it," he said, as she heard him flick through the pages of the movie section.

"Oh, that would be fun. I love foreign movies!" she gushed. "I fell in love with Louis Trintignant in *A Man and a Woman.* Do you remember the music in that movie? It was so sexy! And that scene where he is racing back to her in the blinding rain," she recalled almost breathless, her eyes dancing with delight. "Ooh, I think I fell in love! I was maybe fifteen at the time but I can still see his face. Sure, I'd love to see it!"

"Good. It starts at eight."

Suzy was originally from Europe. She saw Roman Polanski's *Repulsion* with Catherine Deneuve. She never forgot the scene where Catherine slashed the landlord to death, leaving the whole place a bloodbath. It was so gruesome, she had to turn away from the screen. That scene messed with her mind for days. And then in another scene, Catherine was happily humming away while ironing, even though the iron was unplugged, while rats were running up and down the counter tops. The whole thing unnerved her.

And Suzy would never forget Charlotte Rampling in the *Night Porter,* playing the wife of a symphony conductor. As Charlotte's character checked into a hotel with her husband, she had glanced over her shoulder, suddenly recognizing the officer with whom she shared a sadomasochistic relationship while she was interned in a concentration camp. There he was now, the Night Porter. And what a fine actor Dirk Bogarde was.

Paul was not your average, kindhearted fellow. He could be rude and patronizing, with very strong opinions about right and wrong. Suzy could be passive and, depending how the situation hit her and what mood she was in, liked to stir up trouble. She'd get in on the game when Paul went off on one of his tangents. Tonight he was lucky; she just ignored him.

They walked by a chain movie theater one night and he started in with the movie posters. "Who *ARE* these people?" he barked in disgust. "Where is their talent?" He grimaced as if in the throes of pain. "Just trumped up nothings! That's all they are," Paul would declare.

Plastered on one wall was a giant picture of a movie "star" possessing unnatural powers (and an incredibly attractive 6-pack, Suzy noticed) glaring menacingly, brandishing a .357 magnum with warships whirling in the background—you know, like in real life. All the while the crowds excitedly waited in ridiculously long lines that moved like sluggish snakes through dry leaves to witness the wonder of the actors' talent, their superior good looks and awesome special effects.

"Look at 'em," he sneered, shaking his head, "Generation X. That's what we have here." He pushed his way through. "You must have an IQ of minus 100 to actually PAY to see this crap." The crowd shuffled forward, as Paul stepped to the side. "See, see what I mean! God!" His face contorted with disapproval, as if he smelled something rancid. He and Suzy hurriedly quickened their pace as if to avoid any contagion.

CHAPTER EIGHT

"Hey Suzy, my sister's coming into town with her husband this winter, and also my dear cousin and her friend will be coming down soon after. I was wondering if you'd like to meet them? We could meet them for lunch or something."

Despite his misanthropic outlook, Paul was not an only child. His sister, Esther, was a very pleasant lady, and her husband was a decent man, recently retired and enjoying the fruits of his labors in their last days in comfort.

"So you're Suzy," Esther gushed, giving her a hug. "I'm so glad to meet you!" she smiled. Esther was short and round, and her favorite subjects were her two gorgeous grandchildren whom she adored more than life itself.

"So, Paul, where did you find this lovely girl?" Paul was kind of shy in these situations, which seemed strange for a man his age. He just grinned and looked across the room, avoiding the question. Esther looked at Suzy. "We're happy for him; he's a wonderful brother" She patted Suzy's hand under the table and then turned away and went on to her favorite topic, "And Paul, I said to Jenny, 'Look darling, see what Grandma has for you,' and she threw her arms around my neck and gave me a great big hug. God,

I just love them to death!" Her eyes lit up. Being a grandmother was so gratifying to Esther, Suzy thought, smiling.

About a month later more family came to town. "Come over here, Suzy, I want you to meet my cousin; we call her Mimi." Paul looked at her, explaining, "You must speak loudly and clearly. She does not hear well anymore." Suzy turned around and there was Mimi, slowly walking toward her.

"It's such a pleasure to meet you, my dear," said Mimi as she held out her hand. Her beautifully manicured hands were befitting a queen, regal and gracious, with red nail polish. Her unlined porcelain features were of a woman half her age.

Mimi was a grand dame of the arts and had spent many years living in France and Spain. Her husband was a collector of art and enjoyed collecting artifacts from their time abroad. Paul loved his cousin. She was the intellect of the family and introduced him to this world of art, music, and wine at a very young age. She lived in New York City just down the street from the Metropolitan, off 52nd, and would invite Paul to go to the symphony. Mimi knew every opera, knew every diva that played at Carnegie Hall, attended every major event, and was quite the raconteur. She was a connoisseur of the finer things in life, and Paul was a good student.

Suzy was certainly impressed by Mimi's vitality and beauty. "Who would believe she was 85?" she gasped. "We should all be so lucky!"

"Yes, I wish my mother had as much vitality. She's been poorly for so long. It's only a matter of time," Paul said despondently as he turned away.

CHAPTER NINE

I f you lived in Coconut Grove in the 90s there was one place you had to be - The Taurus bar and restaurant. It was tucked away at the edge of the Grove on Main Highway. The Taurus was the local watering hole for anyone in the know. Though just a shack, a hole in the wall, they had the best rock 'n roll, blues, or country and western bands on Friday and Saturday nights. Strictly American, and strictly fun. At the Taurus, one could rub elbows with a roofer, a plumber, an electrician, a CEO, attorneys, city officials, artists, construction workers, or one of those eccentric millionaires that lived in the Grove. It was like an updated Village People and no one cared which character you were. You could wear a suit and tie, a t-shirt and shorts. Nobody gave a damn.

This was where Suzy first met Karen one balmy summer evening. Suzy had just got comfortable when a statuesque redhead sidled up next to her at the bar and ordered a vodka martini. Karen reached into her black leather bag with the famous interlocking double C on it, took out a cigarette, put it between her lips with her long red manicured nails, then fumbled for her lighter. They smiled at each other. "Hi. Here, let me put you out of your misery." Suzy offered her a light.

"Thank you." Karen blew out the smoke above her head. "Hi. Gosh it's getting crowded early tonight! Isn't this a fun place? I'm Karen, by the way."

"Hi, I'm Suzy." She noticed Karen's green eyes, porcelain white skin and upturned mouth and nose. Statuesque, with long, thick, wavy red hair cascading down her back and a deep, rich voice that reminded Suzy of Kathleen Turner's version of Jessica Rabbit in *Who Framed Roger Rabbit* – "I'm not bad, I'm just drawn that way." She was exceptionally beautiful. Young, and so beautiful, with the world at her perfectly manicured fingertips.

"So, have you been here before?" Karen asked as she took another drag, flicking the ash with her perfectly manicured hand while she sipped on her martini. She skewered the olive and delicately popped it into her mouth so as not to smudge her red lipstick, and delicately, slowly, pulled the toothpick from her mouth. She then leisurely chewed the olive. *Very prissy, dainty, very feminine,* Suzy thought.

"Actually, I have never been here before, even though I live close by in the Gables. How about you?"

"No, I've never been here either. I recently got divorced so I am staying with my parents here in Miami Beach. Starting over, that sort of thing, you know how that goes …" She swung around to face the door, "My girlfriend was supposed to meet me here, but I guess she couldn't make it. Oh well!" She turned around and smiled brightly. Obviously she was not too perturbed.

"So, anyway, I work over here at the Mall. I work for Chanel. I love it; I've always worked in cosmetics. I meet all kinds of interesting people. They fly in from South America, or they're the snowbirds. But I find quite a lot of Europeans also visit South Florida. There's a lot to be said for our climate, even though I personally can't stand the heat. Like now." Grimacing, she flipped her mane of hair back and patted her exquisitely made-up face and neck with a tissue as she peered up at the slow-turning fan above them. "Of course, it's never cool enough for me." Picking up a menu that had been left on the bar, she tossed her hair back, feverishly fanning herself.

"Oooh, that's a little better." She fumbled with the neckline of her blouse, while fanning faster. "I love the fall and especially the winter months; it really is the best time. And you, Suzy, what do you do?"

"Well, actually, I'm the manager of a small company. They sell medical equipment in the U.S. and overseas. I enjoy the work and I've been with the company for several years now, so I can't complain."

Suzy was clearly much older than Karen, yet they had an instant bond. Karen was twenty-eight, going on forty-eight, with a lot of insight and worldliness beyond her years, with a zany sense of humor. As she was telling a story, she would mimic the character and flash those green eyes of hers while Suzy grinned in amusement.

"So, you're from England, aren't you?" she inquired.

"Yes," Suzy said.

"My father loves Benny Hill; he's a riot! Not much makes my father laugh but Benny really cracks him up." Karen laughed as she spoke. "He gets a big kick out of Benny chasing all the young chicks with the old man running behind them. When my parents are home they go to bed early and all I can hear from the bedroom is 'He-he, he-he-he, he-he,' as she mimicked her father's deep voice. 'He-he, he-he.' He's probably seen the same re-runs twenty times, but he still watches. Every week, Friday, same station, don't touch that dial."

Karen then mimicked Benny Hill. She had a deep, dirty laugh. Her eyes gleamed and sparkled as she reminisced while waving circles in the air with her cigarette and flicking her mane of red hair.

The two women were deep in conversation when a fight suddenly broke out in the bar. Two young men were fighting over a girl, it seemed, and in no time, they were bounced out of there. Karen and Suzy just looked at each other and grinned. "I wonder if she was worth it?" laughed Karen as she looked around to see the girl in question.

As they went back to their conversation, a deep voice butted in, "Hi ladies. Couldn't help noticing you two." They both turned around to see a tall, lanky, balding man in shorts. Their eyes looked up at his generic face and then down to his skinny legs, tube socks and sneakers, and up again to his face. They looked expressionlessly at each other. Karen cocked her head forward and coldly asked, "Yes? Is there something I can do for you?" as she puffed on her cigarette and blew the smoke out from the corner of her lips.

He stood, stared at the cold, challenging green eyes and red hair for a moment, then mumbled, "Oh, no, no, I er, uh, no," and walked off.

"It's so crowded in here and this is all we get?" She looked over her shoulder at him leaving, her green eyes flashing. "What am I? A freak magnet?" She shrugged. "I didn't want to talk to him anyway! God, where the hell do they come from? Are there any real men around here?" She shook her head slowly, her eyes watching the shiny glow on the back of his bald head as it faded away into the crowd. Karen had an intimidating effect on men thanks to her statuesque beauty. Poor thing. Suzy brought out her air violin and started playing a dirge for poor, beautiful Karen and her quest to find a man worthy of her. Life is so tough when you're gorgeous. They both burst out laughing.

"Testing, testing. One, two, testing." The band was on the edge, ready to amp up. "One, two, three." And the music suddenly exploded throughout the room. They were loud but good.

"Clean shirt, new shoes
And I don't know where I am goin' to.
Silk shirt, black tie,
I don't need a reason why."
Suzy and Karen joined in,
"They come runnin' just as fast as they can -
'COS EV'RY GIRL'S CRAZY 'BOUT A SHARP DRESSED MAN."
The floor was filling up with couples dancing.

"Gold watch, diamond ring,
I ain't missin' not a single thing.
Cufflinks, stick pin,
When I step out I'm gonna do you in.
They come runnin' just as fast as they can
'Cause every girl's crazy 'bout a sharp-dressed man."

Karen threw her head back, laughing, "Don't you just love ZZ Top?"

At that moment, a short, bearded fellow stepped forward, his tie slightly askew like it had been a long week, and looked up at Karen. "Hi, my name is Joe." He grabbed her hand and swept her off to the dance floor, smiling brightly up at her. Suzy watched Karen with her arms and hips slowly gyrating on the dance floor. She was laughing and giving Joe her "bewitched" smile. Many of the guys on the dance floor were noticing her, both shyly and overtly, enviously thinking to themselves, *Lucky bastard!* Yes, Karen was a Prize, a Miss Glamour Puss, while most of the women looked so ordinary next to her. She turned, moved and slinked sensuously, to the beat of the music. Suzy caught the men standing around nursing their drinks, staring at her, and laughed to herself. *Hey! You snooze, you lose!* Other people were jitterbugging, smiling and laughing, while Dutch the Bartender was concocting and serving up drinks while keeping up a lively banter... Dutch was more famous around the Grove than The Taurus itself, and that was saying something. This night he wore a Nixon mask with a Hawaiian shirt and a lei around his neck. Next week he might wear a gladiator, genie, or superhero costume. His favorite was Phantom of the Opera. Of course Halloween was Dutch's "High holiday" when he went all out with a costume more extravagant than the year before. Just part of the Grove...

After the song ended, Shorty and Karen returned to the bar. "Can I buy you a drink?" Shorty asked Suzy as he waved to the bartender. "Make that three."

"So how are you ladies this evening?" Shorty smiled from ear to ear, his eyes dancing with delight as he stared at Karen. She caught his eye, and gave him a perfect, kittenish grin. *He's no doubt melting by now,* Suzy thought and looked away. As she was turning, Suzy spotted an old friend, Chris from the Gables, and waved him over excitedly. He came over and Suzy introduced him around. Chris was Suzy's first boyfriend when she was still new to Miami. At the time they met, he was in the throes of his divorce. The two were once very close over the years but now had drifted in different directions. They were still friends though.

"Suzy! You look great!" he exclaimed, as they hugged each other. "So what's new with you? It's good to see you after all this time."

Suzy smiled up at Chris. "God, it's been ages! How's everything? I hear you bought a publishing company?" She smiled broadly, as they held hands for a moment, remembering what a tender lover he had been. On and on they chatted, catching up. Finally, the overbearingly bright lights flashed on, making everyone squint like they had just stepped out into a sunny afternoon. The band began packing up their instruments.

"Oh my," Karen turned around. "My God, I never realized the time!" She jumped off the barstool, "It was great meeting you all. Perhaps we can get together next week?" With that, phone numbers were exchanged all around.

And now three years later, even though neither one had seen the two men again, Suzy and Karen were dear friends. Suzy appreciated Karen's quick, dry sense of humor. They would often talk in a bar or restaurant, recalling their hilarious escapades each time, usually ending with the two of them in hysterics, laughing with such gusto that it filled the room. People would turn around, curious to know what was so funny, and lean in with a hopeful look in their eyes, a smile of expectancy on their lips, hoping to hear the punch line, which made the two women roar all the more.

Karen had no mercy for idiots; she would dismiss them as if they were to be thrown to the lions. In Roman times, she would have been in her glory: "Off with his head!" as she gave the thumbs down to kill the gladiator. Suzy got a kick out of watching the stream of unsuspecting victims who tangled with this demure-looking vixen every week. It would have been advisable to be equipped with a whip and a chair when they approached her. Some, who were insensitive, who didn't realize that they were shot down, tried again, only to leave, sadly, with their tails between their legs.

"See what I mean? They actually come back for more. I swear, what is wrong with them? These guys love abuse!" Her eyes would widen in total disbelief, as she shook her head. "I'm telling you!" she repeated, "They love abuse! Assholes! I want to meet a real man, for a change. God, please!" She would look heavenward and sigh. "I'm twenty-eight – I'm in my prime. Send me a real man before it's too late. Please God," she begged.

Another endearing trait of Karen's was the fact that she could drink most men under the table, and watch them stagger out the door on all fours when she was just getting started. Looking over her shoulder, watching them stumble out the door, she would exclaim, bewildered, her green eyes flashing, "Now what the hell is wrong with him?"

Still, she would have gladly given all of that up to find her special some-one, have a house with a white picket fence, rock babies to sleep under the shade of an old apple tree in the backyard, and whip up a chicken casserole in the kitchen while baking an apple pie in the oven. All Karen wanted was a strong man she could challenge, who would be able to handle her, like in any John Wayne, Maureen O'Hara movie. A man who could penetrate her Ice Princess façade and have her melting in his arms. Now what was so difficult about that?

"They call her 'hard hearted Hannah,'
The vamp of Savannah;
The meanest gal in town

Leather is tough, but Hannah's heart is tougher;
She's a gal who loves to see men suffer,
To tease them and thrill 'em;
To torture and kill 'em
Is her delight they say.
I saw her at the seashore with a great big pan;
There was Hannah pourin' water on a drownin' man."

CHAPTER TEN

I t was a beautiful Saturday morning and Suzy felt great. She got up, made herself a cup of java, and looked out the window. There was a soft breeze stirring so she decided to open the front door and windows. She idly watched the birds chirping outside on the telephone wire, hopping on one leg and then the other as they sang. The shrill ring of the telephone jolted her. It was Paul.

"So, how are you today?" she asked casually as she sipped her coffee.

"I'm looking through the ads." Paul was in a grumpy mood. His voice sounded flat and weary.

"For what?" she inquired brightly.

"I have to move out of here; this place is driving me nuts!" he hissed.

"Why? It's a beautiful building, and my God, it's on the Bay, off Brickell, and close to where you work. What could possibly be wrong with it?" The view from Paul's apartment was spectacular: a panoramic view of Miami Beach, the cruise ships at the Port of Miami, downtown Miami and the Gables. The sunrises with the ocean fanning out in the distance were pure heaven to see. One could not wish for more; it was like living in perpetual paradise. *We should all be so lucky,* she thought, as she shook her head, glancing around her own place.

"The pipes," he growled, "It's the pipes!"

"The pipes? What do you mean, the pipes, Paul?" Suzy asked hesitantly. It sounded like he was in the midst of a horror film so she talked slowly, not wanting to make any sudden verbal utterances that could push him over the edge. Just kidding—the temptation was far too great. "Are they Scottish? Do they play bagpipes at all hours? Flute, piccolo?"

"The *WATER* pipes," he retorted angrily. "The people! Upstairs!... When they are taking a shower! Like right now!""

"Okaaayyy, the water pipes? Is that it?" She still didn't understand. "And ... so? You should be thrilled they appreciate hygiene."

"I can hear the pipes ... the noise! I can hear the water running through the pipes. I can't sleep. It's ridiculous." His voice rose a notch or two louder and higher as he became more irritated. "I complained to the office, and they won't do a damn thing," he went on, " and then this guy next door has music blaring half the night. It's so friggin' loud that the floor vibrates. Then he has a couple of chicks in there and they're hollering and laughing half the night. Then I hear banging against the wall. They must be having an orgy—bang, bang, bang against the wall! It's total bedlam!"

"Hmmm. The nerve of them! And they never called you?" Suzy was glad Paul could not reach through the phone and strangle her.

"Whaaat?" He was really very irritated by now."Stop it! This is serious. I've complained again and again to the office downstairs, and they still do nothing. I pay high rent here. I just have to move. My lease is up next month, and this place is driving me nuts. It's no use!" His voice became flat and dejected. "I'd leave now if it was up to me." Paul was at his wit's end.

"I hear you. And you have every right to be angry," Suzy offered brightly. "Do you want me to come over and help you find a place on the beach? Start looking in the Miami Herald and I'll be right over." She wasn't sure what to think at this point but wished she had paid more attention in that Psych class in college. Pipes? Hmmm, never heard that one before...

The manager walked briskly in front of them to the corner apartment #510, turned the key into the lock, and said, "This one will be available in about a week." The couple that was renting the apartment had obviously been in a hurry that morning. The bathroom was strewn with towels and the walls were still damp from the steam. Other than that, the place was open and spacious, with lots of floor-to-ceiling windows for unobstructed views of the ocean and best of all, no obvious "crazy" irritations. So far... for Paul's comfort, and his paintings, this would be ideal. The view, now on two sides, was phenomenal. And with nobody on the one side, distractions were cut by a third. It was absolutely incredible. What a find! Hopefully, Suzy thought, none of the neighbors showered and they all belonged to a religious sect that took vows of silence and walked barefoot on their tiptoes. That was the only way he'd be happy. Paul looked pleased.

CHAPTER ELEVEN

K aren flew in the door and headed for a seat by the bar. It was Friday night at the Taurus, and the band was just setting up. It was still quite early, but she looked around the bar to see who was there. Some of the regulars were gathered around in groups, laid back, relaxing, looking forward to the weekend after a hard workweek. Suzy came running in, saw Karen, and hugged her. They had become quite good friends and enjoyed the same whacky sense of humor in their quest to find Mr. Right.

"Hi, sorry I'm late; the traffic was terrible. You know, Friday night on 1-95 is murder," said Suzy as she plopped on the seat beside Karen. Dutch, the bartender smiled. He was wearing his insanely happy clown face tonight, with the lipstick extending almost up to his ears. He was smiling ... or was he?

"Ladies, how are you tonight?" He placed two glasses of Chardonnay in front of them.

"Hey Dutch, nice to see you." Karen and Suzy grinned. "Cheers!" They began to chat about their week at work, and laughed, catching up on the gossip.

"I told you about Steve, right? Steve, the one with the hands like baseball mitts," Karen started.

"Yeah, the one with the big hands and the big hooter to match – that Steve, you mean?" Suzy giggled.

Karen laughed. "Yeah, remember?" Suzy had met him at their Christmas party last year. "He got caught up with a nymphomaniac—can you imagine?!"

"No!" Suzy's eyes widened.

"Yeah, he looks very gaunt, like he's lost a lot of weight. I don't know…" her voice trailed away.

Suzy thought for a moment. "Well, if they're doing the sliding sheets boogy day and night, he's going to lose weight, right? Well, all I can say for the guy is he'd better be big in other places, too!" She howled with laughter, and slapped Karen's thigh, leaning into her.

"Hey!" Her eyes popped as she covered her opened mouth in feigned disbelief. "Just think! What a letdown with those mitt hands if he had a tiny pecker!" Gales of laughter exploded.

"Yeah. It'd be like false advertising!" Karen threw back her head, laughing raucously.

Suzy continued, "You know my ex, Frank, once had an affair with a nymphomaniac!"

"So what's that story?" Karen grinned; she loved stories.

"Well, at the time, he was on a business trip to Colorado, Wyoming—I don't remember, Big Country is all I remember…Anyway, he was with another business associate, a man, and they were having dinner in the hotel dining room. There were two good-looking women having dinner there as well. So they noticed each other, and Frank sent drinks to the ladies' table and the ladies asked the men to join them. Well, the short version was that the older woman was beautifully dressed—you know, the designer clothes, nails, hair and makeup. So Frank asked her out. Well," Suzy drew a breath, "the story was that she had been a nun."

Karen's eyes popped, "A nun? How did that happen?"

Suzy went on, "She was about eighteen, maybe twenty. A very religious young girl, she came from Chicago and felt she had this calling so she became a nun. While she was at the convent, there was a priest who took a shine to her. She was a beautiful girl. So he took the station wagon and went into town and bought her street clothes. They would leave the convent and drive out of the town and into the boondocks. They would then both change into street clothes in the station wagon and he would take her to a motel nearby. They did this practically every weekend!"

Karen's eyes shot up into her head. "Whaaat? That's the first story I've ever heard that didn't involve a young boy. Now that's a change."

Suzy punched Karen in the arm. "That was a cheap shot."

"But true," Karen added.

"Yeah, well anyway, it turns out she really enjoyed the sex. She enjoyed it so much that she began feeling guilty about it. After all, she was supposed to be married to God; he was her husband. So in time, Catholic guilt got the best of her. She couldn't be faithful to God and continue schtupping the priest. She really loved sex, I mean, really loved the sex; she was insatiable, and it was such a torment for her and she felt really bad about the whole thing… She couldn't handle it so she decided that she had to leave the convent and returned to Chicago. So now she's back and got a job as a teacher and so she, you know, is feeling lonely. You know how it is, especially in a big city; it is hard. So she decided to answer a Lonely Hearts ad in the newspaper. Then one day, out of the blue, an older man responded, a rancher from near Denver—I don't know, somewhere there—who was a widower with children. Anyway, they met, he liked her, and he was lonely and she was lonely. She liked him too, and although he was no oil painting, he was kind to her. And before you knew it, he asked her to marry him. But he told her he would only marry on the condition that since he had left his children everything in his will she would agree not to contest it. And so she said OK; I would guess he would leave her a policy or something like that."

"Oh my God!" Karen's eyes widened. "This sounds like something from the *Sound of Music*. Except, you know, Christopher Plummer was nice to look at."

"But there was no nympho nun in that one! The only thing alive was the hills, remember? So anyway, she agreed to marry him. All she knew about him was that he had a ranch. He seemed to be a good man, and that was that. He was just a nice old farm boy." Suzy sipped on her wine.

"OK, then what?"

Suzy spun around. "Oh, yes, he married her all right." She took a drag from her cigarette for dramatic effect, then carried on, "Turned out she was on him before he woke up in the morning; he'd come home for lunch, she'd take care of him again; then in the evening, when he came home for dinner, she was on him again; and then again after dinner, when they went to bed. She wouldn't leave him alone. Yep, he was a very happy and a very tired rancher!"

Karen grinned, her green eyes sparkling at the thought. "My kind of girl. See, that's all I want. Why must it be sooo hard to find? Okay, then what happened?"

"Oh, he croaked!" Suzy looked over at Karen, giggling. "What the hell did you expect, Karen? For God's sake! She blew him away! Literally! A very happy man, I'll have you know – he left this world with a big grin on his face," she continued. "He went from heaven on earth to actual heaven." They both howled with laughter.

"And the best part was, he left everything to her. Everything!" Suzy's eyes widened as she gasped, "I mean, everything! He had the ranch—that was about a thousand acres; he owned about five or six gas stations and all kinds of other properties. Apartment buildings—you name it, he practically owned the town. He changed his will and left it all to her! Now that's one grateful man! He left her a very, very wealthy woman. But she decided to give the children a big piece of the pie. So at least she was good-hearted. And that was his daughter with her when Frank met them."

"So what happened with Frank?"

"Frank? Oh! Well, they did get together quite a bit. She would fly to meet him in New York, Chicago or Las Vegas—it didn't matter where. I mean, money was no object! She liked him a lot. He was very smart and very funny. He liked her, too. She was attractive and always beautifully dressed. Until they got into the room, that is! After the door closed, all hell broke loose! She tore off her clothes, panting, and jumped all over him like a wild tigress on a rampage, eating him up alive. She was insatiable! She would orgasm the moment he laid his hand on her; that's all it took!! She was on fire! But after a couple of days with her," Suzy giggled, "he'd run down to the lobby to send himself telegrams saying he was called back to an important meeting and had get to the office immediately. He couldn't take it; she wore him out! He was so weak, he said, he could barely walk."

Shrieking with laughter, Suzy continued, "I'm telling you, he truly could barely walk! When he left the room his legs buckled, he was so weak! It was like he needed an oxygen tank when he left her back in the room." She tried to catch her breath. "I'm serious. He told me he was so weak, he had to hold on to the walls in the hallway as he staggered out of the room to get to the elevator. He said he had to leave; he was afraid she was going to kill him off too! Can you imagine a nun being a nymphomaniac?" Suzy and Karen threw their heads back, reeling with laughter.

"Mmmmmm, well, I can imagine being one. Come on, ride me, Cowboy! Yeehaw!" Karen hollered, then impishly smiled. "The Climax Queen rides again!! I guess that's what the Mother Superior was singing about in the *Sound of Music*. Climb every mountain, ford every stream. Follow that large penis.. till you find your dream." Both roared, and, as usual, heads turned to look at them, wondering what was so funny, but Karen and Suzy didn't notice.

CHAPTER TWELVE

"Did I tell you my friend from Washington is coming down to visit?" Paul asked.

"No, I thought you said that you were going to visit him." Suzy was delighted.

"I was, but he decided to come down and visit his family before he goes to Europe for business. Do you think we can introduce him to someone while he's here, Suzy?" he inquired brightly.

Paul had met Sarah, a friend of Suzy's, recently. She remembered her girlfriend's remarks after Paul had left that evening.

Sarah was gorgeous—well, at least she had been a few years ago, until the onset of menopause, when she started to blimp around the hips, but fortunately her breasts were now more voluptuous than ever so it kind of evened everything out.

Sarah had the sexiest, throaty deep voice, bordering on laryngitis, and the most fascinating green eyes. Between her expressive big green eyes, the voice, and the huge, full breasts, men would drool on sight, just like Pavlov's dogs when the bell rang. All men except Paul, that is. It took them all of maybe twenty minutes to be at each other's throats.

"I *know* Nixon lied - I *didn't* say he didn't," she hissed at him, her eyes now a deep foreboding shade of dark green as she pointed in the air with her long, beautifully manicured nails. She looked back at them from the rear view mirror as she sped along the expressway. "All I am saying," her voice, suddenly flat, was controlled and low as she carefully spoke, her eyes flashing, "is that other people were *involved,* that's all." She flopped back against her seat and stared straight ahead.

Paul glanced at Suzy, who was purposely looking out the window, pretending she was not there. All she wanted was a pleasant evening.. Not this!

"And all I said was that the man I know in Washington told me that there was no way, that's all." Paul sat up in the back seat, eyeing Sarah in the rearview mirror. Suzy felt uneasy; this was not going well at all.

"They say Pacific Time is a great restaurant," Suzy piped in, deciding to change the subject. The well-lit Metrorail tracks were along one side, while to their other side the multicolored city lights reflected from the tall magnificent slabs of concrete and glass that towered the downtown area as they sped along on their way to Lincoln Road.

"Doesn't downtown look beautiful now that they lit up the Metrorail? It's too bad almost no one uses it," she chimed, trying to change the subject yet again.

There was silence as they approached Lincoln Road and then parked. All three got out of the car. Paul took Suzy's arm. It was a habit that she found very chivalrous and charming at the same time. *Women do like men who think of small but meaningful things like that,* she thought. Sarah walked a few steps ahead.

"Sarah, my God, you look better than ever. You are stunning!" Steven, Sarah's date for the evening, stood with outstretched arms, and she walked right into his embrace. They had been friends for many years, but each was married to somebody else at the time, and yet they stayed dear friends. Now both were single.

They gazed adoringly at each other as they slipped their arms around each other's waists and then proceeded to the restaurant.

Paul smiled at Suzy. "Let's hope dinner will go smoothly. Is she always that way?" he whispered quizzically, his big blue eyes even more saucer-like.

The next evening, when she got home from work, Suzy sat on the sofa, kicked off her shoes, leaned over, picked up the phone and dialed. "Hey, Sarah," was all Suzy could get out before Sarah tore into her.

"Suzy, where in God's name did you find *him*?" Sarah roared down the phone. "I mean, who the hell does he think *he is*?"

Bursting into laughter, Suzy spluttered, "I was hoping you two would get along." Still giggling, she asked, "What happened? I swear to God, at one point I thought I was going to smack the both of you! I'm glad your friend Steve joined us or else I would have left!"

"But I don't understand. What's a good-looking girl like you doing with *him*? You're too pretty! Look in the mirror, for God's sake. All I know is when he goes out with you," she roared, "people think he must have real money; that's got to be it." She sniffed.

"Well, guess what," Suzy, said in a sing-song response, ignoring Sarah's remark. "I have something to ask you."

"And what is it?" Her voice was now at its normal pitch, low but curious.

"Paul has a friend coming down from Washington, who would like to meet you!"

"Oh, yeah, and who is he?" she asked curiously. Sarah was now in a completely different frame of mind. "Mmmmm, and so…" Sarah's curiosity was piqued, "has he been married, or is he still married?" She obviously did not trust Paul.

"Look, he is good-looking, rich and loves to have a good time. He's coming in this weekend and we can get together Saturday night. We'll have dinner at Dinaro's in the Gables at six. And you can thank Paul for inviting you. Oh, and by the way, he is single. Bye!" As she slammed the phone down, she couldn't help but laugh. This was going to be interesting.

CHAPTER THIRTEEN

Suzy and Sarah sat on a bench inside the restaurant, waiting for Paul and his friend Peter. Suzy took a deep breath; she hated waiting for anybody, because they were usually late. She fidgeted with her hands, looked around, her shoulders hunched. Paul and his friend from Washington should have been here ten minutes ago. She looked down at her dress, idly brushed it off with one hand, and sighed.

Sarah eyed Suzy with a stone face. "I just hope he's not going to be a dud…" Her voice trailed. She already had her doubts. Anything remotely associated with Paul made the hairs on the back of her neck snap to attention.

"Look, I have no idea what he looks like, OK?" Suzy was feeling uneasy; she looked down at her watch. It was now almost quarter past 6. Sarah sighed while grimly staring at her. They both looked away. Their blank stares wandered around the room, watching people waft through.

Sarah proclaimed stonily, "They're late."

"Well, all I can think of is the traffic. You know how it is…" Suzy offered. Every minute seemed like eternity, having Sarah huffing and puffing away beside her, making Suzy feel very nervous as she checked her watch for what felt like the hundredth time.

Suddenly the restaurant doors burst open and a backlit, Greek god-like apparition strode through the door. It was as though the heavens had opened and a host of angels were singing the *Hallelujah Chorus* – or maybe that was just in Sarah's mind. The two stared with gaping mouths. Peter wore a dark designer suit, white shirt, and red tie. Standing next to him was Paul, although that hardly registered. He could have been a prop for all she cared. Suzy reached over and lifted Sarah's chin off her chest. "You're drooling, dear."

Peter was tall, tanned, strikingly handsome, and distinguished-looking, with soft, wavy gray hair. He had an air about him; he lit up the room. His masculine cologne permeated the space around them. Paul had long disappeared into the woodwork. The two women turned and looked at each other. Sarah thought, *Oh girl, I owe you one.* And Suzy thought, *You sure as hell do!* Their eyes were speaking volumes.

Peter walked toward them, extending his hand to Suzy, as he smiled and introduced himself. He then turned to Sarah. "I do apologize for the delay. So much traffic at this time of day, just getting over the Causeway was horrendous!" He took Sarah's arm and turned toward the dining room. "If I had known it was you," he smiled, looking deep into her eyes and lowering his voice, "I would have taken a helicopter."

Sarah squealed with delight. They gazed deeply into each other's eyes. She smiled from ear to ear; her green eyes sparkled like 4th of July fireworks, while Paul and Suzy exchanged glances.

So far, so good, Suzy thought, watching them talking animatedly. Sarah smiled as Peter put his arm around her shoulder, leading her into the restaurant. *Wow, she hit the jackpot.*

He was so attentive to her, helping her into the seat, offering to light her cigarette, staring straight into her eyes as they engaged in conversation. As if she was the only woman in the room – only woman on Earth, actually. Sarah was entranced. They were in a world of their own, totally ignoring

Paul and Suzy, who exchanged looks of sheer delight for their friends even though they felt a little redundant at this point.

"Uh, hello, we're still here."

The waiter immediately brought the menus and started to hand them out.

Suzy took the menu, when suddenly there was a roar from the other side of the table.

"How dare you bring us the menus!" Sarah roared. "I want to sit and relax, have a drink. I don't want to be rushed, do you?" Her eyes swept over the others at the table and, with disgust, the waiter.

"Yes, of course, you're absolutely right," Peter piped up quickly, smiling at her. For a split second his eyes rested on her ample, heaving chest. His reward, if he played his cards right. "Take the menus away," he demanded, flicking his hand in the air in several swift movements, scowling, to denote his displeasure. The waiter scooped up the menus and spun around, slinking back into the kitchen.

Suzy and Paul looked at each other, dumbfounded. Where the hell was this coming from? Both were ravenous; they usually ate dinner at six thirty and were ready to eat.

"I have never had such terrible service!" she bellowed, looking at Peter, then at Paul. "I thought this was a first class restaurant," she sniffed.

"Let's order drinks, shall we?" Peter spoke up, as he spun around in his chair and spotted the waiter across the room. "Waiter," Peter called out, waving his hand, beckoning the unforgiveable waiter.

Suzy and Paul were not big drinkers, especially on empty stomachs, so they silently sipped on their white wine while beginning to feel little woozy. Paul spotted the breadbasket, leaned over, and handed it to Suzy as he took a roll for himself.

"I'm starving!" Paul grimaced to Suzy. "How long do we have to wait?"

"Yeah, me too. I never expected this." Both were getting seriously irritated, but kept it to themselves with sheer effort and sat in silence.

They glumly stared at Sarah and Peter, who were now toasting each other, looking deep into each other's eyes as she stroked his cheek, oblivious of the other two... Rude! Paul was so hungry he was questioning the stigma on cannibalism.

Paul and Suzy idly watched the couple at the next table as they paid their bill, got up, and left. A young fellow in a white jacket hurried over and began busing the table. Paul leaned over and glared at Suzy. "I just want you to know," he cleared his throat, "that they came in after we did."

She glared back at him. *Oh, now it was all her fault, was it?* She turned and stared into the distance.

After what seemed like an eternity, Peter looked up, turned around and waved to the waiter, who, along with the menus, was now allowed back to the table. He carefully took all their orders and once again slunk off into the background.

Paul eyed his watch; it was almost eight o' clock. Suzy noticed he was paler than usual, his big blue eyes lowered. "Be lucky to get to eat by dawn, at this rate," he mumbled. "Do you think we can eat soon?" he murmured anxiously as his eyes surveyed the table for crumbs. They had eaten the rolls about an hour ago. Suzy caught Paul eyeing the leaves on the table's centerpiece; even they were beginning to look appetizing.

From out of nowhere, the waiter returned to the table, carefully placing the plates in front of Sarah and Peter. Paul reached out to the waiter, who had his in his hand. Just as the waiter was about to place it in front of him, another roar blasted out from the other side of the table.

"Take it back." Sarah's chest heaved convulsively. "It's cold. I hate cold food!" she shouted.

The waiter snatched the plate from Paul's outstretched hand and, after he hurriedly gathered up the others, he darted back into the kitchen. Paul's jaw dropped in disbelief as he muttered gibberish, his blue eyes popping out of their sockets, and Suzy heard a definite sob. Suzy and Paul mouthed words to each other and waved their hands in the air like some angry sign language as their eyes followed the waiter carrying their dinner back to the kitchen.

"I can't *believe* it!" Paul finally found his voice. "Can you believe this?" Eyes flashing, he shook his head from side to side as hunger made him oblivious to social mores, and his hands balled into clenched fists as he grimaced.

Sarah and Peter smiled beguilingly at each other. Suzy watched as Peter's gaze once again lasciviously wandered quickly down to the heaving mountains of Sarah's creamy breasts with a gleam that he, though trying to be a gentleman, could not hide. The Sarah magic was in high gear; now it was his turn to drool.

The waiter finally made his way back to the table with the plates. Paul was so hungry he felt like a man coming across a mirage in the desert. As soon as the waiter approached, Paul tore the plate from his grasp, plunged his knife into the steaming hot, juicy steak, and stuffed a chunk of meat into his mouth like a ravenous dog. It was no mirage and Paul wasn't going to let it get away from him this time. Chewing voraciously, his eyes darted menacingly around the table as he swallowed quickly and again and again attacked the steak, his knife and fork clenched in his hands standing up in the air, his eyes throwing lightning bolts, daring anyone to try to take his food back this time. It all depended on how much they wanted to keep their appendages. Suzy watched in silence as she, too, ravenously wolfed down her Veal Marsala… It was hot and so good.

Sarah turned away from Peter for a moment and looked over at Paul and Suzy as if they had just arrived.

"Now," she said crisply, "is everybody happy? I hate cold food, don't you?" she cooed.

Paul and Suzy didn't answer. They couldn't hear Sarah over their own maniacal mastications as they swallowed quickly and rammed home another chunk and then another, chewing like two ravenous dogs that had been starved for a week, ready to snarl and kill if anyone dared to come near.

Paul angrily plunged his fork into the juicy steak but hit the bone, causing his knife to slide across the plate, catapulting his baked potato fully loaded with sour cream, butter and chives across the table, hitting Sarah squarely on her ample breasts and chest. He thrust himself back into the chair, shocked, his big blue eyes popping out of his head as he almost choked on a half-swallowed mouthful of steak.

"Oh my God!" he gasped, wide-eyed. Sarah yelped and shot jagged daggers at him while Peter immediately grabbed his napkin and dove into her big breasts, tenderly wiping the white mass over and over, as if it were a magic lamp that would grant him three wishes. He already knew what he'd ask for.

"Waiter," Peter called as he flung his other arm up and repeatedly snapped his fingers.

"There, there," he said gently with a lustful smile, bordering on lecherous. Well, men are men, after all. Sarah impatiently brushed Peter's hands away, scowling at Paul. "Look what you did!" Sarah bellowed furiously in horror. "My dress is ruined. It's ruined!" she wailed while Peter reached up and again dabbed vigorously with one hand between her breasts, which flung off bits of potato and sour cream that landed on the carpet and table.

"I just bought this last week from Saks. I can't believe you ruined it the very first time I wore it!" she bellowed in rage, as she sat back down.

"I'll have it dry cleaned for you." Paul offered pitifully.

Peter shot him a look of disgust and patted her chest once again for good luck. Globs of white sour cream and green chives continued to dribble down Sarah's black lace dress. "Of course you will, Paul," said Peter as he comforted Sarah.

She stared fiercely at Paul and growled, "Dry cleaning will not fix this dress! I need a new one. Dry cleaning won't cut it." She stabbed her long manicured fingers in the air in disbelief. Shaking with anger, she scooped off some sour cream that had splattered on her shoulder like bird poop.

Suzy was petrified in her seat. This entire scenario was simply too embarrassing. Diners from other tables were watching.

Paul glared at Sarah. It usually took quite a bit to anger him, but at this point, he had reached a controlled boil. Leaning forward, he looked her straight in the eye, lowered his voice, paused, and said, "Now, I just want to ask you one more question." Sarah glared back at him, silent. "I am asking you this question, and then I'm leaving. Would you like anything else on your baked potato? Maybe a few bacon bits?" Paul slowly rose, threw a $20 bill on the table for the dry cleaner, never losing eye contact with Sarah, grabbed Suzy's hand, and proceeded to the door.

As they stood waiting for the valet to bring the car, they turned, glanced at each other, and burst out laughing. Suzy smiled to herself. *Well,* she mused, *I wonder who's going to be the winner tonight—Peter or the potato? Will the genie grant his wish?*

CHAPTER FOURTEEN

After what became known as the Flying Baked Potato Incident, Paul never forgave Sarah. It was best to keep them apart. From that evening on, when Suzy and Paul met, Sarah was nowhere in sight – that is, until the trip to the Miccosukee Casino. Suzy had to really hold onto the leashes of these two ferocious Rottweilers. Just one look sideways and they were ready to fly at each other's throats.

Sarah loved to gamble; she was as bad as Paul, maybe worse. Paul had fallen, tripped over the pavement downtown and hurt his elbow, and his arm was in a sling so he could not drive.

One lazy afternoon, Suzy gave Sarah a call. "Why don't we go to the Miccosukee Casino and play bingo or something?" she suggested. Sarah loved to. Suddenly, Suzy couldn't resist an afterthought. "By the way, Paul whacked the crap out of his elbow and can't drive so just once, could we please take him along, just this once?" Suzy begged.

Sarah grimaced at the thought, then remembered what a hot date Peter was. He was planning to see her again the next trip to sunny South Florida, he promised, so she reluctantly gave in. "Well, as long as he doesn't start, that's all I'm saying. I guess I'll put up with him but only because of you,

you know that." Still, Sarah's eyes sparkled with the anticipation. "Yeah, come over to my house around six, and we'll go from there. But if he starts," she warned, "I'm going to throw him out of the car. Even if I'm on I-95, at 70 miles an hour, one word out of him and he, I promise you, will be out! I'm letting you know that *now*!"

The ride to the casino was a little tense, but even so, the two managed to quell their differences and be mostly invisible to one another.

"I'm going over to the poker," Paul tossed over his shoulder, as he headed off to the other side of the casino and disappeared in the crowd. Suzy and Sarah stood at the entrance and looked at each other. Sarah glanced over in the direction Paul had absconded as if she was seeking assurance of the fact, and then she looked over at Suzy.

"Thank God, and I hope he stays there all night. Keep him out of my sight. Come on!" She grabbed Suzy's arm and the two made their way over to the bingo tables. The bingo section was crowded and smoky. After several hours, just as the two were winning a little and the big jackpot was drawing near, suddenly a voice behind them said, "Hi. Any chance of us leaving soon?"

Sarah spun around in her seat, scowling with her fangs bared at Paul.

Paul looked down at Suzy. "I said," he repeated, ignoring Sarah, "any chance of us leaving soon?"

Sarah spun back in her chair, giving Suzy a short, knowing stare, and then went back to playing the current game. As they played, he stood behind them. They were too aware of his presence. *What a Ball Breaker,* Suzy thought. Their irritation with him as a distraction became evermore annoying and they began losing. After ten minutes went by, Sarah turned to Suzy. "Let's leave."

There was silence as Sarah drove. Suddenly, Sarah flicked the radio on and turned it up loud. Paul hated pop music, and she knew it.

"Why don't we stop and get a little bite to eat?" he called out over the blasting radio. It was about 11 pm and they were near 8th Street. They all agreed and she drove to her favorite Latin late-night restaurant.

Sarah walked ahead of Paul as they entered the restaurant, and the waiter led them to a table. It was a busy night, as they watched the waiters whizzing by with their orders. As they sat down, the waiter handed each of them a menu. The conversation was strained. Sarah looked away in one direction, while Paul looked to the other side of the room, both avoiding each other. Paul and Suzy sat across from each other while Sarah sat in the middle. Propping their menus in front of their faces, Sarah looked over at Suzy and caught her eye; Suzy noticed the sheer distaste in Sarah's grimace. Sarah's eyes darted toward Paul as she smirked and stuck out her tongue. Suzy looked up quickly. Paul was studying the dessert display near the wall, frowning, bored, distant. The waiter came to take their orders.

Paul shot a glance at Sarah. "You go ahead." He buried his face in the menu.

"I'll have the cafe con leche with the tostados, and I want the milk hot - caliente - OK? - in a glass," as she pointed her long manicured finger at the glass on the table. "Aqui." She looked up at him. "No cup, OK? And I want ..."

Just then Paul spun around. "Look," he growled, "if you start again, I'm walking out this minute. I'm just letting you know - OK?" He shot her a menacing glance and looked down at his menu.

She jumped back in her seat; her eyebrows shot up to her forehead as she looked over at Suzy. Dumbfounded, her green eyes now black and stormy, she looked down at the table cloth and then back up to Suzy, who was by then hiding behind the menu as she stifled her giggling. The more she suppressed it, the more she wanted to howl with laughter.

Wiping the grin off her face, lowering the menu, Suzy said, "Oh, and waiter, I'll have the caffe con leche and a Cuban sandwich, por favor." The waiter nodded.

"And I'll have the turkey on rye," Paul said stonily. They all ate in silence, after which Paul wandered off to inspect the dessert display in person.

"Well, did you hear what he said?" Did you?" Sarah was filing her beautiful nails. She looked up, and pointed the emery board at Suzy. "You remember what he said, don't you?" Sarah narrowed her eyes. "He said that every time he goes on vacation with a woman, they wind up in the loony bin - that's why he's single. Now," she looked up, rapping the board on the table, "why do you think that happens?" She had that knowing look in her eye. "I'm telling you right now, I figured that one out from day one! Wait and see." Sarah glared up at the ceiling again, rolled her eyes then stared straight at Suzy.

Suzy giggled. Sarah was so neurotic herself. Suzy enjoyed her company but only in small doses, and she would certainly never, ever double date with her again. They would still occasionally go out with some of their other girlfriends, but that was every now and then, and even that became ever less frequent.

A few weeks later, while Suzy and Paul were driving down Brickell Avenue, sitting in the car, waiting for the light to change, Suzy mimicked Sarah's conversation about Paul. In an overly serious, lower-registered voice, she repeated, "Every time he goes on vacation with a woman, she winds up in the loony bin." Despite herself, she smirked knowingly at Paul. "Every time," she repeated with a solemnity only befitting a judge.

Paul collapsed laughing. He got a big kick out of this. She grinned, thinking how well he could accept a joke against himself, which she thought rather unusual.

CHAPTER FIFTEEN

I t was July, Paul's firm was swamped, his caseload was backbreaking, and Suzy saw him only occasionally. However, it was also his birthday soon and Suzy had been thinking about it.

"Hi. How's your work load coming along?" she asked him, after calling him on a whim one evening.

"I'm so bogged down. I hope I'll get a break soon."

"Well, your birthday's coming up, so let's plan for next weekend."

She had found him a lovely watercolor painting in one of the galleries on Ponce de Leon and was excited to give it to him. Paul had already made reservations in the Gables at one of the French restaurants he loved. They met about six, and dinner was as usual, a pleasant interlude. They sat upstairs, where they overlooked the restaurant and watched and listened to the pianist while relaxing with a glass of Chardonnay. Dessert, of course, had the usual candle and cake with the waiters singing as an embarrassed Paul squirmed in his seat. At what seemed an appropriate moment, she presented the gift that she had beautifully wrapped to him.

"Aah!!" His eyes widened as he held the painting. He was enthralled. "What a delightful, thoughtful thing to do," he said as the waiter brought them each a glass of wine.

On the way home, he decided to drive past downtown, going to Miami Beach via the Venetian Causeway. Suzy felt pretty good; the evening had been so pleasant. She laid her head back, closed her eyes, and relaxed, a little buzzed.

Paul, not too familiar with this particular route, came to a little bridge on what he thought was the way to Miami Beach. He slowed down. "Jeez!" he exclaimed while he squirmed, stretched, and squinted as if he needed glasses, looking up at the street sign name, muttering, "No friggin' street lights. You'd think we were in a Third World country." He twisted around, peering up. "What does that sign say? Where the hell are we?"

Suzy turned sleepily, forgetting to put on her glasses, and with one eye open slightly, she cocked her head forward and proclaimed, "Oh! Yes! Yes, I see the sign…" She bent forward, squinting. "Oh! Yeah, here we are! We're at Dildo Island! " she said proudly, amazed that she could read the sign from across the road without her glasses.

"What? Oh my God, my God!" he screamed, suddenly shooting up into the air and bouncing around as if his ass was on fire. "It's Di-leeee-doe Island! Di-leeee-doe Island, Suzy! If *that* wasn't a Freudian slip, I don't know what is," he shouted, as he grimaced, and shook his head violently. The Brillo' pad he called hair was damn near standing at attention. "Jeez," he said, as he bounced around again. "I can't believe what you said," he spluttered while still shaking his head.

"Wow, chill out! What? Are you afraid of a little competition?" Suzy smirked to herself. "Well gee, don't have a stroke over it!" she laughed.

"Stop talking. I don't want to hear anymore about it," he snapped at her.

Suzy glanced sideways at Paul and then found herself stifling a case of the giggles as if she was at some church service. She turned toward the window, covering her mouth, inwardly giggling. *Gee,* she thought wickedly, *if he gets that worked up, maybe I should do this again ... and often.* Was he really *that* old fashioned? Hard to believe.

Next stop, Dildo Island.

CHAPTER SIXTEEN

It was a warm Sunday morning. Let's face it, in southern Florida every morning is a warm morning. Suzy got up early with the expectation of having brunch with Karen down in the Grove. She sipped her second cup of coffee while reading the paper. The shrill ring of the phone interrupted her tranquility. It was Paul.

"You won't believe this. I have bad news. My mother, my mother," he repeated quietly. "You know she hasn't been well for a long time, and she has decided to leave me her apartment in New York. I have to go up there and take care of her affairs so I just wondered if you would drive me to the airport this afternoon?"

"Oh God, Paul! I'm so sorry. I hope everything will be all right. Is your brother going to meet you?"

"Sandy will be there at JFK, so we'll go into Manhattan, and I'll stay with him. I can't stand his wife, but I guess we can tolerate each other for a few days," he sighed. "God knows what he saw in her. He is such a good-looking guy. He's tall and very handsome, even today. They met in college. He was very shy, and she took a shine to him. All I can think of is, she was the first woman he dated (the first time both got laid, especially in those days, is what he meant, Suzy surmised) and I feel like she made him marry her. She probably made him feel guilty, so he married her. My mother always said she grabbed him before he knew what had happened."

"But isn't your brother a judge?"

"Yes, he is now. All I know is, he could have done a lot better."

"Yes, too bad…So what time shall I pick you up?" Suzy asked, changing the subject as she swallowed the last mouthful of her coffee.

CHAPTER SEVENTEEN

It was eight o' clock Friday night in the Grove. Karen ran into the Taurus and grabbed two seats at the end of the bar, which happened to be the closest to the band. Dutch, behind the bar, walked up with a grin. He placed a napkin on the bar before her, which she immediately snatched up and used to pat her brow and cheeks. "Whew!" she exclaimed as she patted away the sweat. She pulled her collar away from her neck and then flipped her long hair away from her collar. Glancing up at the fan above, she noted it was churning fast. Even though it was on full blast, the air was so thick with humidity. Dog days. Summer in south Florida was hot, humid, blistering, with a hint of mystery amidst the discomfort. Especially on a Friday night.

"Hey Karen! The usual? Is your friend on her way?" asked Dutch as he set down another napkin. Today he was wearing a top hat and makeup, a circus ringmaster ready to call out the elephants, acrobats and clowns. Dutch's outfit sure fit right in. Karen looked around the room. *Damn, sure are enough clowns here tonight already. What was that song, send in the clowns—was that it? Yep,* she frowned. *Don't bother, they're here... That's just what I need, more clowns,* she thought sarcastically. What she needed was a hot lion tamer. Once again, she prayed for a live one to walk through the door, for a change, and rescue her from her biological clock, which was chiming so loudly it was giving her a headache. *Is hot sex with a hot man really that difficult?* She said a little prayer to herself. It seemed with each passing week, she was becoming more and more religious.

'Hey Dutch, how are you?" Karen smiled and nodded to confirm her drink order. She turned to glance at the door, just as Suzy came bustling in.

"Hi, sorry I'm late! The damn traffic—you know how it is Friday on 95. A truck was hanging off the side of one of the overpasses, hanging right there in mid-air! I couldn't believe my eyes. I wonder what happened to the driver? The expressway was backed up for miles," she spewed out as she plopped herself down. Her hair was a little tousled from the rush to meet Karen. As Suzy sat down, she tried to brush it with her fingers to get it under control, sighing with relief, and took a long sip of the Chardonnay that Dutch placed in front of her.

"Cheers, Dutch!" they both called out to him and he managed to wave to them despite his focus on the several shot glasses he was juggling to the delight of the bar patrons..

"Boy, have I got something to tell you!" Karen bent forward. "Remember that girl I used to work with last year at Chanel's?"

"Oh yes, that tall, slim, gorgeous girl with the big blue eyes?"

"Yes. That's her. Did I tell you about her boyfriend – the married one?"

Suzy moved closer and nodded expectantly. The band was setting up behind them, warming up for the night. "Testing, testing, one, two, testing," their lead singer intoned as he tapped the mike.

"Yeah, that one, well, apparently he was over at her place last Friday night. She still believes he's going to get divorced and marry her." Karen paused to smirk and take a quick sip from her drink. "God, how naïve can you be? Five years! Yeah, sure, in your dreams, lady," she sniggered. "Anyway, apparently, there they were, lying on the bed after sex and he's sprawled across the bed, snoring, dead to the world! She's lying on the other side, listening to him. After a while, she got bored. She poked him, but he didn't move a muscle. She called out his name, and still nothing. She went into another room. Now, I have no idea how she got the thought, but she went and got a permanent magic marker. And since he's lying on his side with his ass practically in her face, she decided to draw a big smiley face on his ass with two big eyes and a big smile. Even drew some teeth in. Just to make it more happy looking!" Karen was cracking up at the thought. "And he still didn't move! About ten minutes later, he suddenly woke up. He looked around, realized he was at her place, jumped off the bed, and said, "Oh, my God! What time is it, hon?"

She looked up, turned to the clock by the bed, and replied, "It's midnight, sweetie."

"Oh my God!" he wheezed, as he jumped into his pants and shoes at the same time while he threw on his shirt, grabbed his tie and ran out the door. "Call you tomorrow," he yelled as he flew out the door.

Suzy smiled widely. "There must be more to this story, huh?"

"Oh yes, ooooh yeess!" Karen laughed, as she threw her head back, her eyes gleaming with devilment.

"So what happened, you say? Well the next morning, as usual, the little red rooster, after showering, came sashaying into the bedroom to get his underwear. His wife was sitting up in bed watching the morning show, sipping her coffee. So, as he walked in front of her to get to the dresser and as he bent over to get his underwear out of a drawer, she did a double take at his ass!

"'What's that?' she said, her voice cold and accusing. Her eyes shot bullets at him.

"'What's what?' he asked quietly, completely unaware, shuffling around in the drawer.

"'That,' she icily said, pointing at his behind.

"He turned around to look at her. 'What?' he innocently asked.

"He hadn't a clue; he turned toward the mirror to see. And with that, the wife leapt out of bed as the husband lunged to get his pants and shoes and grab his underwear. He ran, pranced, leapt around the bedroom while trying to get his clothes on. Next he hopped around like a one-legged kangaroo as he tried to get his socks on. The wife grabbed one of his shoes away from him, whacking him with it. All the while he was yelling, 'Oh, come on now; come on, stop it' She pummeled him over and over again on the head like she was Hercules, with strength she never knew she had. It was feeling quite therapeutic for her, it seemed. Hell hath no fury, like they say. "Hey! Cut it out, will ya!" while ducking, dodging, jumping over the couch, he furiously fumbled to get his shirt on. Finally he ran out of the room."

'You were with that whore again? Huh! You were with that whore!' she screamed, spun around grabbing a heavy glass ashtray and, surprised by her own strength, hurled it at him like a pitched baseball, just missing his head crashing into the wall, glass shards splattered across the hallway.

Suzy watched Karen, wide-eyed. "Oh my, and they call this marital bliss?"

Karen went on recalling. "'You low life!' she screamed as she chased after him, down the hallway, into the kitchen, lunged toward him. 'You son of a bitch!' she yelled, banging him across his head again with his shoe, then on the shoulders, while he ducked and bobbed around the chairs in the kitchen, grabbing his shoe away from her.

"You think you are soooo fucking hilarious! Smiley face on your ass - after a piece of ass, is that it? Was it that good? You rotten bastard!' she screamed, chasing him into the garage, where he jumped into the car, put it in gear and hauled ass out of there!"

Karen shrieked with laughter, obviously enjoying the retelling, "And then wifey ran out into the street after him, picked up a curb stone—can you believe this?" Karen's eyes widened. "And when he stopped at the Stop sign, she heaved it through the rear window!" Karen took another sip and went on,

" And guess what!! Who should be outside mowing the lawn, but her next door neighbor! He was doing a double take!! He was standing there with his mouth wide open!" Karen threw her head back and laughed. "Yeah, and when he watched her throw the rock, he ran back into his house to hide!"

Suzy laughed, "Oh my God! And wait till he gets home later—I'd hate to be in his shoes!"

"Or shoe, as the case may be," laughed Karen.

All of a sudden, the band started,

"I'm a thousand miles from nowhere;

Time don't matter to me.

I'm a thousand miles from nowhere;

And there's no place I wanna be.

I got heartaches in my pocket,

I got echoes in my head,

All that I keep hearing

Are the cruel, cruel things you said..."

And, once more, the Grove came alive.

CHAPTER EIGHTEEN

Suzy had moved to Fort Lauderdale. Paul was busy at his office; there were many ends to tie up before leaving for New York, and the now not-so-small medical equipment company Suzy managed had moved to its new, upscale location in Ft. Lauderdale and was swamped with orders from countries from Bahrain to Brazil, and all points in between, keeping her busy maintaining a tight ship.

The little old lady realtor fumbled with the locks until she finally got the door opened. "There hon, I think you're going to like this one. It's got the ocean view you wanted."

Suzy walked straight through to the balcony, opened the sliding door, and stepped out. She was instantly immersed in a strong ocean aroma and the sight of the darker blue-green sea meeting the lighter blue sky, forming a horizon where several freighters awaited entry to Port Everglades, just a little farther down to the right of the coast. She stood in silence, her heart racing. She looked down, watching the cars slowly drive by, flanked by swaying palm trees in the median. A soft breeze blew her hair around; she brushed it off her face. Turning, she watched the bridge go up at the Intracoastal, as a sleek, multi-million dollar yacht glided by on its way to an unknown destination, either North along the Atlantic coast, or to the Caribbean, who knew.... It was all so overwhelmingly enchanting, so exciting. Her heart was racing, and beating so hard, she could hardly catch her breath. Oh, how long she had waited for this moment. All those years of struggling were finally paying off. This was her dream come true—her new address, Fort Lauderdale. By the beach.

She tried to act cool, calm, collected, but her excitement threatened to bubble over. If she had been into tantric sex, she would have climaxed ten times by now. She stepped into the living room, then checked the kitchen and the cupboards. The realtor watched and followed her silently as Suzy leisurely walked through the rest of the apartment.

"Take your time, hon," the realtor offered. Suzy had already worked out where all her furniture would go.

Her new office was in the heart of downtown Fort Lauderdale and her staff was a nice group with which to work, all seeking to please while being pleasant. A good job, and a new apartment with an ocean and an Intracoastal view. Life was good. She loved sitting on the balcony watching the moon slowly rise above the horizon and gleam over the ocean. The shining, rippling waves became hypnotic. Mesmerizing. She remembered a number of years ago when she and her now ex-husband rented a house by the water in Bermuda. The sun would rise and the shimmering waves were breathtaking and at night, when the moon rose, the ocean wavelets would light up with a rippling, sparkling, intriguing effect that somehow made her feel high, intoxicated. Drunk with beauty. It's no wonder the word 'lunatic' pertains to the moon, the Latin word for moon being Luna. It was all very powerful, even spiritual. *This is livin' the Dream; how lucky I am,* she realized.

Suzy loved her job, but she needed to brush up on certain computer programs being used in the new office. She liked being sharp and ahead of the game, and it would also be an added accomplishment on her resume.

She checked the *Sun Sentinel* newspaper ads and found, "Need help with IBM-XT, etc? All your computer needs. Call Juan." She dialed the number.

She heard a light knocking on her door. She looked at her watch. Three-thirty. *My, exactly on time*, she thought…

And Juan strode in. "Hi Suzy! How you doing today?" he asked as he put his bag down. Tall, tanned, slim, and gift-wrapped in tight blue jeans and a coral-colored, form-fitting, Ralph Lauren Polo shirt, he seemed to float on air as he moved across the room on the balls of his feet, lithe, panther-like. Gracefully, he sat down in front of her computer. She stared at him. My, my, Juan looked Juan-derful. To be sure. Was she not supposed to think this? And why not?

Hot damn. She cleared her throat, pulled up a chair next to him, and watched his hands glide over the keys, his long, jean-clad legs stretched out before him, yet his muscular body upright, erect, as he explained the newer software to her.

She nodded; he leaned closer to the screen, typing, eyes straight ahead, while she scribbled notes on her yellow pad. He turned to her, explaining, and their eyes locked. She noticed his velvety brown eyes, and his perfect features topped by brown, softly wavy hair.

He looked directly into her eyes as he spoke in his warm, Latino-accented voice.

"Let's change seats, and we'll go through this together," he offered as he sprang smoothly out of his chair. As he sat close to her, she felt his animal heat, hotter than the mid-day Arizona desert in August. She fanned herself with her notepad. The panther is a beautiful animal. Her mind raced. Though he was making her dizzy, she worked at being nonchalant. *Act cooool, lady,* she reminded herself. *What's going on?* The air was electric. A tug of war was straining her brain. *He is too young, for God's sake; what am I reading into this? Is this my imagination?* Thoughts swirled in all directions; she was having a hard time concentrating…

He checked his watch, "Oh, I guess the hour is over." Suzy looked up, rose, retrieved her checkbook, and wrote out the check. She bent forward as she wrote.

"So, Juan, is it possible for you to come in the evening or Saturday?"

"Sure, how about 5:30 Wednesday? I have an opening then."

She watched him, with his panther-like movements, gather up his bag and head to the door. Swift, silent, and confident, he vanished.

Suzy flopped down on the sofa, a little dazed. Damn, that was unnerving. Wednesday rolled by; she slipped from the office a few minutes early and rushed home. Juan would be on his way by now. There was a soft but firm knock on the door.

"Come in!" she called out. "Door's open!" In a flash, she was seated at her computer. As he entered, his light cologne permeated the air. It was fresh and pleasant.

She sat next to him, notepad in hand. Every now and then, he looked at her with those big, beautiful eyes of his that were so innocent but knowing. She could feel the thoughts behind those eyes. He could so easily be a poker player, she surmised, feeling an air of mystery and intrigue about him. Was he as intrigued by her? He spoke softly, patiently taking her through the programs while explaining the different ways they were operated. He answered her questions patiently, even kindly. Bending forward to share the screen with him, she felt their hands and thighs touch and felt his animal heat intoxicate the very air. His eyes pierced deeply into hers, speaking volumes to her silent longing.

Is *this really happening?* she wondered, struggling to catch her breath. His words tumbled out. She nodded in what seemed to be the appropriate places without hearing a word.

Suddenly he leapt from the chair, had her make out the check, then paused at the door and kissed her lightly on the cheek. "I can be here Saturday; will that be OK?" She nodded, smiling.

The next day, she called him from work just to get some refresher points, as she was actually stuck while trying to use one of the new programs.

"You can call me anytime; you know I'm happy to help you out," he insisted. He really wanted to hear from her, she was certain. No, it was not her imagination; she was sure he had the hots for her. But so young! He oozed sex; it exuded off him like a flashing taser and she found it so very flattering as she fell under its spell. His line that he was always 'happy to help out' could be interpreted in different, delectable ways. She smiled and laughed softly as she walked out the door.

The receptionist glanced up from her desk, "Something funny, Suzy?"

"Maybe. Just maybe. Funny and good." She struggled to suppress a giggle. "Goodnight."

Saturday, Suzy peeked at her watch. He was due at half-past three. Good, time for a quick nap. She had just gotten back from the gym, taken a quick shower, and put on a soft cotton T-shirt and loose fitting shorts. Now, she lay on the couch, her legs spread-eagled, one leg propped on the glass coffee table. Nuzzling into the pillows, she took a deep breath and sought a quick 20-minute nap. The door was unlocked; she wouldn't have to get up for him.

"Hellooo!" She heard his gentle, deep male voice as she slipped from her sleep. His muscular body and long legs stood in the middle of the room, smiling down at her.

"Oh. You're early, sorry," she said as she rose from the couch. And with that animal stride of his, he was at his seat and setting to work on her computer. She sat next to him and watched in silence. They locked eyes several times.

Who could have eyes like this? she wondered. They were like a hypnotic drug, consuming and controlling her. However, she could feel the proverbial pea under the mattresses; their age difference really bothered her. Yet, his taut, suntanned body was so close to her. His light cologne floated around them and it all seemed so natural. She felt so very comfortable sitting there with him as he explained the images on the monitor's screen. But then, suddenly feeling as though he could read her mind, she tore her eyes away from him as he glanced over at her. Her eyes were locked on the screen as he sprang soundlessly to his feet and slipped from view.

"Take off your lipstick," said his unexpectedly husky male voice, now behind her.

How bossy, how demanding, she thought. *Kind of nervy.* But she liked it.

"Whaaat?" She spun around, as if unsure if she had heard him right, and looked up.

"Take off your lipstick," he repeated, now in a self-assured, deep, testosterone-laden voice. Demanding, yet soothing. Her heart missed a beat; she caught her breath. She looked at him, dazed, as she meekly reached for a tissue. Like a little girl, she obediently wiped it off. She stared at the lipstick-smudged tissue. *I can't believe he said that to me. And I did it!* Her mind was racing in overdrive. *Who the hell would believe this?* She felt flattered, amused, and slightly fearful too.

She slowly stood up from her chair and faced him. Their eyes met and with an urgency, a hunger, he reached out to her. She felt a thrilling surge of passion as he wrapped his arms around her, pulled her into his taut chest, and kissed her repeatedly. The faint stubble on his otherwise smooth face felt like a hundred pinpricks, so painful but so delicious she felt like crying out, but she knew she couldn't stop now. The world stood still, so perfectly enchanting. He smiled as he gazed down at her.

"I wanted to do this the very moment I saw you," he confessed roguishly as his smile elongated into a grin. "I'm sorry if this is awkward for you, but I just can't help myself."

"But Juan, I'm much older than you and, and I, I mean, I, I'm very confused…it, it's so unexpected. But so very sweet, actually," she added as she looked up at him and smiled.

After she had given him the check, he kissed her tenderly on the cheek and they walked to the door together.

"See you soon. Just call. OK?"

After he left, she sat down and unscrambled her thoughts. Oh my God! It was all a little shocking, but oh, so enjoyable. Her lips tingled and seemed slightly swollen; her chin burned from the stubble. She couldn't stop smiling. It certainly beat the 6 o'clock news.

For the next couple of days at home, at work, and in-between, she thought of him. She waited for a couple of weeks. Then, she picked up her phone.

Juan strode in like a vibrant energy flowing through the room. He was so light on his feet, moving animal-like with such muscular precision. It was fascinating to watch him. The testosterone was bouncing off the walls. His long legs and supple body moved with determination, swiftly, purposefully, confidently. Silently, she sat next to him, and they began. They chatted and laughed as they stared at the screen. They were relaxed; the naturalness of their closeness felt as if they had always known each other, She didn't know the how and why of it, and she didn't care.

Springing to his feet, he gathered up his bag and, after receiving his check, headed toward the door as she followed. He turned and leaned into her, his arm around her neck, kissing her sweetly at first then deeply, his chest pressed upon hers. His hand then moved toward her breast and covered it. She took his hand gently, to cup and fondle her breast, "Like this, you mean? Is this what you like?" she asked hoarsely.

He buckled and panted "Oh!" while grabbing her hand and placing it on his bulging pants. "Oh," he repeated with a tinge of self-consciousness, a touch of feigned embarrassment. "Now, see what you made me do?" His eyes glistened with anticipation.

She led him into the bedroom. "I'll be right back," she said softly, shyly, again hoarsely as her voice cracked. She spun around, stepped into the bathroom, and closed the door behind her. She undressed quickly and wrapped herself in a towel, stepped back into the bedroom and sat on the edge of the bed.

There he stood, by the side of the bed, naked in all his aroused male glory. He was so perfectly hung, like the proverbial horse. What a beautiful body; everything was so—so flawless… She couldn't have wished for more, or better. She looked into his eyes and not a word was spoken. He bent forward, and in one nanosecond, snapped off her bra. *My, this one's obviously had plenty of practice; no fumbling around with him,* soared through her thoughts as he stared at her full breasts. She extended her hand to him; he bent toward her as she took his hand and placed it on her breast.

"Here, it's all yours," she whispered as he buried his face on her chest while easing himself on top of her. He was kissing her wildly as she guided his hand down her body, as each thrust was more exciting, arousing such scrumptious pleasure as she gyrated her hips with each move of his. She couldn't get enough of him.

"Oh," she panted, "oh, my …." She felt so heady as she moaned and writhed. He twisted her around and entered from behind, thrusting rhythmically, she rocked with every move, now faster and faster, gasping, fell back against the bed. . Slowly rolling over, they lay there, breathing rapidly, panting, and feeling so wonderfully spent. He lay slightly on top of her, breathing heavily on her neck.

"Mmmm, delicious," she whispered, kissing him deeply. "Wonderful," she sleepily sighed, stroked his hair and brow, murmured, "Wow. You *are* some hot man." She felt so relaxed, so content, nuzzling close, tasting his skin. He was delicious. "You must come again."

"Really?" he laughed softly. "I can arrange that if you give me a few minutes!"

She realized what she had just said and tousled his hair. "Oh!" she laughed. "That's not what I meant, you bad boy." He bent forward, cupped her breast into his mouth. "Ooooh, that feels so good,…don't stop…"

She lay there in the darkness and heard the bathroom door open, sleepily glanced at the clock by the bedside..A quarter to nine. She yawned, relaxed, and slowly rose, following him to the door, as he gently kissed her.

Mae West was right. "It's not the men in your life, but the life in your men."

* * *

"So you're moving to New York. Do you think that's a wise move? Do you think you can live with that weasel? I mean, like day and night?" Karen asked, as they sat in the front sidewalk section of the open café on the main drag on A1A, across from the beach, idly watching the young boys and girls rollerblading by. Sunday brunch at the beach. Life felt like one big vacation since she moved to the beach. The ocean and sky were both flawlessly blue, one a slightly deeper shade of sapphire than the other, while palm trees swayed and rustled in the breeze. Just a perfect, heavenly day.

Suzy smiled as she sipped her coffee. "Well, we've known each other quite a while. And he really doesn't have anybody as far as a support system goes, and I don't have any family here. Plus we like a lot of the same things: theater, art, and museums. He's quite generous; isn't an alcoholic, or a womanizer. Sure, nobody's perfect, but he is good company, always interesting. I must say he's the best date I ever had. He always takes me to nice places. He can be really funny, and equally kind. I mean he's not going to abuse me, sell me to the white slave market in Marrakesh, or anything." She laughed.

"Are you trying to convince me or yourself?" Karen interjected.

Suzy continued without missing a beat, "Paul is decent, he's cultured—actually knows a Manet from a Monet. And knows how to spend some mon-ee!" She giggled, "And of course, I have met his sister and her husband and some of his friends. They all seem like honorable, nice, decent professional people, so what could be so bad? He's never beaten me; he's not the type. Maybe he's a little quirky, sometimes a little nerdy, and yes, little eccentric and—."

" A little?" Karen's voice went up two octaves as she slowly shook her head, eyes popping.

"Well, no one's perfect, after all! And I do enjoy his mind. I know you're not crazy about him but I've never, believe it or not, ever had an argument with him. We actually get along fine. He's bright. And he's a lawyer to boot."

"And what are you going to do about your apartment?"

"Oh, I've already taken care of that. I'm renting it out to my neighbor's family who come down for the winter every year. So that's taken care of."

"I dunno. The big question is, do you really think you can live with that weasel day in and day out?"

Paul was not one of Karen's favorite people. Personality-wise, they clashed. Karen was tall, at least six feet in her heels, and looked down on him, literally and figuratively; they both could be quite opinionated, always coming from different directions and inevitably clashing. Paul saw everything in black or white. Period. When he made a statement, that was that. No grey area. No opening for discussion. Typical lawyer.

Suzy buttered her roll, took a bite, then chewed reflectively. "Oh, Karen, I'm sure it's going to be fine! You're behaving like he's the Count of Transylvania "– deepening her voice, mimicking, 'I'm going to suck your Bluuuuud' - or something!" giggling, as she went on, "Actually he has been very kind to me."

"That weasel," Karen went on…Suzy giggled inwardly; it was beginning to sound like that was Paul's real name—she said it all the time."… has no patience and gets irritated at the drop of a hat. Also, he's never been married. Think about it …" She gave Suzy a long, knowing look, looking deep into Suzy's eyes, before continuing, "If he was such a catch he would have at least been married and divorced by now, don't you think!" Her eyes widened, looking into the distance. Suzy saw her disapproval of the whole thing "I just don't know … " her voice trailed off and she shook her head from side to side as a Harley roared by.

"They should ban those noisy bastards!" they both said, irritated, blocking their ears as they scowled in the direction of the Harley.

Just then, a young, thin thing, a skinny, stringy blonde with a 50-Z chest, sauntered by. Her breasts jutted out like two watermelons under her mini bikini top while her skimpy cut-off shorts exposed her ass cheeks. Waddling alongside was the bald-headed, three-chinned, 300-pound boyfriend wearing a T-shirt that read Superman across it, and denim shorts, who couldn't have been a day under 65. Suzy glanced around the café. A sea of male eyes stared, all doing a double take, wondering what the blubber old Baldy had that they didn't. They were drooling, with their tongues hanging out like dogs on a summer's afternoon. Their female companions stared at their partners disapprovingly with stone cold, steel eyes set in faces of granite, lips pursed... *Oh-oh, I'll bet none of them are getting any nooky tonight,* thought Suzy.

"Look how idiotic he looks with that young cheap-lookin' chick," the plain–Jane, overweight wife at the table next to them sneered as she took a huge bite out of her bacon, ham and turkey double-decker sandwich. She looked as if she had just stepped out of K-Mart's clearance sale, the Blue Light special worth all of $30 for the entire color-coordinated ensemble covered in swaying palm trees and parrots, and, to accessorize, don't forget the palm tree earrings to match. All she needed to do in that outfit was stand in some grass, and dogs would automatically lift their legs.

"Yeah," her unwashed husband sniggered, with a dirty gleam in his eye, still following the couple down the street. "He may look like an idiot, but he's bangin' that!" He punctuated his thought with the dirtiest gutter laugh they had ever heard.

Karen looked sideways at him disapprovingly, cupped her hands in front of her mouth, and grimaced. "What a low-life pig. I feel like I need to take a Silkwood shower," she said in hushed tones.

Suzy nodded in agreement. "Yeah, an absolute sleaze ball—who the hell would want him?"

"Yes sir," he went on, still with that dirty gleam in his eye, carried away, having visions of the chick doing a pole dance in some sleazy dimly lit out of the way bar for him, "one cunt hair can pull a Mack truck from here to Denver!"

"Did you hear *HIM?*" Karen exploded. "Waiter! Waiter! Bring me the check. Let's get out of here!"

CHAPTER NINETEEN

P aul turned the key and unlocked the apartment's door. Jose, the building's plump, gold-toothed, mustachioed Puerto Rican porter, was trying so hard to keep up with Paul's rapid, confident stride, wheezing, as he trundled down the dimly lit marble hallway, pushing the heavily laden luggage rack. Suzy's garment bags were neatly stacked on the luggage rack, as were her leather suitcases with their yellow tassels that bobbed back and forth as Jose pushed the luggage rack into the apartment. Suzy followed them in. Paul handed Jose a scrunched up ten-dollar bill after he had finished putting the garment bags and suitcases in the bedroom.

"Gracias, Senor, muchas gracias!" Jose's his eyes lit up as he smiled broadly, exposing a front gold-capped tooth. With his tooth and his greased-down black curly hair and beads of perspiration, Suzy couldn't help but imagine a brothel keeper in Tijuana, as he quietly closed the door behind him. Suzy had a wild outrageous visual mind at times… "He's probably a sweet fellow," she smiled. .

Suzy ran over to the window that overlooked Third Avenue. On her right was the Chrysler building, the Empire State Building, and in the distance was the East River; beyond that, the twin towers of the World Trade Center.

All the twinkling lights that danced before her in the night seemed like a sea of sparkling diamonds. Below, the yellow cabs and honking traffic hustled and bustled toward Germantown. The people looked like ants as they scurried along Third Avenue. There, before her, was a fairyland that was absolutely magical. Yes, New York was an incredible sight to behold. You could feel the electricity in the air.

She was overwhelmed. Her eyes lit up; clapping her hands to her face, she exclaimed, "Isn't this exciting?" Paul was smiling, as he felt her excitement. Then Suzy noticed an open penthouse window in the building across the street. A woman lay on a bed while watching TV. The drapes were wide open, exposing her and the brightly lit room. Suzy thought of the James Stewart movie *Rear Window*, where he could see into all the apartments in his complex. As Suzy watched, the woman moved her arm behind her head, shifting her body slightly. It was like looking at a live mannequin in Macy's shop window.

"Why doesn't she close her drapes?"

Paul laughed, embarrassed. "I dunno; she never does." Suzy noticed how easily Paul got embarrassed. *How funny*, she thought.

When Suzy awoke, she felt exhilarated as she looked around the room, hearing the roaring traffic below. Paul was reading the paper in the kitchen.

"Good morning!"

"Sleep well?" he offered.

"Yes, thanks."

She wandered into the living room. A feeling of newness, a fresh beginning in a new city, swept over her. The apartment was a one bedroom unit, with beautiful hardwood floors, Chinese rugs, cove molding along the ceilings, and hot water radiators like those in the old buildings that she remembered back in England. The living room was hung with so many paintings that they covered the walls. Most were paintings and sketches: New York City scenes rendered in oil, tempera, watercolor and pen and ink.

One was a scene of a child looking up at the Statue of Liberty; his eyes shone with awe as he held a hand to his cheek while his scarf blew back behind him in the breeze. She moved closer and recognized the Chrysler Building and the Guggenheim Museum in several of the works; she bent forward and spotted a lithographic print of the Brooklyn Bridge, and above that was a sketch of Broadway and Radio City Music Hall. There was an exquisite watercolor of a nineteenth century couple enjoying a carriage ride through a snow-covered Central Park with snow-covered trees above. These were gems that Paul had found over the years. He had a keen eye for beauty, and a delicate flair for recognizing originality in the works of unknown artists. Against one wall was a beige couch, above which hung a late eighteenth century oil painting in an elaborate frame with a special light above it. She surmised it had been found during one of his trips to France. Two high-backed chairs with a mahogany coffee table added a nice touch. She found it all so charming, warm and inviting. So really lovely.

Down the hallway was Paul's bedroom. He bought the Empire-styled sleigh bed from his dear friend who owned furniture stores in New Jersey. The immaculate bathroom was old fashioned with a claw-foot, stand-alone tub and black and white tiling, all very charming.

Although there wasn't a lot of closet space in the apartment, there was just enough for the two of them, with a lot of forethought and planning.

Opening the fridge, Suzy saw only a few items, mainly milk, bread and eggs, some oranges, peaches, and Fuji apples, but that was about it. Some frozen food items—organic perhaps; she couldn't quite tell—but no meat or vegetables. *A real bachelor's pad,* she thought.

Suzy checked the cupboards. Plates, cups, saucers, a teapot, a tin of tea, and vitamins, lots of vitamins, vitamins packed and stacked everywhere. More than enough to make a wimpy, paltry boy into Hercules. She examined a small selection of the bottles: Saw Palmetto, Vitamin B, B6, B12, C, D, Selenium, Potassium, Astragalus, Yohimbe, Vitamin E, Zinc, L-Carnitine, to name a few. My God, he had a fortune invested here. *Why the hell does he look so sickly?* She put the bottles back in the cupboard.

"What do you want for breakfast?" she called out as she stood outside the bathroom.

"Two boiled eggs and tea, please."

"How many minutes?"

"Three minutes and twenty seconds!" She glanced around for the egg timer.

Breakfast was on the table as Paul sauntered back from the bathroom, wearing his robe, socks, and slippers. Sexy. In a *Father Knows Best* kind of way. He flung open the cupboard, grabbed a bunch of bottles, emptied the pills into his hand, and gulped them down with orange juice. He poured himself another glass of orange juice, selected another batch of vitamins, repeated the whole process. And then as she stood there, her mouth agape, dazed by this illusion, he repeated the process once again, including the orange juice, all with a mechanical precision that was robotic.

"Are you all right? Isn't that a lot of pills? You're not sick, are you?"

"Oh no. I take these vitamins every day. I feel great; been taking them for years!"

"Jeez, you should damn well feel fantastic after all that! It's amazing you don't choke on all those pills. Here, have your breakfast. The tea is over there." She stepped back into the kitchen. "I couldn't find any coffee." She peeked into the cupboard under the sink.

"Never drink coffee!" he snapped. "It is bad for you! It's the worst thing you can do to yourself!" he barked at her. Suzy flinched at his tone, at the crisp brittleness of it, and wondered how she'd managed to miss Paul's aversion to coffee, and all the health advice, in all the time she had known him.

"I thought that was smoking? Isn't that the worst thing?" He ignored her. Again, her wit went over like a lead balloon with Paul so she changed the subject. "I think we need to get some food. Perhaps we can go shopping," she suggested.

"Yes, there is D'Agostino's just around the corner. You can take care of it."

Suzy put on her shoes and grabbed her purse, heading toward the door. Paul, busy on the phone, sprang from the couch, felt in his pocket and handed her two twenties. She looked at them like they were a couple of dog turds.

"What's this? You're giving me $40? What, to buy a week's worth of groceries? For two people?" Suzy stared at him. "Are you kidding?"

Paul was indignant. "That's plenty!" He was irritated with her.

Shaking her head, she walked out the door. Once at D'Agostino's, she bought what she thought Paul would enjoy: a little chicken, ground beef, some vegetables, and canned goods. Suzy brought them home, put them away, then decided to search the newspaper want ads. After all, she was not on vacation. She circled positions that might be interesting. This was going to be a time of adjustment for both of them; it was all new and there would definitely be some ups and downs, but for now Suzy was concentrating on finding a job.

"I guess I'd better turn in," Suzy said late in the evening, after dinner. She slowly got up from the sofa. "It's been quite an exciting day. I hope I get some phone calls soon!" she said lightly and walked to the hallway closet. She put her shoes in the closet, grabbed the nightdress from the hanger, went into the bathroom to change, washed her face, and prepared for bed. She was exhausted.

Putting on her nightdress, Suzy came out of the bathroom and slipped under the covers. Paul was already in bed; the radio was on an AM station, some health program. She listened for a few minutes, kissed him goodnight, and turned toward the wall. He then rustled around, putting in his earplugs, and turned the dial to another station—now it was the BBC from London.

He flopped back down; she turned around to check the time. It was after midnight. Sighing, she tossed and turned, while the buzz of the radio kept her awake, but eventually she fell into a fitful sleep.

Suzy could have sworn she heard a voice in the distance. Who was he talking to? Who was here?

"I am very disappointed in you. I can't believe you did that!" Paul's loud, biting voice started to cut through her stupor. He was standing in front of the bed.

"What? What?" She tried to sit up but her head was fuzzy from lack of sleep. "What's wrong?" She was having a hard time understanding what he was talking about.

"I am very disappointed in you," he repeated. "I can't believe you did *THAT* - is what I said."

"I, uh, I don't get it. I don't understand. Whaat? What did I do?" she whispered, brushing her hair out of her eyes, still trying to get her brain caught up with the conversation. Unless the house was on fire, mornings and Suzy did not get along well. At all.

"*THIS!*" He hissed loudly like an angry cobra, pointed to a can in his left hand. "*THIS!!*" He looked accusingly at her. "Why would you buy this?" His eyes turned icy grey.

"What? What? I…what the hell are you talking about?" she repeated in a whisper, while now sitting upright, rubbing her eyes.

"You bought *CANNED* fruit - canned fruit! Was there no fresh fruit in the entire grocery store? How dare you!" His slitted eyes shot daggers at her.

"Oh! No problem. I'll take it back," she offered, still not quite sure of the terrible crime she had committed. *Did Paul really mean to wake me up over canned fruit? Surely not.*

Mornings were not Suzy's favorite time of day; she had to be gently cajoled into the day and treated with kid gloves until she could make it on her own, which usually took a few hours to get her into kick-butt mode, and then it was Watch out, world! *Hmmm, I hope he doesn't do that again,* she thought. Little did he know he was treading on thin ice and that would not be good.

Suzy decided to make Paul one of his favorite dishes as a peace offering for buying *gasp* canned fruit. Paul's favorite food was meatloaf. All men liked meatloaf for some reason; maybe it made them think of their mother's home cooking. Homemade meatloaf with mashed potatoes and gravy, a salad and broccoli. Very nutritious. And high protein. That should please him.

Suzy heard the key turn in the door. She turned on the TV for him to view the 6 o'clock news while she put the salad dishes on the table.

"Hi there, had a good day?" As he walked in, she was breezily placing the dishes on the table, pouring the water into the glasses.

"Oh, hi, yes, everything was fine." Looking at the table set, he seemed pleased. "Mmmm, something smells good!" He turned off the TV.

Suzy spun around. "Oh, I thought you would like to watch the news!"

Sitting down at the table he explained, "I don't like a lot of extraneous noise when I'm eating. I learned this when I was in Japan. They look upon the meal as a ritual to enjoy and a time to talk softly, to quietly discuss the day," he said quietly.

Suzy put the plates out and sat down across from him. "Oh! That sounds nice, interesting!" She served him the meatloaf.

"Mmm, this looks wonderful. I see I kept you busy today!" His face lit up, looking at the spread in front of him. Being a bachelor all these years, it was obviously quite a treat for him to be served a home-cooked meal after a long, hard day.

"Thank you, Paul, I hope you like it," she smiled cheerily as she poured the wine. She placed the meatloaf on her fork, raised it in midair, and as she was about to take a bite, it started! Chomp, chomp, chomp, slurp, chomp, chomp, chomp, as he smacked his lips with every mouthful. She watched in disbelief. Oh-oh, glass raised to mouth, slurp, glass put down, fork in hand, chomp, chomp. Suzy stared, horrified. *Holy Mother of God! What the hell is this!* The stillness of the room echoed and amplified every mouthful, tenfold.

"Well, I said to my boss at lunch," he started, paused, looked out the window, and then at his plate, "I was hoping for a better position…" His voice droned on although Suzy didn't hear a thing he was saying. She was too engrossed in listening to the lips smacking, another swill of water and the open mouth chewing. He had the manners of a mastiff.

"This is unbelievable," she said under her breath. "Who would have thought that someone so refined, so educated would eat like a complete slob?" Sure, when they ate at a restaurant on a date, there was the noise of the patrons along with the bustle of the staff, to drown out the noisy and obnoxious mastication of the meal but Suzy suspected that he was self-conscious in public and watched his manners. She played with her food, deep in thought, looking across the way. Paul noticed her quietness.

"Anything wrong, Suzy?" His head was cocked to one side; his fork, held in mid-air, had a large wad of broccoli embedded in its tines. He noisily devoured the broccoli, then scooped up the mashed potatoes and gravy and slurped them down, mopping a drop of gravy from the corner of his mouth. "Mmmm, the mashed potatoes and gravy are delicious." He scooped another mouthful. Chomp, chomp, chomp … he was in seventh heaven.

Suzy looked up. "Huh? Oh, no, I'm glad you're enjoying the meatloaf!" She smiled wryly, got up and started putting the dishes in the sink.

CHAPTER TWENTY

S uzy had been in New York for several days when Paul set up a dinner-date night out. He had a variety of dear friends and tonight Sam, his cousin, was picking them up. Paul and Sam were cousins from the Bronx; they had gone to high school together at one time, and then stayed in touch all these years. He owned several liquor stores in Manhattan and New Jersey.

"You'll like him; he knows every good restaurant in New York." Paul paused, then lowered his voice. "He just married this, this young Latina girl. I don't know why he goes for them." He shook his head; his blue eyes stared off into space. "His ex-wife was beautiful and very elegant. I have no idea why he married this one. He's had a lot of beautiful women but…this one especially. I can't figure it out, but you'll see!" he warned.

The bell rang in the apartment. Paul leapt over to answer it. "Come on! Sam's here!" Paul called out to her. "And he's probably double parked!" They flew out the door and ran to the elevator.

Sam stretched out his hand and smiled. "Welcome to New York! Nice to meet you, Suzy."

Carita, his new young wife in the front passenger seat, looked up, smiled, waving to her. "Hi! How are you?"

Sam opened the rear door for them. "We thought you might like a ride to Chinatown. They have some excellent restaurants there. Hey Suzy, you'll love this place, won't she, Paul?"

Suzy smiled as Sam glanced at her in the rear view mirror as he got behind the wheel.

"I'm sure I'll be impressed. Paul has told me all about you! I hear if you don't know a good restaurant, then nobody does!" She laughed lightly to punctuate the thought.

Paul lurched toward her as they rounded a corner unexpectedly. "See, see, see what I mean?" He shook his head vigorously; his big blue expressive eyes widened. His hairpiece bounced about with every bump on the road, as if it were trying to escape through the open car window. Suzy struggled not to laugh aloud. Lowering his voice, Paul said, "This, this - is what he wound up with! She looks like she comes from the Andes mountains." Scowling, he spoke quietly. "She doesn't know how to dress. She doesn't speak the language, and she was a maid at his father's house, for God's sake! I tried to talk him out of it, but he wouldn't listen. It's no use!" He went on, teeth clenched, his hissing whisper barely audible, "And wait until she gets older and starts to blimp out, you'll see!"

Suzy looked on, aghast. Thank God, Sam had the radio on and was chatting with his wife.

"So, Carita," Paul suddenly addressed her. He spoke to her loudly and slowly as if she were deaf and a lip reader, "How- is- the- English- coming -along?"

Carita was certainly no beauty. She had short, straight black hair, a brown complexion, and the flat features of an indigenous Indian culture, and she was a little plump. Nonetheless, she was a pleasant girl. Carita turned around, smiled and softly spoke. Her voice sounded like tinkling glass, crisp and delicate.

"Aaahh, si, I- am, ah- doing good! I go ah, - to- school- aver -rree- week," She laughed pleasantly while Sam looked over at her adoringly, as he drove past Delancey Street.

"Eh, bueno, mi amore!" Sam was delighted at her progress. "See, my honey is doing great, huh, Paul?" He reached over and affectionately squeezed Carita's shoulder.

Paul slid back down into the back seat and stared at Suzy. "Oh yeah, she'll be conversing with you in no time!" he called out to Sam. He then turned his head toward the window, and smirked.

It was a storefront type restaurant, nothing fancy, but there were long lines to enter this establishment. It was one of those excellent restaurants catering to the local clientele, a gem not known to the rest of the tourists. Dinner was certainly a gastronomical experience, as promised, of succulent dishes that were brought to the table. Sam adored food as much as he loved women. He was a great host, insisting that they try several of the house specialties as he baby-fed his Carita a lobster morsel. "Here honey, try this!"

This time, he fork-fed her a cube of prime pepper steak as another platter arrived. The waiter laid down another steaming hot dish. This time, a huge black fish overlapped the dish, staring glassy-eyed, with a gaping mouth, directly at Paul.

As the waiter laid it down, Paul took one look, screamed, flew back into his seat, turned twenty shades of green, flailing his hands up vigorously as if trying to protect himself from the horror, while rolling his head back in disgust, screaming, "Take it away! Take it away! Jeez, I can't bear to look!" He shuddered in disgust, squirming, clutching his chest. His hairpiece slipped down, poised to take a swan dive into his soup. "Jesus, I can't. Take it away, waiter, take it away!" He sounded like a squealing pig, covering his eyes. "At least chop the goddamn head off! I can't stand it looking at me!" He whined, once again he squirmed in his seat. "It turned my stomach! Ugh!"

Upon hearing the screams, the waiter dove into the middle of the table swept the platter up hastily, whisked it back to the kitchen.

Hearing Paul's screaming, all the patrons of the restaurant stopped in silence, turned and stared, heads bobbing around to see. Sam, embarrassed, then recovering, began to grin and waved and nodded to the sea of eyes surrounding them. Geez, take a bow already. Light laughter then danced around the room as everyone went back to enjoying their dinners, though still eyeing Paul from the corners of their eyes.

"What the…?"

Carita and Suzy looked at each other, then at Paul, and then back to each other. Neither had seen the fish in the first place; they missed it all as they were concentrating on eating what they had on their plates, and the sudden outburst from Paul, screaming and floundering around, unnerved them.

"What the hell happened?…?" Their expressions were solemn, quizzical. But then, simultaneously, they both put their hands over their mouths as they strived to stifle their laughter and the more they struggled to hold it back, the worse it became, until they both exploded into convulsive laughter. Paul scowled at them, but they couldn't stop. The more he scowled, the harder they laughed until both had tears in their eyes.

"Sorry. I didn't mean to laugh," Suzy wiped her eyes with the napkin, "but you looked so funny, we couldn't help it!" She cupped her fingers with the napkin around her eye and pulled a face, grinning at Carita, then both of them convulsed into laughter again. She then picked up her fork, regaining her composure, and helped herself to the duck. "How about some of this for you?" she asked Paul consolingly.

Sam turned to Suzy. "So Suzy, how are you enjoying New York?"

"Oh!" She deftly patted her lips with her napkin. "It takes getting used to, I guess, but it won't take me too long, I hope!" She smiled.

Carita looked at her. "Si, when I come here, eet take me long time more! Beeg town!"

Sam comforted her, "Don't worry, you're doing great!" They certainly were a likeable couple.

CHAPTER TWENTY-ONE

P aul had gone for several job interviews. He was taking his time. After all, he was in early retirement and in no rush but still, reading the *New York Times* was limiting and there was only so much running errands he could do to take up his time.

"Guess what! My brother Sandy told me there's a position as a judge in the Health Department at the courthouse and I could qualify. You know I don't want anything full time, and this job is only three days a week!" he said brightly.

"Oh, Paul, I am excited for you!" she said with all sincerity. "I think it would be great for you. After all, you're too young to just sit at home. So when does the position start?"

"I should be able to start within a month, after a bunch of formalities—hoops to jump though first. But it's doable."

After getting ready for bed, Suzy lay down, straightening out, and tried to relax. Paul lay next to her like a stiff in the morgue, eyes closed, arms at his side.

Sharing the queen size bed was fine even with his ersatz rigor mortis, except that Paul forgot to tell her that he listened to the radio all night, in between catnaps. All night! And every night! The buzz of human voices was terribly distracting as he flipped from one radio station to the other. She didn't want conversationalists' busy-bee buzzing at midnight, 2 a.m., or 4:30 a.m. She heaved and tossed and turned relentlessly, even with the covers pulled over her ears. Sleep was what she wanted, wonderfully refreshing sleep, as she was getting very cranky due to the lack of it. However, this was Paul's nightly ritual. Another thing he forgot to mention to her. She tossed and turned but no matter what, she couldn't drown out the sound. The constant buzzing of the radio turned her night's rest into a living nightmare. She needed complete quiet to sleep. And to get up in the morning and make appointments for job interviews was sapping all of her strength after being awake most of the night with Dr. Upton and the BBC World News with talk show after talk show throughout the night. She could not care less about the state of the economy, what was happening in Washington, how Bill was doing in the polls and what Hillary was up to, and if Vincent Foster had been killed or committed suicide. Any time between 8:30 a.m. and maybe midnight was OK, but after that, she didn't want to hear it. In the mornings, she felt so tired, as she stumbled out of bed and got dressed, while still stifling yawns.

Every week, Suzy got dressed, and ran from one end of town to the other. Between getting lost, the rough push and shove mentality of the city, and the constant walking up and down the different avenues in high heels, her feet began to hurt.

Another hot, sizzling day in the Big Apple. Suzy dialed the number, pen in hand, newspaper on the kitchen table. "Yes, I am calling about the position you advertised in the paper...And where are you located, please? What time? And who shall I ask for? I'll be there, thank you." This was her new mantra. And off she went, scurrying to all corners of Manhattan, across town on a bus and cab rides across to the West Side through the park. Down into the belly of the subway, up and down escalators, shooting up to the 80th floor in these skyscrapers, down into dingy basement offices. "Over here, lady!" the man would say gruffly, chewing on a stogie, grabbing her resume from her. "We'll call you next week!"

Manhattan is only about thirteen miles long and approximately two miles wide, with a population of 1.5 million. What was the problem? she wondered. She spoke well, she was neat, her clothes were pressed and coordinated, she didn't have a revolving third eye on her forehead, didn't have green teeth, or dragon breath.

By this point, New York had certainly lost a lot of its glitter. Resume after resume... "Oh, yes, that would be fine. We will make our decision early next week and let you know" with their phony icy smile. Yes, it's true, Frank Sinatra was right. "If you can make it there, you can make it anywhere, New York, New York." How well she was beginning to find out. All she wanted was a frigging job. She wasn't going for CEO of Chase Manhattan bank, or running for Mayor of New York, for chrissake!

Suzy actually went for a job interview at the famous diet doctor Dr. Upton's office and factory. The same Dr. Upton that was on the radio, Paul's guru. She walked into this magnificent building with polished marble floors and ornate columns. To the right was the Apothecary section with white lab-coated gentlemen dispensing all kinds of potent pills and potions to cure and revitalize the body. Everything was white, the walls and the floors, very sanitized. And very opulent. Her eyes widened in admiration No expense spared. So very impressive.

She took a seat opposite the straggly-haired interviewer, who went on to inform Suzy the position was for 37 1/2 hours a week and "your salary, of course will be commensurate with your experience," blah, blah, blah, blah.

Really ... to be a receptionist? Thirty-seven and a half hours a week!

Suzy stopped listening at this point. Words were being mouthed, but they were soundless. She must have had a silly grin on her face and nodded eagerly, while envisioning herself saying, "Oh yes, I'd LOVE to work 37 and

1/2 hours each week for you, O God Almighty," swooning at the prospect, falling to her knees and kissing the ground of the O Hallowed One, the greatest doctor in Manhattan, and dare I say, modestly perhaps, the world!

Oh, I see, it's not a 40 hour week, so that means I will not be entitled to healthcare insurance. You penny-pinching misers! Oh, I know what that means, I'll have to buy your vitamins to stay healthy. Is that your MO? But how could I pass up this golden opportunity to be a pauper, as you rake in millions with your books, products for a Slimmer You, vitamins to cure most maladies, and radio show? Wow! Just think, with that salary, I could live very comfortably under a bridge by the river in a cardboard box (maybe two if I'm lucky – a doublewide) with the rest of the homeless. The interviewer went on and on until Suzy, dazed, snapped back into the conversation.

"Uh, Miss Grant," the interviewer said in a crisp, efficient voice, looking over the top of her glasses at Suzy, pen in hand, "as far as your goals are concerned, where" - she stressed the *WHERE* and sniffed -, "do you want to be five years from now?"

Suzy looked squarely at her. Smiling sweetly, she gushed, "Oh, that's easy, I'd like your position!" There was a deathly silence for a second. The interviewer glared grimly and rose from her chair. "Thank you for coming; we'll let you know," she said icily, and pointed to the door. "Next!"

Needless to say, Suzy did not get the position. Nor did she expect to, or want to.

After numerous interviews with a variety of companies, she had decided to use an agency. On Thursday the phone rang. "Suzy, I just spoke to Andrea," gushed the young man from the agency, "and they really like you. They're going to make their decision today, so why don't you give me a number where I can reach you later?"

"I'll be home; you can try here!" She was thrilled. She wanted to work; her bills were depleting her account back home, and funds were really low at this point!

"It looks real good, so I'll call you later!" He sounded excited and his excitement was contagious.

Suzy had errands to run, but she decided to wait at home for the phone call. She looked at her watch; it was only 10:15 a.m. She finished ironing Paul's shirts and a couple pairs of pants, and decided to have a cup of tea. As she sat down by the window in the kitchen she peered at the clock on the wall; it was almost 1:00. Sipping on the tea, she glanced outside the window. The weather looked a little on the gray side, probably going to get cooler. After all, it was November. Across the street, in the next building, as usual, the body in the penthouse was flopped on the bed watching TV. Suzy shook her head. The woman never seemed to do anything but stay in bed and watch TV. No matter whether it was morning, noon or night, if you looked over at her, there she was, sprawled out on the bed with the room's bright light blazing as she stared at the TV in front of her, with the drapes flung wide open. Never had she seen the body even stand up! It was all too weird. She wondered if the woman was an invalid. Well, if she was, then wouldn't someone be taking care of her, at least occasionally? But no, there was never another person around. She had to eat, didn't she? She never saw her eat. The terrace was very pretty with trees and potted plants, but once again, nobody ever watered or tended them. She needed Jimmy Stewart with his binoculars from *Rear Window* to solve this mystery. He knew everything going on in those buildings. And I mean, *everything*! Anything moved, he was on it!

She looked at her watch; it was now 2:15. Suzy walked slowly into the living room. She sat down on the couch and flicked through the New York Times, barely comprehending the headlines, let alone the news of the day. She sighed, slowly glancing at her watch; it was 3:20.Time for some fresh coffee, she thought. Maybe that would cheer her up. Slowly getting up from the kitchen table, stretching her back muscles, she sauntered into the bedroom and glumly stared at the phone. Her eyes looked wearily around the room. She flopped on the bed then turned on the radio. Schubert's piano concerto filled the air; it was soothing yet it did not lessen her anxiety. She picked up the magazine by the nightstand. *Time* magazine, another country's leader's face on the front cover with military planes and their flag in the foggy distance. *Jesus,* she wearily thought, *I am overdosing on politics today.* She flicked through another session of world events, quickly glancing over at Paul's travel clock on the nightstand. It was now ten to five. Suddenly, the phone rang. She leapt up off the bed, her heart racing.

"Oh, thank God!" She excitedly picked it up. Just as she uttered "Hello" the phone clicked dead on the other end. "Damn it!" Looking up to the ceiling, she blinked back the tears and sighed.

CHAPTER TWENTY-TWO

Paul loved the horses, which didn't surprise Suzy in the least since he could be a real horse's ass at times. Since horseracing was the sport of kings, Paul often (wrongly) fancied himself a descendent of some medieval king, causing him to anticipate his week in Saratoga each summer like a child awaited Christmas. Paul's friend Arnie and his wife Beth also went to Saratoga every summer, so all four of them got together for a weeklong party filled with betting, drinks, meals, and good times with good friends. This particular year, they would attend a concert by the one and only Miss Diana Ross.

Arnie and Beth had a house in the Adirondacks near Lake George where they spent summers and invited Paul and Suzy to join them there as well. Arnie was a tall, handsome professor from Columbia University. Suzy and he had met briefly several times on the West Side, at Arnie and Beth's apartment. Arnie, as hard as he tried, could not resist touching Suzy. She intrigued him. Whenever she walked into the room, his eyes lit up and he rushed over. "Oh, hi, Suzy! How are you?" he exclaimed in a delighted, expectant tone. He would always pat her on the top of her head lightly as if patting a dog, as she patiently waited for him to stop. It was really annoying, but she didn't have the heart to tell him. It was sweet, really innocent, in its own way. He just couldn't help himself. And although he had the hots for her, he always restrained himself; she knew he was totally harmless. Oh, let him his have his naughty fantasy, she smiled inwardly. She wondered if at night he would fantasize about her while making love to his wife. Perhaps knowing that Suzy was taboo made it more exciting. Who knows what runs through a man's head? Hey, it happens every day. Even holier than thou President Jimmy Carter, who is devoted to his wife Rosalynn, confessed he had "lusted in his heart." So why shouldn't Arnie? Men are men, after all. Arnie's wife Beth was a warm, cheery lady, kind of artsy-fartsy. Suzy liked her very much and she enjoyed chatting with her. They would go for long walks together in the Adirondacks, shopping and to lunch while the men stayed behind reading their papers in the garden.

It was decided that Paul and Suzy would meet up with them after the races in Saratoga, where Diana Ross would perform that evening at the Saratoga Performing Arts Center, an outdoor amphitheater close by. Suzy was thrilled. At least, despite all their problems, she always appreciated that he took her to nice places, so there was some compensation.

Saratoga, also known for the Saratoga Springs nearby, was just delight-ful, very picturesque, and charming. It's the oldest thoroughbred race course in America, which opened in 1863, and the first horse to win there was Lizzie W. Saratoga was home to the Travers Stakes and many famous horses like Gallant Fox, Kelso, Cigar, Alydar, Fourstardave, Longfellow and Sea Biscuit had won on this course. Notably Secretariat and Man O'War, two of the greatest thoroughbreds in history, had shocked punters by losing there, after Secretariat's glorious record of winning the Kentucky Derby in less than two minutes and being the first horse to win the Triple Crown in twenty five years, and Man O'War, who had won Aqueduct where he was a two and a half length winner, won the Preakness Stakes and the Belmont Stakes by a mindboggling twenty length lead in less than two minutes and fifteen seconds but who lost to Upset at Saratoga, which was now known as the graveyard of champions.

It was also the site for a James Bond movie, *Diamonds are Forever*, starring Sean Connery. Gee, Paul had a mountain of knowledge regarding this subject, she thought. She wondered how much all this knowledge had cost him in losses from the track.

As they approached the entrance to the race course, Suzy was enthralled to see the statuesque white fountain surrounded by jockeys in different colors and the white latticework on the walls of the building with the boxes of red and white geraniums surrounding the buildings. In the midst stood a bronze statue of Sea Hero, the 1993 winner of the Kentucky Derby and The Travers Stakes here in Saratoga.

It was a sleepy, hot, sultry day, and yet there was a buzz of excitement in the air as they strolled through the grounds. They watched the horses canter in the distance as they exercised on the track. It was just gorgeous! Suzy was entranced, so excited, as she looked around. Suzy and Paul sat on a bench in the shade, facing the art show, eating an ice cream. It was early yet when Paul brought out the racing form and studied it. She lazily watched him; he was totally absorbed. He wore his cap over his eyes with his binoculars hanging from his neck. She studied his profile. Oh no... Before her very eyes, the "other" Paul, the evil twin, emerged. She watched the transformation with horror. His jaw jutted out, his eyes glazed over. The determination to pick the winners was real. *For a change,* she thought, as he slowly began to furiously scratch and underline each race. He wasn't bad looking—not great looking, but not bad looking. Not wanting to disturb him—for a fortune was riding on these precious moments of sheer concentration, she hoped—she slowly ambled over to the art show display ahead, where there were some interesting pieces from past winners. To her right, the Victorian stadium was beautifully dazzling with its ornate white woodwork and a sea of boxed geraniums and billowing bougainvillea, all in sun-drenched, vivid hues of red, pink and purple. *It's so beautiful here!* She marveled at the loveliness; everything was mowed, trimmed and freshly painted. It was all picture-perfect.

Saratoga was a work of art in itself, and the art show was just a distraction as she walked back over to Paul and sat down next to him. The visor on his cap pressed low onto the top of his sunglasses. With his head bowed, pencil poised, while maintaining a continual muttering to the unseen gods, he squinted into the racing form, totally engrossed. Picking out at least two winners by now, she hoped.

"What time is it, please?" she heard a soft, feminine voice next to her ask. The woman had soft brown eyes, a big straw hat perched over one eye, wearing a blue pantsuit, a newspaper spread out on her lap.

Suzy looked down at her watch. "Almost 11:30," she answered. The two women started talking. "It's so beautiful here!" Suzy gazed as she noticed the cascades of flowers surrounding them. Splashes of red, pink, white, purple and yellow billowed beautifully from each railing.

"Oh, yes, this is the oldest track in the country, I believe!" she answered. "I've been here many times over the years, my husband was a jockey. I'm Maria Hernandez." Suzy looked at her, noticing her soft, lyrical accent.

Upon hearing her name, Paul perked up and looked over. "Are you related to Johnny Hernandez?"

"Yes," she said quietly, nodding, "that was my husband."

"Was he from Puerto Rico? A jockey in the 60s, if I recall," he went on. "Yes, a very fine jockey". Paul looked up into the distance. "Yes, didn't he win the Belmont in 1969?"

"Yes!" Maria was delighted that he remembered. "Yes. That's right!" Her eyes sparkled and her hand flew to her face in awe. "I can't believe you remembered! I am so impressed! We also came here in the season for many years, but then he retired, as you know."

Suzy sat there, listening. Curiosity always got the better of her. Turning to the woman, she asked, "So what brings you here today?" The woman didn't look that old to have a husband that retired in the 70s; here it was the 90s—how old could she be?

Maria laughed softly, "Ah, now my son! He's an apprentice. He's riding today. Pancho Hernandez - he's running in the fourth and tenth races today." She smiled with pride.

Suzy was thrilled for her. "Oh, how exciting! You must have been to all the tracks all over the country!"

Maria smiled.

"Yesterday, there was such a terrible accident," Suzy said and her eyes widened as she spoke. "They took one of the jockeys to the hospital and they had to shoot the horse! Right there; I saw it!" She pointed to the other side, way over on the other side of the track.

The woman glanced over as she spoke. And with that, Paul cleared his throat noisily and nervously shifted from side to side, slapping the racing form on his thigh. Suzy looked over to him, noticing his face had turned to granite. He sprang to his feet, hissing. "Suzy, can I see you a minute?" His eyes had turned to two steel bullets in his head.

She looked up, bewildered, as he held her arm firmly while he strode into a clearing. Looking quickly from side to side, making sure nobody heard him, he hissed, "How dare you talk like *THAT?!*"

His eyes were blazing, his nose almost poking hers. "Why are you telling her this?" His face contorted in fury. "She does not want to hear this! Do you hear me, do you hear me???" he hissed louder. "I, I, I…" Now he began to stutter in fury. "I don't understand you," he went on. "You just say anything that comes into your mind! Anywhere, anyhow! It makes no difference! I really don't understand *YOU*!!"

Suzy stood there, her heart beating faster and faster. She felt sharp pains, as if a dagger was hacking repeatedly into her stomach, while he carried on, repeatedly berating her, "I really don't understand you!"

Watching his mouth, contorting and twisting as he spoke, somehow it seemed like it was as big as a 50-foot tall Imax screen, battering her brain and beating her with every word and motion. On and on he went; there was no stopping him. Everything was a blur to her now; her head was swimming; she felt weak and exhausted.

"Do you hear *ME?*"

She looked up, dazed. "What?" she whispered.

"I asked, did you hear me?" he demanded.

Her mind was fogged; she didn't know what the hell he said; confusion reigned. She blocked out his voice ten minutes ago.

Stunned, she nodded wearily. Anything to shut him up.

"I'm going to the seats now!" He glared at her. "And if I don't see you, we'll meet by the gates over there at five. Remember, we're meeting Arnie tonight!" Turning on his heels, he tore off toward the crowd.

In a hollow, dejected voice, she muttered, "I'll see you later." Her eyes followed him as she watched his head bobbing up and down as he passed through the crowd. She had wanted to smack him in the worst way. Looking at her watch, it was now 12:30, post time. *God, another five hours to go; hopefully he'll cool off by then.*

Later, when they got into the car, Paul was silent. They both avoided eye contact. At a local grocery store they grabbed some cold cuts, potato salad, and some sandwiches made from freshly baked whole grain bread and some sodas. Despite Paul's current aloofness creating an uncomfortable vibe between them, she was becoming ever more excited at the thought that in a couple of hours, the great Diana Ross would be performing live in concert at the amphitheatre. Suzy loved glamour, and Diana Ross was the ultimate glamorous star throughout the years. She looked like a star, she acted like a star, she was a star.

Suzy recalled the first time she saw Diana Ross. It was in the early hours of the morning at London's Heathrow airport back in the 60s, the flight arriving from Detroit. This frail, skinny waif wearing a thin, simple cotton dress leaned against a column in the baggage area. Her eyes were sunk into her tired face; her body was weary, seemingly exhausted, as it curved against the concrete column as she waited patiently for her luggage coming down the conveyor belt. There was no one from the record company to meet her and assist her. She was just another passenger in a sea of businessmen and tourists. Nobody recognized her. The Supremes were just starting out then with their first hit record. But tonight, thirty-odd years later, she would hear the words, "Ladies and gentlemen, here she is—the Great, the Glamorous, the One and Only - Miss Diana Ross, in all her glory!" Suzy could hardly contain herself. Paul was in no way, shape or form going to steal her thunder tonight.

"Arnie!" She waved. "Look Paul, they're over there!" she called out as she made her way across the hilly lawn surrounding the amphitheater.

Arnie introduced them to their other friends while Beth was emptying out the Styrofoam cooler. She handed out the sandwiches, cookies and all kinds of goodies, and everybody happily munched away. "Have a cookie, or would you like a piece of cake I made?" Beth handed Suzy a plate.

"Ooh, that cake looks good, I'll try that, if you don't mind, thanks," and she took the piece, and tasted it. "Mmm, absolutely delicious, don't you think?" she asked as she turned to one of the other friends.

They nodded in agreement. "Oh, yes, Beth is an excellent cook. She makes the best."

Suzy handed out the sandwiches and sodas. "You must have one of these. They are absolutely delicious! We just had them made before we came so they're very fresh. The bread just came out of the oven!"

They munched, oohing and aahing over all the tasty goodies. Suzy looked around. The place was getting crowded, and there was an air of excitement in anticipation of the show.

There were seats in the auditorium, but they were expensive. Anyway, their group was having a picnic, and it was such fun sitting on the ground.

Suzy looked around. "Paul!" she shouted. "Why are you up there?"

He was sitting on a low chair that Arnie had brought for him, munching away. Everyone else was sitting on blankets, as there were only a couple of chairs to go around. The setting sun was bathing everything in a beautiful light.

Beth followed Suzy's glance up and over to Paul. "I hope you brought yourselves something to wear," she said, "You know, it gets very cool at night here. Even in the summertime it has gone down to the fifties!"

Paul was rubbing his shoulders; he was getting chilled already. "No, we didn't - maybe you have a spare sweater or a towel, perhaps?" he said.

Beth rummaged around in her pile of clothing. "No, sorry Paul." She rummaged through her bag, trying to find something for him, and lifted up a piece of clothing. "All I have are these leggings if you'd like them." Beth tossed the leggings up to him.

Grateful for anything to keep warm, Paul looked at the leggings as if they were a sweater for an octopus. He decided to lay the larger part, the waist area, on his back and to his neck and then folded the legs around his neck and arms so it looked like he had been jumped from behind by a stilt walker's yoga pants.

Suzy watched quietly for an instant. "Gee, Paul!" she shouted up to him – she couldn't help herself – "Just what you've always wanted! A pair of women's legs wrapped around your neck! Aren't you the lucky one?" She threw herself on the ground, convulsing with laughter. It felt good to get even.

Rolling his eyes heavenward, Paul cringed, turning pink, yellow, orange, and purple simultaneously. He shook his head vigorously from side to side, his coarse scouring pad hair flopping in the breeze.

Sitting bolt upright, Paul began spluttering, and out flew his mouthful of sandwich like someone had just given him the Heimlich. He prayed nobody had heard Suzy's comment, especially his dear friends Arnie and Beth. Suzy felt a tad nervous, thinking Paul might fly, arms and legs outspread, and take her down like a wrestler. But just then, the universe shifted slightly in Suzy's favor.

"Hey you, you son of a bitch!" growled the burly, bearded biker as he leapt up out of his chair when the slobbery sandwich bit hit him on the back of the neck. "What the fuck do you think you're doin'?" He then threw the bite of sandwich back at Paul and watched as it landed on his forehead, the lettuce and mayonnaise dripping down his cheeks like big gloppy tears.

Suzy reeled again. She could see Paul waving his hands around rapidly, begging, as the biker, who was probably on his second six-pack by now, lunged forward.

"It was an accident, I tell you! Hold it! It was an accident. Hey, I'm sorry!" His voice had gone up four octaves by now, sounding like a frightened little girl as he looked up at the gorilla pushing his face into Paul's face as the condiments, now mixed with beads of sweat, were running down his face. He noticed the brute had three black teeth as his lips curled around them in some sort of freakish smile.

Glaring menacingly, the near toothless giant stopped for a second. "Hey, you pansy ass, I'll break your head with one hand. See this?" He curled up his tattooed right bicep, the size of a ham-hock, and balled his hand into a fist. "The next time you'll be eating a knuckle sandwich, got it?"

As the biker spoke, beer and onion-smelling saliva sprayed Paul's face and chest. Blinking as each word sprayed him, Paul turned ashen, his stomach queasy, as he begged for mercy. And with that the gorilla turned away quickly and sat down. His biker friends shot a menacing look at Paul, grinned and toasted him with their beer cans.

Hmmm... Suzy stared as she watched Paul squirm. *I guess what goes around, comes around,* she thought. *Lovin' it,* she smiled to herself impishly.

At that instant, the lights flashed on the stage and a hush came over the crowd. Suzy could hardly breathe, she was so excited. "And now, ladies and gentleman, here she is, the One ... the Only ...Let's hear it for Miss Diana Ross!" The crowd leapt to its feet, whistling and cheering. As the curtain rose, out stepped Diana Ross wearing a stunning red dress, her hair cascading over her shoulders—a marvelous vision of glitz and glamour. She waved to the crowd as she walked to the stage-front microphone as the orchestra played "Ain't No Mountain High Enough" and her backup singers, coming out behind her in the background, swayed with the music. The dazzle effects of the swirling blue and pink lighting flooded the stage from above and below. Suzy sat there, transfixed, breathless, excited, entranced, her eyes gleaming, a rush of joy swept over her. The crowd roared, cat whistling. Thankfully, the day had finally ended on a happy note.

CHAPTER TWENTY-THREE

P aul liked flowers so Suzy stopped by a little florist shop and bought a bouquet. Fresh flowers cheered up the apartment; that's what he said. She really enjoyed walking up and down Madison Avenue. That was her favorite street. She loved all the little boutiques; they fascinated her. There was Zsa Zsa Gabor's mother's jewelry store, Jolie, with all the beautiful baubles in the window. And there were so many designer stores, with the latest fashions in men and women's wear, antiques, the finest beautiful leather shoes, handbags and boots, and jewelry…Myriads of diamonds, sapphires, emeralds galore in all shades and colors. Sparkling rocks mounted as bracelets, rings, necklaces, earrings and watches.

Suzy's dream had always been to have a Piaget watch, with a diamond bezel and Florentine finish. Oh, God did she dream about it, seeing it in magazines and on other women over the years, made her so envious. She remembered walking into a jewelry store in Florida to admire the exact watch in the counter showcase. There she stood, hypnotized by it, her tongue hanging out like a dog looking at a juicy steak, transfixed to the spot.

The handsome tanned salesman watched her and stepped up to the counter. "Hi, how' ya doing?" he smiled at her, looking down at the watch. "So you like it, honey?" he asked in his Southern drawl.

Shyly, she said, "Ooooh, yes!" She was so excited, eyes gleaming.

"So why don't ya try it on?" He bent down and helped put it on her wrist. "There, what do ya think?"

She couldn't believe her eyes! The watch that she always wanted! And finally, after all these years of longing, it was now on her wrist. She had dreamt of this watch over and over, always promising herself that one day she would own one like this. She slowly turned her wrist back and forth; the whole thing was diamonds—bright, twinkling, sparkling diamonds on a white gold strap. She paused, caught up in the moment. She brought it up to the light. Ooooh, her heart skipped a beat. What a masterpiece of Swiss ingenuity this was before her. The price tag hung from it; she daren't look at that—she knew the watch was in the thousands.

"It looks good on you!" the salesman said, smiling, "Real good, honey!"

"But—" she suddenly noticed, rather disappointed, "there are no numbers on it! Only hands!" She looked at the young man; her bubble had just burst. "How can I tell the time?" she wailed, looking sad. Like she could afford to take it home today, gift-wrapped!

He smiled. "Now, honey," he laughed, "when you wear a watch like this," eyeing her, "you don't neeed" - he emphasized the *need* - "to know what time it is!" Gee, what a concept! I got it! She smiled to herself as she remembered the salesman's face.

Passing more stores, she felt quite envious. All this high-end, luxurious merchandise was getting to her, as she pressed her nose against the window. *Gee, wouldn't it be nice to be rich and just buy anything I wanted,* she thought wistfully. Just whip out a credit card and say, "Charge it! Price no object." Then get the chauffeur to put the packages in the limo. Suzy smiled wryly at the thought. One can only dream…

She walked up the street. Her feet hurt, and there was a burning sensation as the bone rubbed on her shoe. It felt as if she was developing a bunion. Suzy was almost home, thank God. She opened the door to the apartment with a sigh of relief, and quickly kicked off her shoes.

"So, how was your day?" she airily said as she arranged the flowers she bought earlier that afternoon. She liked carnations best because they lasted longer, with baby's breath.

"You'll never believe this!" Paul threw his coat and hat on the bed, his briefcase by the chair and came out into the living room and plunked himself down on the couch. His position at the Health Department was certainly keeping him busy, it seemed. "Well, I heard this wild case today!" he muttered into his chest. "This one was a real doozey! This couple has alligators." His big blue eyes widened; he threw his hands up in the air on either side of his head. "Friggin' alligators! Here, in Manhattan. Not one but several. And the wife even sleeps with one! Look, here's the picture!" He was spluttering, as he gave her the photo.

"Alligators? I've slept with some sharks myself – and a few snakes! And let's not forget a few rats, too! Do I know that feeling!" How well she knew. Fortunately the comment went over Paul's head.

"Unbelievable! Here, look at these pictures." He could hardly control himself.

"What!" Suzy's mouth gaped. "No way! How could that be?"

"It seems they have a loft, downtown, off the Village somewhere, and they have these alligators in a huge Jacuzzi and they just flop in and out of it. Then they sleep on the bed. Look at 'em! Can you even believe this?" His eyebrows shot up into his head.

"But how did they get them up there?"

"They must have gotten them as little babies or something and now they have three or four."

"But how could they keep them? I mean, didn't anybody else ever see them? I mean, you can hardly walk in without seeing these mothers! Jeez!"

He scratched his head, shrugging his shoulders. "I think they had them in the attic. Can you imagine? Alligators in the attic in Manhattan! Jeez, this really takes the cake!"

"My God, they look enormous! How many feet are they?" She studied the picture closely. "They must be at least seven or eight feet, don't you think?"

"Must be!"

"So, what do alligators eat?" Suzy was intrigued. "Aren't they carnivorous? What do you think they feed them? They have to spend a fortune on food. Maybe they were eyeing the couple as a possible snack. Boy, the man will be a tasty leg for an appetizer!" she cringed at the thought. "Ok, Ok, I know what they drink. Don't tell me. Yes, I got it...But of course—Gatorade!"

"Let's eat! I have a nice chicken stew for you" She put the plates on the table.

CHAPTER TWENTY-FOUR

I t was the summer of '94. The Adirondacks were about four hours away from Manhattan by Amtrak. The train wound its way past the Hudson River, passing the wine country and the magnificent palatial estates, dotted around the hillsides as they chugged along.

Suzy gazed out the window, impressed. "Just look at all these mansions!" she squealed. "I wonder who lives there?" She pointed upward, while Paul glanced now and then while reading the New York Times from cover to cover. Having taken this trip many times over the years, he was very familiar with the ride, but to Suzy, this was such a thrill. Paul's friend Arnie had invited them to his and Beth's house in the Adirondacks for the weekend. The house was perched on a hillside, and Lake George was farther down below, on the other side of the winding country road.

As soon as Arnie heard Paul's voice in the living, he strode in, his face lit up like a Christmas tree, patting Suzy affectionately on the head. She flashed him one of her smiles; he melted and patted her softly again. He had that sad, longing expression on his face, like a forlorn puppy. She wanted to giggle in the worst way, but stepped back instead.

Beth was busy helping Paul with his bag and showing him their room.

"Bucolic, simply bucolic," is how Paul described it as they watched the boats leisurely passing by. It was an idyllic and relaxing afternoon. Paul and Arnie were reading magazines sitting on the Adirondack deck chairs, beers in hand, catching a few rays while Suzy and Beth went for a walk in the woods nearby.

During the summer, the Adirondacks were so delightful—warm, very pleasant, but at night, the temperature dropped into the 50s or cooler. That first night they were going later to a quaint little restaurant for dinner where Beth enjoyed their famous steaks and a vodka martini with olives.

Suzy sat on the bed, waiting for Paul. She did a double-take as Paul came out of the bathroom. He was dressed and ready for bed, wearing long johns and a thick T-shirt under his flannel pajamas. He also had on wool socks, a thick wool robe with a scarf around his neck and a ski cap covering his head. *He was wrapped up like an Egyptian mummy from the Sphinx!* she thought. "We're not in Antarctica for God's sake." Eyeing the ski cap, "You're not planning on robbing a bank tonight, by any chance?" He ignored her, kicked off his slippers, got into bed, and pulled the covers up to his chin. They lay in the double bed together. With two blankets and a bedspread, Suzy was comfortable, and warm.

She looked at Paul lying there like a corpse, rolled her eyes, and thought, *How in God's name did I wind up with this Sexpot?* She lay in the dark, looked up at the ceiling, and questioned some of her life choices as she watched the car lights reflected on the walls as they passed by. She was glad there was no radio for a change while listening to Paul's rhythmic, light snoring. Shaking her head and sighing, Suzy turned slowly onto her side. Her mind began to wander to the good times she enjoyed as a sweet young thing.

It was London, in the 60s, the Swinging Sixties. What an exciting time. London was sheer magic in those days! One could almost see the electricity in the air. The fashion world of Vogue magazine, Harper's Bazaar and Vanity Fair had page after page of the bouffant-teased beehive hairdos, the smoky dolly eyes, the miniskirt, and the high boots. Young, Free, and Fabulous! Mary Quaint, Jean Shrimpton, and Twiggy were on practically every other page. And then Vidal Sassoon created the geometric and asymmetrical hair cut, which also became an instant hit.

Then there was the music: the Marquee Club on Oxford Street spawned bands like the Rolling Stones, Pink Floyd, David Bowie, Cream, The Who, the Moody Blues, Eric Burdon and the Animals. *"Oh Lord, please don't let me be misunderstood."* Georgie Fame was the big star of the Flamingo Club on Wardour Street, and all the clubs down in basements like the Whisky a GoGo in Soho and Knightsbridge and Kensington where all the stars hung out—it was all there for her. Herman's Hermits, Brian Poole and the Tremeloes, Gerry and the Pacemakers were part of the Mersey Beat. Dusty Springfield's *"You don't have to say you love me"*, Cilla Black, Lulu, Petula Clark's *"Downtown"*, Cliff Richard and the Shadows, Adam Faith and of course the Beatles were exploding on the scene - *"Can't buy me love, can't buy me love"*... *"She's got a ticket to ride"*... *"Help! I need somebody."* Liverpool would never be the same again. The British Invasion was about to take America, and the world, by storm. The trendy Italian restaurants in London—the San Lorenzo and the Terrazza to name a few...

Suzy remembered when she had her first "sexual" experience. God, when youth is too stupid for words. *How sweet, and so innocent we were then*, she thought. If a man held your hand and gave you a shy, quick kiss, was the extent of a really hot date. Virginity was a Badge of Honor in those days, something to be held in high esteem and not to be relinquished until you found Mr. Right and only then to be lost on your wedding night. All that Catholic guilt was stuck in our heads. She still could see her mother's wagging finger and menacing looks of disapproval at the thought. You held on to your virginity for dear life, no matter what, something on the likes of Fort Knox. Totally impenetrable at all costs. Yes, she was going to the altar chaste, untouched by man or beast.

She remembered the date at the Hilton in London many moons ago. It was in the summer. She tapped on the hotel door. It had been left slightly ajar.

"Come on in," the sexy masculine voice inside called to her.

Nervously, she opened the door. She was wearing her black miniskirt, black patent leather pumps, and black stockings with a black lacy blouse. Her dark hair was softly wavy with the flip style, which was popular then. And of course, no British dolly would be caught dead without her eyelashes! Those big doe eyes and porcelain skin made her look even younger than she was.

Suzy's date for the evening reeked of cologne, as if he had bathed in it. He was tall and slim, with a swarthy complexion. His dark hair was slicked back, and he had a cigarette dangling from his hand as he ushered her into the room.

"Come overrr heeeeeerrre, darrling." He stretched his hand out to her and softly held hers, as he looked deep into her eyes. His voice had a strong Middle Eastern accent. Suzy noticed he pronounced the letter "R" with a trill so strong it sounded like the noise playing cards made when sticking it into the spokes of a spinning wheel of a bicycle. He smiled at her while they sat by the window. She could see Green Park and the tall buildings of the city in the distance.

She noticed his suit, a gray silk. The jacket was thrown across the bed. He wore a crisp white shirt with a garish print tie. He took a drag from his cigarette as he studied her.

"So, darrling, your name is Suzy, eh?" He took in her long black-stockinged legs and round, firm breasts that stood at attention. His deep, dark eyes devoured her quickly. She blushed nervously, batting those thick, big eyelashes as she quickly looked down at the floor and nodded.

"Yes, and you are George. It was funny how you chased me up the stairs at the airport to give me your card." She laughed coyly, blushing, embarrassed at his audacity.

"Arre you frrom London, darrling?" he asked, taking another drag from his cigarette then blowing the smoke out the side of his mouth. She noticed his perfect white teeth surrounded by full, voluptuous lips and the trimmed moustache, as he watched her intently.

"Yes, I've lived here for some time now but my family came from the South of England...and where are you from, George?" she asked politely. She looked hesitantly at him. He had very dark eyes that seemed to look right through her. It made her feel uncomfortable.

"Oh, my family is from Beirut. We have a house there and we have another house in Paris. I live in Paris. It's such a beautiful city." He suddenly jumped up. "Would you like a drreenk, darrling?" Moving over to the bar, he offered her a Scotch. He reached for his glass as he poured himself one.

"Oh no," she exclaimed. "No, I don't drink, but thank you. Maybe a Coca-Cola. That would be lovely, thanks." She smiled broadly.

He looked over at her as he stuck a cigarette in the side of his mouth as he carried a drink over for Suzy. "Whew! London is so hot this yearrr. I do believe this is the hottest summerrr for a long time!" He wiped away beads of perspiration from his brow. He took a swig of Scotch, while still staring at her with what seemed like a knowing look in his eyes. "I thought you would like the Beachcomber. It is a verrry nice restaurant. I like it verrry much, darrling." Suzy nodded in agreement, smiling coyly, batting her eyelashes. After all, she was all of eighteen years old now – almost an adult. Taking another sip, George turned to her. "Come, we will be late forr deeeennerrrr." He grabbed his jacket and headed toward the door.

Suzy put her glass down immediately and ran down the hallway after him to the elevator. She got to the elevator just as the doors opened.

The Beachcomber at the Mayfair hotel off Piccadilly was an exotic restaurant with waterfalls and a Hawaiian theme, with tropical drinks and exotic dancers wearing leis and brightly colored skirts and flowers. Many times she had walked by the restaurant.

"And you, madam, what would you like to order?" The handsome Italian waiter with the deepest brown eyes bent forward, flirting with Suzy. His eyes blazed down on her like two hot, burning coals in a sea of creamy brown skin. He flashed a smile of perfect white teeth and soft full lips. She blushed, embarrassed, and batted her eyelashes. George looked up and caught him staring at Suzy. His deep brown eyes clouded over, looking at her and then looking back at him. She sat demurely, not sure what was going on, sipping on her Coca-Cola.

"She will have the beef and fried rice, here," he pointed to the menu, "the same as me." He growled, "And bring me a Mai Tai! Make that two Mai Tais!" He glared at the waiter.

George looked disapprovingly at Suzy, but she was oblivious. He lit another cigarette, snapping the lighter shut. Suzy stared at the lighter; it was a Dunhill with his initials monogrammed on it. It was exquisite.

"What a beautiful lighter." She picked it up as she reached into her bag for a cigarette. George took the lighter out of her hand, reached forward, and lit Suzy's cigarette. In a few minutes, the waiter arrived with their dinner on a silver tray and placed it in front of them. Suzy looked down and did not make eye contact this time. She did not want to upset George.

"Dinner was just heavenly, thank you, George!" Her eyes shone with excitement as she sipped away on her Mai Tai. She felt a little woozy and giggly. George by now was telling her a tale about a lady he had met who invited him back to her place, when they heard footsteps down the hallway.

"And then what did you do?" she giggled, covering her mouth, embarrassed and looked at the tablecloth.

"I had to jump out the window because the husband was coming after me! Thank God it was the first flooorrr."

Gales of laughter exploded from her. Suzy again covered her mouth with the napkin, holding back the laughter. The man at the next table looked disapprovingly at the two of them, while his wife sniffed haughtily, like she smelled something unappealing, and then looked away, appalled at the behavior of Suzy and her date. George paid the check, and the "stiff upper lip" couple watched as they exited the restaurant.

"So, darrling, come and have one leetle drreenk, yes?" he begged, as he led her through the lobby and toward the elevator.

"Oh, yes, I'd like that, George." She was feeling good, quite mellow. *Why not? It's not that late,* she thought, in all her innocence. His lips curled into a big smile, gleaming lecherously at her, as he took her hand.

Unlocking the door at the hotel, he went over to the bar and brought her a Coke and a whiskey for himself. She slipped off her shoes and sat on the bed, sipping on her drink, fanning herself with a menu. It was a little warm in the room even though the windows were open.

"I will be right back, darrling. Make yourself comfortable, heh, darrling?" He smiled lasciviously, as he proceeded to go into the bathroom.

Suzy waved slightly, smiling. She was feeling kind of relaxed and sleepy. She sat cross-legged on the bed. She was enjoying the evening, up here in the clouds on the sixteenth floor of the Hilton with the whole of London twinkling below. She had never been on such a high floor before in her life. It was so dreamy. *Oh! How exciting!* She thought, closing her eyes, smiling to herself.

The bathroom door opened slowly and George called, "Ready or not, here I come." Suddenly, out of the corner of her eye, Suzy caught a glimpse of – *OH MY GOD!* What the...??? Her eyes popped wide open; she flinched and accidentally flung her drink into the air as she jumped off the bed. He was naked! Not only was he naked, but what was ...

"Oh no, *OH HELL NO!*" she screamed in horror. This – this *THING* was peeking around the bathroom door like a submarine periscope and it was aimed right at her. Suzy jumped up like the Road Runner, feet pedaling backwards on an invisible bike in mid air – meep, meep! Holy Mother of God, he was naked! Suzy had never seen a naked man before in her life!.

"Oh no," she cried hysterically. "Help, somebody help me!" She was tearing around the room, dodging George and his ginormous manhood. She grabbed her shoes and handbag and, too scared to turn her back on the scene, she hurriedly backed up toward the door, grappling nervously for the handle behind her back. Suzy found it hard to breathe as her throat closed up. She tried to scream but nothing came out, as if she was in a dream (please God, let it be a dream) and she felt her heart racing. She could even feel her heartbeat in her ears.

Finally, Suzy got the door open and ran as fast as her legs could carry her down the hallway toward the elevator, terrified that George would run after her. She punched the button frantically for the elevator, hurriedly putting on her shoes. "Hurry up, please God, hurry up!" Her heart was pounding and it seemed like an eternity before the doors finally opened.

Suzy jumped in and pushed the "Close Door" button incessantly until it closed. She threw herself against the back wall, panting, her hair disheveled, and beads of perspiration ran down her forehead and neck, as if she were a potential murder victim trying to outrun her tormentor. Shaking, she fumbled in her bag for a tissue and patted herself, and finally, as the doors of the elevator opened, Suzy flew out of them like a bat out of hell and tore across the crowded lobby, ducking and weaving like a boxer. People were staring but she did not see them; she sprinted across the lobby, jumped into the revolving door, spun around like a Cuisinart in full throttle, and found herself catapulted out and smacked right into the tall, burly, braided doorman with his top hat flying in midair.

"Now, now, missy, are you all right?" he gently said, as he firmly grabbed her arm. "Something wrong, miss? Want a cab, lovey, do yer?" He seemed like such a nice, caring man.

Shaking, she blubbered, "Yes, please," and he hailed a cab and opened the door for her.

She flung herself into the back seat. Suzy wanted to yell, "Step on it," but she was still gasping for air after the agility course through the lobby. The cabbie was watching her, alarmed, from the rearview mirror.

"Are you all right, miss?" he asked, turning around, a concerned look in his eyes.

"Yes," she wheezed, as her chest heaved like bellows. What an ordeal! She bowed her head and slumped in the back seat, her entire body exhausted. Sweating profusely, she was unable to believe she'd just witnessed a naked man—not only a naked man, but one who was chasing her around a hotel room with a pecker twice the size of a salami, even bigger than Max's Delicatessen sold! Oh my God, the horror! Shockingly, there was suddenly a stirring in her. Deep, deep, way down within her, a pulsating sensation and a gushing dampness she had never experienced before...

She lay there, listening to Paul's soft snoring, turned on her side, and sighed...*Where was George now, when you needed him?*

CHAPTER TWENTY-FIVE

Being a judge for the Health Department was quite fascinating. At least it gave Paul some good stories. He had some of the strangest cases or better still, they had a strange effect on him was more like it. He was often reduced to giggling like a silly, shy schoolboy whenever he told a story concerning the different women who stood before him in the courtroom.

"Yes, it was interesting today," he laughed nervously. "I had this young girl, maybe twenty, twenty-two, somewhere around there, pretty young thing, with long blonde hair cascading down her back..." He shifted in his chair as he spoke, a bit uncomfortable and continued, embarrassed. "Anyway, I had to fine her for the violations. The kitchen was filthy, you know, the usual, she and her husband were running this joint in the Bronx." He looked up at Suzy quickly, and giggled nervously, "And really, I would have been a little lenient, but that's the law! She was standing there nervous and shifting, you know what I mean?" He bowed his head to the side, recalling this sweet young thing, trying to restrain his excitement, turning red.

"I er, really don't know how to explain it," he giggled once again, embarrassed.

Suzy looked over at him. No, she didn't know how to explain it either. What kind of a man-child was this? What the hell was the matter with him, and why had she never seen this side of him before?

"I er, really don't know how to explain it." He covered his mouth as he looked down at the table, then fiddled with his tie, clearing his throat.

"Try using some words. Why did you feel that way?" she asked, not sure what the problem was.

"Well," he wriggled in his seat again, "she was just - I don't know." He started giggling nervously. "She was, er, I guess, it was her feminine, you know, little ways." He laughed, embarrassed, and looked to the ground.

Oh my God, did he refer to his penis as his pee-pee or weenie? Use your big boy words, Paul. Suzy rolled her eyes and slumped back in her chair, smiling, "Aaahh! Now I get the picture!"

She moved her shoulders coquettishly, batting her eyes slowly, tilting her head slowly from side to side with her pouty, provocative lips, slowly playing with her hair to one side, then moving forward in her chair, slowly, seductively looking into his eyes, nervously touching her neck and hair again, elbows on the table, then looking him directly in the eyes.

"Is that what happened? Those feminine wiles, you mean? " she asked in a low, whispery voice. Paul watched and giggled nervously, grinning from ear to ear.

CHAPTER TWENTY-SIX

S uzy loved sleeping in on weekend mornings. She could wake up when she felt like it, rested and refreshed with her earplugs. It was sheer bliss. The sun was peeking through the shades. Looking over to the clock by the bedside, it read 9:30. Yawning and stretching, lying still for a minute or two, she heard Paul in the kitchen, opening the cupboard. Getting his vitamin supplies ready for the day, no doubt. The kettle was whistling.

A thought crossed Suzy's mind. With a wild gleam in her eyes and a mischievous smile, she slowly crept out of bed, and on tiptoe, taking long strides and ever so quietly stepping on the wooden floor, sidled against the hallway wall just outside of the kitchen. Pressing her body flat along the frame of the door, trying desperately not to breathe loud, she waited. She heard him turn on the gas stove. Slowly, she peeked around the corner. Paul had a pot on the stove, boiling his eggs—three minutes and twenty seconds, not a moment more. He was such a creature of habit.

He stood in his robe with his scrawny white bird legs that ended in slippers, bed head, staring deeply into the pot as if it were a crystal ball, totally engrossed in his thoughts. His wooden spoon stuck straight up in the air, like a soldier on guard duty, rifle in hand, ready for combat. Suzy wondered what Paul was thinking; he seemed mesmerized, in another world. She knew he did not hear her.

Suddenly, Suzy leapt out in front of the kitchen doorway and screamed at the top of her lungs, *"AAAAAAHHHHHH!!!"*

Paul spun around screaming, *"AAAAAHHHH!!!!"* He shot up to the ceiling, while doing a triple axel, his hair shooting straight up, still screaming *"AAAAAAHHHH!!!"* and frantically waving the wooden spoon in the air as if swatting a swarm of flies. His face was twisted in horror with a wild look in his eyes. *"AAAAH!!!"*.

"Oh, my God, Oh my God!" wheezed Paul, looking deathly pale. "Jeez, jeez." He doubled over, clutching his heart, staggering to the counter for support, still vigorously swatting at imaginary flies. "Oh God." His eyes were bulging; he was still wheezing. "You almost gave me a heart attack!" He tried to catch his breath, groaning. "Jeez, you could have killed me!" His chest rose and fell rapidly, heaving as he frantically tried to catch his breath while his eyes rolled back, a pained expression on his face as he slumped into the chair, wheezing uncontrollably.

Suzy watched him for a moment. Sprawled out on the chair, his hair standing up on end, and his scrawny legs askew, he finally dropped the wooden spoon, gulping mouthfuls of air. As she leaned on the door, she couldn't stop herself from collapsing into torrents of laughter. She clutched her stomach in agony, then in the next moment, turning purple as she tried to stifle herself seeing how pitiful he looked, she once again keeled over, pressing herself against the doorjamb, in uncontrollable shrieks of laughter.

"Good morning!" Suzy said, spluttering away, holding her stomach, "I am proud of you! I never knew you were so athletic! Oh, and that triple axel, Paul, was fabulous! Definitely a 10 - You've won the Gold!" She headed to the bathroom. Her bladder was bursting.

CHAPTER TWENTY-SEVEN

It was a Tuesday morning, another foggy, wet day in the Big Apple. Suzy stepped into her galoshes and raincoat, and just as she was about to walk out the door, she heard the shrill sound of the phone and ran back in to answer it.

"Suzy!" the young man from the placement agency babbled quickly. "Sorry about the other day, but we had a call this morning from a Dr. Johnson's office and I immediately thought you would be perfect for the position. Yes!" She heard him thump his pen on the notepad in front of him. "This is a lovely office down on 34th and Park. The office manager will expect you at 5:15. Her name is Michelle. She's really nice; you'll love her!"

Suzy's heart pounded. "Oh, oh, thank you so much!" she wheezed as she hung up. She felt a bit of relief. What if this was the one?

"Remember," said the girl at the agency, "always look professional for an interview, and never be late! These are the Golden Rules for interviewing."

What? No see through blouse and short shorts, tube tops, or Miller Light?

The office was tucked away down a basement entrance. Michelle was a young lady from the Bronx, a plump, cheerful girl with soft brown eyes.

She and Suzy chatted away. "Now, the doctor expects you to take care of the front desk and make sure you call the patients the day before their appointments. The doctor does surgery on Wednesdays and Fridays, we do all the billing, and it's my decision as to who works here. The doctor leaves it all up to me!" she said brightly. "So I'd like you to meet her, and I'll call you next week sometime!"

With a big smile, Michelle led Suzy through the office and to the front door. Suzy was delighted. "Oh yes, that would be wonderful! Thank you!" And off she went to find the subway uptown.

In the afternoon the phone rang. "Suzy?" It was Michelle. "Hi! The doctor would like to meet with you on Wednesday night at 5:30, when she's done with the patients."

What an angel Michelle was! she thought. Finally, a decent job!

"Yes, yes, I'll be there!" Suzy said excitedly.

She prepared dinner before she left to meet the doctor. The roast and potatoes would be ready about sevenish, and the vegetables were parboiled, so they would not take too long when she got back.

Suzy flung on her coat and headed for the subway.

The office was brightly lit and she walked down the steps into the belly of the beast. When Suzy slowly opened the door she heard a bell ring in the distance. She heard Dr. Johnson's muffled voice in the back with a patient. Michelle popped her head around the corner.

"Hi," she grinned. "She won't be too much longer; take a seat, OK?"

Suzy nodded nervously. She looked at her watch. It was twenty past five. On the coffee table before her were the requisite out-of-date magazines. Bending forward, she grabbed one and began to flip through it slowly. She heard the faucet run in the back. There was a tape playing; more muffled sounds from the back. Thumbing through another magazine, Suzy glanced at her watch it was now twenty past six. She shifted around in the seat, uncrossed her legs, put the magazine back, and selected another. And another. And another.

"How to make him want you - *ALWAYS!*" screamed the headlines, with a provocative, busty blonde lying on the bed with a come-hither, sexy smile. Suzy flipped through the pages slowly. Somehow, at this point, she really didn't care. She looked up at the clock on the wall. It was 7:15. Finally, the patient, with prescription in hand, hurriedly walked past Suzy and out the door.

Suzy cleared her throat. She heard footsteps. And there, finally, before her stood Dr. Johnson: middle aged, average height, with short, graying straight hair and bangs. One of those prissy, mousy types of women, wearing glasses—you know the type…a workaholic, sour on life, and mad at the world. She barely managed a smile, and in a quiet voice said, "I'm Dr. Johnson. Would you come this way please?" She walked toward her office. "Won't you sit down?" She motioned to the chair across from her, not looking up.

"Oh, thank you, Doctor." Suzy proceeded to sit across from her. Glancing up, she noticed a painting on the wall beside the desk. It was from some exotic island, Bora Bora or Tonga.

"Isn't that beautiful—where is that, Doctor?" she asked brightly. Maybe the doctor was having a bad day, she thought. Perhaps she misjudged her.

"Oh, it's from Papua. I went there on vacation," she said quietly. Noticing some papers on her desk then looking at Suzy, she paused for a moment and went on, "Well, we are seeing some more people, and we haven't made a decision yet. Thank you."

With that, she rose from her chair. Suzy stood up. Speechless and stunned, she walked to the door in a daze. Her head was swimming,

What the hell was that? She walked into the street in a daze, as if a train had hit her. She walked as if in a trance to the station. Passersby eyed her sideways hurriedly, whispering to their friends, but she didn't see them.

"Well, we are seeing some more people, and we haven't made a decision yet!" The doctor's voice echoed in her head over and over again, like a broken record. Suzy stepped into the street still replaying the interview, if you could call it that, in her head when she heard screeching tires and a lot of honking as a taxi almost hit her. "Hey, watch where you're goin', lady! What are you – drunk?"

The incident barely registered with Suzy. "I make the decisions around here," Michelle's bubbly voice giggled in the background. That bubbly little bitch dragged Suzy around by the nose because she saw how badly Suzy wanted the job. Her mind was racing. She traveled forty blocks to sit in a waiting room for almost two hours, and was out the door two seconds later. Not even an apology for keeping HER waiting - a common courtesy! Suzy was beyond mad! She was furious, livid, fuming, enraged, and every other synonym she could think of! She stumbled onto the platform; the train pulled in; she stepped up and slumped on to the seat, placing her elbow on the armrest and shaking her head with a glazed look in her eyes, staring wearily at the floor.

CHAPTER TWENTY-EIGHT

S uzy smelled the lamb as she got out of the elevator. "Oh no!" she gasped
and hurriedly put the key into the lock.

Tearing off her coat and flinging it across the sofa, she ran over to
the stove. Oh my, the potatoes were crispy brown; she tapped one, and it
exploded, belching out ash before collapsing. A mere ghost of its former
self. The meat was well done, too. Char-burned.

*If only Paul was a little domesticated, he could have taken it out 20
minutes ago!* she thought. She grabbed the plates and started to put the food
out. Strains of Beethoven filled the room. He had been lying on the bed,
relaxing, listening to classical music in the semi-darkness, as usual. How
in the hell did he not smell the food burning?

Popping her head around the corner, she shouted, "Dinner's ready,"
and turned away to place the plates on the table.

"Aahh, this looks great!" exclaimed Paul, rubbing his hands with glee
as he sat down across from her.

She sat down and looked at the plate of food. It looked appetizing, but
she had no appetite! She hadn't had anything to eat since lunch, which
was about two. It was after eight now. Suzy sliced a small piece of lamb

and scooped the potato ash onto the fork, bringing it up to her mouth, and chewed the food slowly. She chewed and chewed; it was just a tasteless mound. The more she chewed the bigger it seemed to get.

Looking out of the window, she felt her heart begin racing. She felt nervous and frustrated—what if the food kept expanding until it clogged her throat and she suffocated? Suzy looked over at Paul, who was chewing away without a care in the world, cutting off another chunk of lamb. Chomp, chomp, chomp, popping another in his mouth, swilling it down with some water. He was heartily chewing away; she heard the smacking of his lips once again. Chomp, chomp, swill, chomp, chomp, swill. She sighed. *What a damn day! Running around for nothing. Once again!* she thought.

"So, how did it go?" he looked expectantly, plunging into the lamb, another mouthful again. "This is just delicious!" Adding more gravy to his potatoes, he zestfully took another bite.

"Glad you like it," she replied flatly. Suzy was still looking out the window, still chewing on the first mouthful, and felt she was ready to burst. "I cannot believe what the hell happened to me!" she blurted. She had held it in, and now that Paul brought it up, she couldn't hold it in one more second. "I went back to meet the doctor. I thought I had the job; Michelle said so! That bitch of a doctor made me wait almost two hours. I sat down in her office for two seconds— TWO seconds—and then she said, 'Well we haven't made up our mind yet!'" Suzy mimicked the doctor's flat nasal voice. Suzy threw her hands up in the air, lips trembling, tears welling up in her eyes, raising her voice in frustration, wailing, "I can't believe that frigging bitch!" as she covered her face, sobbing.

Paul's eyes turned to steel bullets and they were glaring right at Suzy. His face became hard and cruel.

"How dare you!" he hissed. His knife and fork were now sticking up in the air perpendicular, his hands balled into fists on the table like a baby in a high chair. "How many times do I have to tell you not to raise your voice when I have my meal? I want to eat in peace and quiet. I don't want it interrupted," he yelled. "Don't you ever ruin my dinner *AGAIN!* You do it all the friggin' time. I have told you time and time again, *I DO NOT WANT MY FRIGGIN' DINNER RUINED BY YOUR YELLING!* I feel sick! I can't eat! How many times do I have to tell you?" He jumped up. "Here, I can't eat anymore!" He slammed the dish into the sink. "I can't have half an hour of peace around here! You're always doing this to me!"

She looked up bewildered, in shock, her mouth wide open. "What the hell? You asked me how the interview went. If you didn't want to know, then why even ask?" Jumping up, she picked up her plate full of food, and screamed, "Here, I can't eat, either!" and slung hers into the sink with his, although she would rather have thrown it at Paul's head.

"Keep your voice down! The neighbors can hear you!" he yelled.

"What? I can't hear you!" she wailed, tears running down her face. "I can't believe you!" she said, crying uncontrollably. "Here I expected you might understand, and instead I get yelled at! Are you the only one around here who deserves sympathy?"

Suzy threw her arms on the table, covering her head, sobbing. What the hell is wrong with men? All she wanted was a little understanding. Suzy had had a bad day; she wasn't asking him to change the world – just listen! She didn't try to ruin his dinner. She actually didn't want to talk about it, but once Paul asked, he triggered her ire, and in turn, then went ballistic! She was always there for him, always a listening ear, to help. *I guess it only works one way in this household,* she thought.

Suzy thought about a calming influence in her life – Emily. Emily, with her soft voice. Dear sweet Emily, Suzy wished she was with her now. She loved her so much for her goodness, for just being there. Emily would understand perfectly. Suzy remembered how they would sit down together at dinnertime and discuss what had taken place that day, and Emily would sit and listen, and have some kind of insight, some kind of solution to

Suzy's problem. They used to help one another. It didn't matter what was bothering either of them; they were there for each other, concerned, and always caring. But living with Paul was becoming difficult and she had no friends in New York. It was so God-awful lonely to be here with no one to turn to. The loneliness and isolation from her friends in Florida made the situation worse.

Shaking and forlorn, she ran into the bedroom and flung herself on the bed, sobbing hysterically. Paul was in another world, and she didn't know how to deal with him. He made everything so difficult. There was no reasoning with him; what was the matter with him? How cruel and insensitive could he be? It's no wonder Paul had never married. Suzy had never met anyone like this before and she hoped she never would again. All these thoughts swarmed around in her head like bees.

After a while, she'd calmed down but was exhausted. Suzy slowly got up, reached into her prescription bottle, and took a Xanax, then crawled back into bed and went to sleep. She did not know if Paul was in the apartment or not. He could have dropped dead, and Suzy wouldn't have cared. She began to hate him for his cruelty and insensitivity toward her. All he was concerned about was himself.

When they had these ridiculous fights, Suzy was afraid to go to the apartment for fear of Paul lashing out at her. She recalled sitting in the small kitchen. She would be in the middle of a conversation with him and suddenly hear, "How many times have I told you not to talk so loud?" as he grimaced, putting his fingers to his ears. Wow, hypersensitive much? As far as Suzy was concerned, she really didn't realize her voice was so loud.

Am I going deaf? she asked herself, but nobody else had ever complained. She looked down, pursed her lips, and looked out the window into the distance, wishing she was a million miles away.

Another time, in the middle of telling him how excited she was when she went to the top of the Empire State Building on a Saturday afternoon, he snapped, "All right already, I heard you the first time!"

"Lower your voice already, I want to enjoy my dinner!" he would impatiently scowl at her again, while she was trying to make polite conversation. *How rude!! Taking a vow of silence like a Carmelite nun would be the perfect woman for him!* She was fuming... *How many days to the First of April, again??* Her snowbirds would be going back up North the last week of March and she could finally go home.

Another time she was gathering the pile of New York Times newspapers to dump in the chute down the hallway. She bent down to pick up the stack of newspapers while Paul was on the phone and then an angry voice belched from the sofa.

"Will you stop making so much damn noise?" he lashed out. Suzy looked quizzically in his direction. She must have said WTF to herself at least ten times per day. The newspapers remained in the pile until Paul had gotten tired enough of walking around them every day and finally took them to the chute himself.

But the most hilarious time was on the weekends, which were horrendous for Mr. Extra Uber Sensitive Ears. Any time sirens neared, he'd press his palms to his ears in agony, scowling, jumping up and down as if he were a tortured prisoner.

"Jeez, the sons of bitches! Kept me up half the night again."

He would flip a crazy switch when he heard the police sirens and fire engines screeching by blowing their horns, tearing uptown to the hospital all night.

Holding his ears with both hands, Paul stood by the window, a pained distorted expression on his face, like Edvard Munch's subject in The Scream. "These goddamn people, making all this goddamn noise!" he'd grimace, shouting at them, as the police and fire trucks tore up 2nd Avenue.

LUCIA MILLER

He reminded Suzy of a terrier yapping away at the window, and the strange thing was, Paul's apartment was just around the corner from Lenox hospital. Now seriously, why would somebody live on the main street if you could not stand noise? And even if you inherited the apartment from your mother, why not sell it and look for a quieter street, and buy there? Also, where in New York can you live where there is no noise? Suzy found this very perplexing. Maybe Paul was not the sharpest crayon in the box, but with the 64-pack there was a sharpener in the back. She was still pissed off about the dinner incident and in a case of passive-aggressive revenge she started screaming, "*I DO NOT WANT MY FRIGGIN' SLEEP RUINED BY YOUR WHINING! And that fucking radio of yours every damn night! I can't sleep! Man up, Paul. God, how many times do I have to tell you?*" That didn't go over very well, but it sure felt good.

CHAPTER TWENTY-NINE

P aul was propped up against the bed's headboard, staring at the newspaper, and said, "So, um, why don't you sleep on the sofa from now on?" Suzy lay on her side facing the wall and ignored his comment.

"So why don't you sleep on the sofa from now on?" he repeated in a flat voice.

Suzy couldn't believe her ears. She slowly rolled over and looked at Paul. She had just come in from one of her fruitless interviews, feeling despondent and defeated. New York was a cruel and callous city, and so was Paul's bedroom apparently. The only reason Suzy came to New York was because Paul had asked her to. She had done it for the sake of a friend. Or she thought he was her friend.

She looked hard at him for a moment, then lowered her eyes to the bed for a moment. "Yes, that's fine." Her voice was flat and controlled as she quietly turned around and went to sit in the living room. She stared out the window, still and quiet, but her mind was racing – the fucking nerve of him!

Well, damn. She couldn't go back home since she had rented out her place until April and even the women's shelters charge rent, so she really had no place to go at that moment. To make matters worse, she was now exiled from the comfortable bed and given the sofa! The sofa bed, for God's sake. Like she was a dog. Sofa beds are notoriously uncomfortable, not to mention bad for your back.

That insulting son of a bitch! Suzy had no friends here and felt very homesick and alone. She put on her coat and took a walk over to a coffee shop she found on 1st Avenue. Actually, it was the only place she knew where the waiters said "Hi" and the people were friendly. There, at least, people treated her better.

Paul never became physically abusive, but his words were scalding and sharp like a switchblade. Or things could go the other way. He would be deathly silent and one would have to wait in terror for the real explosion. Either way, Suzy decided not to buy into the bullshit. Instead she was going to avoid Paul and the apartment as much as possible. As she walked by the apartment, she glanced upward and saw the lights were on. It was chilly that evening. As she trudged along the street, passersby hurriedly pushed and weaved through, making their way uptown, while the cars and taxis zoomed along, angrily blowing their horns, everyone in a frantic rush. Walking slowly along the street, peering into different stores, she stood for a moment, and observed the products before her, killing time. She decided to go to a diner and have a snack and a cup of coffee, and kept walking until she found one.

It was well after dark when she crept into the apartment, took the cushions off the sofa, set them on the other chair, and pulled out the bed. But the bed filled up the room, making it hard to walk around. She decided to put the bed back. In the dimly lit hallway she saw Paul lying in the dark, the radio buzzing as he listened to another talk show. They ignored each other; it was best, she thought. She opened up the linen closet, took out the sheets and blankets, and brought them into the living room. She looked down on the sofa. There was a big iron bar in the middle of the sofa bed. *How the hell can*

I sleep on this? she wondered. It looked like some kind of medieval torture device. You'd think they would have improved the dynamics by now. Suzy decided to cover the bottom of the sofa with a blanket, folded in two, and again, for some cushion against the bar. She then covered the blanket with a sheet, put the second sheet over it, and put the pillowcase on the pillow. Her new sleeping quarters – Paul really knew how to entertain. Suzy then folded the blanket in two, and laid it on the top of her new bed. Suzy threw the pillow down, and now her new bed was complete. Hey, beggars can't be choosers, she mused as she moved around trying to get comfortable. But try as she might, that goddamn bar stuck in her back. She turned on her side, and maybe there would be a little relief. If she could only position herself, maybe it wouldn't be so bad. It was okay for a little while, but then again, she could feel it sticking into her bones. Tossing and turning did not help. She sighed. If only she was in her own bed back home, her queen size bed with the firm mattress, she could spread out to her heart's content, safe and snug. Ironically, Suzy's bed was Paul's old bed that she had bought from him before he left for New York. She gave up, finally, and fell into a fitful sleep.

It was really getting cold now. Winter had arrived—the winter of her discontent, she thought. Bring it on! The sooner winter blew through the sooner she'd be able to go home.

The following evening, she walked by the apartment building. Glancing up, she hesitated as she saw the lights were on in the apartment. Her stomach tightened. It was cool; she shivered, pulling her coat closer. She had nowhere to go particularly and she was exhausted from her lack of sleep. Barnes and Noble was too far; the closest one was about fifteen blocks away. She decided to have dinner at a little place off Second Avenue.

As she went around the corner, she looked into the window of the Irish bar, O'Hara's. It seemed warm and inviting, not too crowded, and she decided she may as well go there, closer to "home," and not wander the streets half the night, until Paul went to bed. Home in this case meant nothing more than a dog kennel, a roof over one's head, and little more.

"Hi!" the cheery bartender said brightly as he placed his hands on the bar in front of her and smiled. "What'll it be?" he asked with a twinkle in his eye.

"Oh, I'll have a Chardonnay, please." She looked straight ahead at him and turned to read the blackboard with the specials beside them. *How nice to feel welcome,* she thought to herself. "And I'll have the shepherd's pie as well."

It was still early in the evening, and not too many people were around. Since Suzy was the only one sitting at the bar, she struck up a conversation with the bartender. He was an out of work actor and told her about his girlfriend and all the different auditions that he had gone on. He had made a couple of commercials to tide him over for a while. He was really a nice fellow, she thought.

She glanced at the man two seats over who had just come in, pulling out his paper to read the headlines, turning page after page. He ordered a drink while waiting for his dinner. Must be a bachelor or divorced, she mused, turning her head around and seeing the big fireplace and all the huge copper pots and pans and hanging plants adorning the walls and pictures of the different cities and castles of Ireland. Sunny pictures – of course, taken in a fleeting moment when it wasn't raining. The walls were a rich deep green felt, with wooden beams on the ceiling. She looked at the rows of different beers and whiskies behind the bar, all neatly placed, the lit mirror wall adding sparkle to them. The bar had a lovely cozy atmosphere, warm and inviting. She felt safe there.

The waitress went by with a big steaming shepherd's pie, two Guinness bottles and glasses on her tray. She smiled up at Suzy as she headed to a couple's table.

The bartender placed the glass in front of her, "Here, hon." He smiled and turned to the couple next to her. "Yes, sir! And how are you tonight?" he asked as he took their orders.

At this point, anyone who smiled at her was a welcome relief. She wondered about her girlfriends in Florida, since she hadn't heard from them. And Paul did not like her to call long distance, especially when he paid the telephone bill. She hated to be in a bar, but where else could she go? Then out came the shepherd's pie, hot and steamy, and all else was forgotten for the moment. Suzy took out her paperback; the print was kind of large. Obviously easy reading material, nothing too complex, she thought, and sipped on the wine as she began to read. It was a light comedy. *I really needed this,* she thought and turned page after page, oblivious to the people around her. Finally, after reading six chapters, she decided to go back to the apartment. Looking at her watch, it was now a little after ten—yes, it was past her bedtime.

As she turned the corner, looking up to the apartment, the kitchen was in darkness but Paul's bedside light was still visible. She knew he was lying on the bed, with his ear cocked in the direction of his little radio on the night stand, with Dr. Upton spewing out more reasons to take more of his vitamins to combat everyday maladies and make Paul stronger, fitter, more energetic, and boost his non-existent libido. Since his pecker didn't stand up and salute, Suzy was not interested. She wasn't about to revive the dead, that's for sure...*you go to Lourdes for a miracle,* she thought, *not Suzy Grant.* Then on to a political talk show, then the BBC from London, and so on, to the early morning hours when he would be taking cat naps in between.

Turning the key ever so gently in the lock, she saw the shadow of the night light on the bathroom wall and listened to the buzzing sounds of the AM station as she hurriedly undressed in the dark and quietly took the pillows off the couch and popped into the bed. The steel bar of the couch, as usual, stuck in her spine, even after she tried covering it over with an extra blanket folded in four, and tossing around did not give her any relief. She lay still. There was no sound from the bedroom except the next caller on the talk show. Thank God, she sighed, and fell into an uneasy sleep.

CHAPTER THIRTY

"**S**uzy! Great news!" the ever-ebullient young man from the employment agency told her. "I just spoke to Miriam at Dr. Kravitz's office. He'll see you at 5:30 sharp on Tuesday, OK? Oh, and don't forget to call me Wednesday morning and give me the feedback. So everything is set. Good luck!" He cheerily hung up.

Suzy was excited. *Please God, let him like me,* she prayed. She had been very depressed without a real job. The endless, fruitless hours that she spent going from one interview to the other were all in vain. Working part-time with Dr. Finkelstein, the famous dermatologist whose clients were the cream of the crop on television, a short distance from the apartment was certainly not what she had in mind, but it was convenient and the bills back home were being paid with her pittance of a salary. Suzy stretched her dollars so tight she could hear the dead presidents cry out in pain. Her budget couldn't budge anymore. Thrift stores were her answer to Lord and Taylor. It always amazed her to see so many elegantly fur-clad women, dressed to the nines, dripping in diamonds and flashy Rolexes and living in the best addresses of Manhattan, rummaging around for a bargain!

She ran into Lenox hospital and glanced at her watch. It was 5:14, to be precise. *Thank God,* she thought as she hurriedly looked up the doctor's name and suite number on the board. *I'm nice and early.* She jumped into the elevator. She was feeling a little apprehensive, a little nervous.

I hope to God he isn't tied up with patients, she thought.. Flashes of spending another disappointing evening of sitting and waiting like she did for Dr. Johnson crossed her mind; that was all too daunting for her. *Suite 505, oh, yes, to the left.* She walked down the long corridor. The place was freakishly quiet, she thought, for a hospital. Turning the corner, she saw the tall, lanky maintenance man mopping the hallway. She stuck her head around the corner, wondering if she was in the wrong office.

Yes. Suite 505, Dr. Kravitz, the sign read.

"Hi, is this Dr. Kravitz's office?" she asked, peering into the waiting room.

"Yes, ma'am," said the maintenance man as he pushed the pail out of the way. "Why? Who do you want, ma'am?"

"I have an interview with Dr. Kravitz. They said he would see me at 5:30!" said Suzy, getting more and more anxious as she glanced into the office. It was deserted.

"Oh no, miss." He shook his head. "Oh no, not Dr. Kravitz. Why, he just left!" He continued to mop the floor.

"Whaaat?" Her mouth gaped wide open. "But I had an interview at 5:30. He couldn't have gone!" she wailed.

"Well, miss, I just saw him ten minutes ago and he had his briefcase with him, so I guess he left for the day."

"No! But I was told to be here at 5:30! I got here at 5:20!" She looked forlorn. "Do you think he went to see a patient?" She was on the verge of tears. *Another wild goose chase,* she thought.

"Uh-uh," he shook his head. "He never said nothin', so I reckon he's gone for the day. See, there ain't nobody here!" he said quietly, as he stared at the office ahead of them.

"But I was told that he would be here!" she insisted, as she held back the tears. "What shall I do?" She fidgeted with her bag.

The maintenance man felt sorry for her. "Well, I don't rightly know, miss, but there ain't nobody in here!" He mopped the waiting room floor. "But you can go in there and see if maybe somebody might be back there in those offices," he offered. He was really feeling sorry for her. He could see the disappointment in her face.

"Dr. Kravitz!" he called out. "Dr. Kravitz!" They peeked into the office down the hallway. On the wall, she noticed the various photos of all the famous football players that had been treated by the doctors in the group. She spotted Joe Namath and Jerry Rice in a couple of them. Some had their leg in a cast, some had their arm in a cast, and some were hugging the good doctor. Some were at the stadium with the doctor, their radiant smiles of victory so vivid that one could almost hear the cheering crowds in the background. *Gee, this doctor must be very well known,* she thought.

So he's the doctor for the Jets, Suzy thought as she wearily walked back to the elevator, dejected and rejected once again. Like a robot, she walked out into the street and headed home, too stunned and too worn out, her mind a blur, the blood drained out of her body. In the apartment she turned on the hallway light, slowly took off her coat and curled up on the couch in a fetal position, hugging her knees in the darkened room, in the silence. How much she had set her heart on this job. Now the world felt as if it was crashing in on her shoulders. She was too exhausted, too disappointed to even cry.

CHAPTER THIRTY-ONE

"O h! By the way, some doctor called you - the number is by the telephone," said Paul as he flew out the door. "Call him."

Dr. Mojag was short, with wisps of gray hair. He called her name and ushered her into his office. He wore glasses that sat on a nose that was so long and pointed, it reminded her of an anteater's snout. My God, she stared at it. What could be worth more, a million dollars or Dr. Mojag's nose full of nickels!!

Flipping through her resume, he looked down his glasses, past the end of his nose, with his beady eyes and then looked up.

"So I see from your resume that you have worked for many doctors. Hmm, so plenty of experience." He eyed her, the snout quivering as it took in gulps of air. "I have a very good clientele, and I have to have somebody who can handle them, you understand. I also have friends in the movie industry that come here," he smiled. As his thin lips parted, his teeth reminded her of the long, pointed teeth of a rodent.

She smiled brightly. "OK."

"Yes, look over there on the wall—see who that is?" He smugly pointed to the wall. She turned her head to the wall next to her. There were photos of him with the famous movie director Woody Schwartz dining at '21, smiling into the camera. She noticed more pictures of the two of them in several famous cities, one of them in front of the Eiffel tower wearing matching berets dipped over one eye, grinning from ear to ear. Another in front of the Parthenon in Greece. Another in London with the Changing the Guard ceremony outside Buckingham Palace. Another walking down the red carpet smiling and waving to the crowd at the Cannes Film Festival. Another of them waving from Onassis' yacht, in the middle of the Mediterranean smiling, wearing their huge sunglasses, looking like an ad for Ray-bans. Miles of smiles all around. The good life must be really good, she mused. Too bad they weren't good looking.

"Really?" She acted impressed.

"Yes, I'm in his next movie, see me over there?" He pointed, gloating, to a photo where he was lounging on a sofa with three well-known actors she recognized, with cameras and lighting strobes in the background in a scene from the latest movie that Woody was making.

"Oh really?" she smiled. "How exciting!" She flashed her sexiest smile.

"So anyway," he went on; she could see he really wanted to impress her with this information, "let me give you my hours."

She was delighted; at least this man could make a decision for a change, she thought.

"Well, I need someone who can start this week—is that possible?"

She did not want to act too enthusiastically. God knows she needed the money badly enough, but at the same time, she didn't want to appear too eager.

"So," he looked slowly at her, "so, er, why don't we start Friday, just to see how it goes?" He eyed her carefully; she noticed his nostrils quivering. Probably getting fatigued from all that weight, she surmised.

She looked up at him. "Sure, why not? Thank you, Doctor!" They shook hands, and she turned, walked past the waiting room packed with applicants, and swept out the door.

Waving down a cab, she threw herself into the backseat and heaved a sigh of relief as a smile made its way across her lips. Friday at nine-thirty sharp, she knocked on the door. Dr. Mojag buzzed her in. She gingerly looked around the office. Was she the only one there besides him? Where was his nurse? she wondered. The place was a morgue, deathly silent. She looked around and hung up her coat. *Ouch,* she winced. *Damn, my foot is hurting like hell,* she thought.

"Er, Suzy," the doctor's long snout peered around the corner from his office, obliterating the rest of his face, "by the way, if anybody calls, let me know, OK? Oh, and help yourself to some coffee." He pointed over to the corner where a pot was set up. Limping, she sat down, and looked at his appointment book for the day. There were three people scheduled. Hmm, she thought, only three people. That would be simple enough.

The phone by her desk rang; she answered it. "Dr. Mojag's office. Good morning!" she trilled down the phone.

"Yes, my name is Diane Krumpet. I want to cancel my appointment for 11:30 on the second of January. I'll be out of town and I'll call to reschedule when I return, all right?" Mrs. Krumpet asked.

She quickly flicked the page to the second, saw the name, and erased it. "Yes, Mrs. Krumpet, thank you for calling."

Just as Suzy hung up the buzzer sounded, buuurrrrr! "Uh, Suzy," the muffled voice of Dr. Mojag could be heard, "was that a phone call?" She detected a note of irritation.

"No, Doctor, it was just a patient calling to cancel her appointment. I took care of it," she airily answered into the intercom.

"Er, didn't I tell you to let me know if there were any calls?"

"Er, yes...?" She was bewildered.

"So, er, why didn't you?"

"But I didn't think that you wanted *THAT* kind of call!" She looked around slowly, in amazement, wondering if she was on *Candid Camera* or *Punked*. No doctor ever wanted to take calls for an appointment; if it was about some problem with the patient, yes, but not those types of calls. She shook her head and looked over to his office. But the voice carried on, "I said I wanted you to let me know if there were any calls, OK?"

She was perplexed. "Yes, doctor," she meekly said.

Another phone call. This client wanted to come over to buy some lotion for her acne. She buzzed the doctor. "Yes, but make sure she pays, OK?" he warned.

She went back on the line, "Yes, Ms. Johannsen, you can come now, and it'll be $59.90. Are you paying in cash or credit card?" Ms. Johannsen would be paying with credit card.

The buzzer sounded once again, buuurrrr! "Suzy … Are you there?" He controlled his tone.

"Yes, doctor," she replied timidly.

"I just want you to know that was a girlfriend of mine; she tries to get this for nothing, you know. Make sure she pays, all right?" he confided in her.

About twenty minutes later, she heard the front door buzzer.

"Who is it?" she called out.

"It's Enke Johannsen."

And in came this tall, leggy blonde, cute in a hard way. She sidled up to the desk, blowing her hair out of her eyes."Hi, I came for the lotion," she said in her thick Swedish accent. Suzy noticed her skin was flawless, glowing, baby fresh.

Suzy went into the examining room where the doctor had all his products displayed and brought out the pink lotion, putting it into his specially designed gold and red monogrammed bag for her.

"That'll be $59.90 please," said Suzy, and with that Enke fumbled in her purse and brought out the card. She swiped it through and quickly signed. She grabbed the bag from the counter and made her way to the front door. Suzy watched her leave, wondering if Dr. Mojag really dated her or not. Maybe he said that to impress her, she thought, men have such goddamn egos. Most times bigger than they are ... Enke was at least three feet taller than he was. But then again, hey, it's been known to happen. Suzy shrugged her shoulders. It reminded her of the joke of the 4'2" jockey that married the 6'2" model. When they were nose to nose, he had his toes in it, and when they were toes to toes, he had his nose in it. She wondered how many times he had his nose in it... A dreadful thought.

The phone rang; she picked it up. "Dr Mojag's office - Good Morning!"

"Yes, this is Mrs. Gromsky ... Now you tell that doctor the stuff he gave me for the warts—well, as I opened it, it slid out of my hand and splattered the dog! Now my dog has a huge bald spot right on his head! After running around the kitchen ten times, my husband thought he was rabid!" And then Mrs. Gromsky hung up!

The phone rang again.

"Oh yes, hello, I have a two o'clock appointment for today, please cancel it. I will call back later; the name is Camille Brown, thank you!" and Camille hung up without giving Suzy a chance to speak.

The phone rang. "Yes, it's Mrs. Klein. I just wanted to tell you, the big bottle of cream that Dr. Mojag prescribed..."

"Yes, Mrs. Klein," Suzy said, "so what happened?"

"Well it accidentally fell out of my bag and smashed on my hallway floor. Oy, what a mess! Splattered all over the floor! Oy vey! So I went in the kitchen to get some paper towels to clean it up, my husband came home and slipped on the cream, and shot through the living room like a greased pig, crashed through the patio doors, and ended up in the pool! Oy vey!" She continued, "It's about 20 degrees out there, you know; he was chilled to the bone. I was afraid he was going to have pneumonia! He's OK now, but he had to have twenty stitches in the emergency room. Can the doctor please give me another prescription?"

Once again the phone rang.

"Yes, I have a three o'clock appointment today; please cancel it. I will call back later to reschedule. The name is Cindy Feinstein, thank you!" and she immediately hung up without giving Suzy a chance to speak.

The buzzer again sounded, buuurrrr!

"Was that the phone?" Dr. Mojag asked, in a sardonic tone.

"Er, yes, Doctor." God he was an annoying little fucker, she thought, shaking her head, looking heavenwards.

"Who was that?" The words rolled off his tongue in a slow, stunted tone.

"Well, the first one was Camille Brown for today, but she cancelled."

"Didn't I just tell you to check with me first?" the voice went on.

"Yes, you did."

"So why didn't you?"

She stared and shook her head. "Because as soon as she told me, she hung up - she did not wait for me to say anything! She hung up as soon as she gave me the message, that's why!"

"But I told you to check all calls with me; didn't I tell you that?" His voice was irritated.

"Yes, I know, Doctor," she insisted, "but there was no time. Do you want me to call her back?" she glared down at the buzzer light, as if she was looking at him.

The phone rang; it was a rep from the pharmaceutical company. She buzzed the doctor, and he took the call.

The front door buzzed again. She pressed down the speaker. "It's Anne Abbot for my 11:00 appointment," the voice shouted.

The tall, statuesque redhead took off her coat, and Suzy ushered her into the room. She buzzed Dr. Mojag. "I'll be right there!" he called out.

He went into the room, when the phone rang. "Dr. Mojag's office. Good morning!"

"Yes," the voice said, "this is Mr. Steinberg." He whimpered, "Uh, the other week I saw the doctor and he gave me some cream to put on my bald spot."

"Yes, Mr. Steinberg, how can I help you?"

"Yes," he went on, "you know this cream, I don't know what's in it, but it attracts flies to my head. And my wife is swatting the flies with the newspaper. She killed about 30 the other day! What should I do?" he sighed, almost on the verge of tears. "She's giving me a headache! I don't know what to do!" He sounded so pitiful.

She looked into the phone as he spoke. "Well, maybe you need to wear a helmet," she suggested.

"A what?"

"A helmet, like when you ride a motorbike—that should help," she suggested.

"I'm going to sit in the house with a motorbike helmet on?" he said, incredulously.

"Well, yes…That should solve the problem—I mean, no flies, no headache, right?"

Again, the phone rang. She answered.

"I would like an appointment for next Tuesday, something in the morning—is that possible?"

She looked through the book. "Er, yes, how about 10:15? Will that be OK? What name, please?"

"It's Michaels, Josephine Michaels."

"Yes, Mrs. Michaels, I have you down for 10:15. And may I have your phone number, please?" she asked as she penciled in her name.

"Sure, it's 898-0404."

"Thank you, we'll see you then," Suzy said, then hung up the phone.

The door to the examining room opened and out came Mrs. Abbot. Her face was all red and blotchy, as she fumbled for a tissue. She wrote out a check and Suzy made her a follow-up appointment in the book, while handing her the appointment card, as Mrs. Abbot threw on her coat and walked out the door.

She sat down to check the rest of the appointment book.

The buzzer at her desk sounded - buuuuurrrrrr!!!

She looked down hurriedly, pressing it. "Yes, Doctor." Her patience was wearing thin.

"Didn't I tell you, heh, heh," he whined. "I want you to heh, heh," his phony laugh really aggravated her now, "put all calls through to me?"

"Yes!" She was getting irritated. She looked up to the ceiling, grabbing the sides of the desk, then clenching her fists on her lap. Her voice was firm to him.

"Did you get a call while I was in the room?" His whiny voice was so irritating to her.

"Yes, I did," she said curtly. She shut her eyes tight, clenching her fists again.

"Well, why didn't I speak to them?"

"Because you were with a patient. And the caller wanted an appointment! That's all!" she replied, rolling her eyes to the ceiling again.

"And what did you do?" he whined like a sick puppy.

"I made the appointment!" Looking at the lack of patients in his book, he should have been thrilled, she thought.

He laughed helplessly. "I, er, want to speak to every person that calls. Do you understand?" His tone was now more and more abrasive.

She shook her head. *This is a fucking nutcase! Why doesn't he just pick up the goddamn phone himself?*

He walked into the office and looked at his watch. "Oh my, it's already 12:30! Why don't you go to lunch, and be back in half an hour. There's a pizza place around the corner," he offered, as he leaned over her shoulder.

Suzy looked up at him as he spoke. The nostrils were almost at her eye level, quivering like the end of an elephant's trunk as it took in huge gulps of air. She slowly rose from the seat and nodded, as she threw on her coat.

Suzy was glad to be out of the office, away from that goddamn whiny voice. God, one of her pet peeves with men was a whiny voice. Urrrhgh! What a turn-off! Her mind was racing as she chewed hungrily on her slice of pizza. Glancing at her watch, she had five minutes to go back to the Torture Chamber. Running down the steps, she tore off her coat and listened for him. She just knew he was going to buzz her.

Sure enough, the buzzer rang- buuuurrrrr!! She winced.

"Er, Suzy, would you come in here please?" She was being summoned by her master.

She knocked gently on his door. He looked up from the papers that he was reading.

"Come in." She noticed his nostrils flaring rapidly in quick succession, as if he was smelling the air like a dog.

Dr. Mojag beckoned her to sit down. He moved around in his chair as he stared down his anteater nose at her, his hands resting on his chin, staring coldly at the wall for a moment, and then back to her. Suzy looked straight into his eyes.

"I, er, don't think this is working out," he said, looking down the snout at her. His beady eyes were cold and cruel. "So, er, what do you think?" He moved closer to the desk, taking in gulps of air.

Suzy's heart was beating faster; she was nervous but at the same time, she welcomed this.

"Yes, Doctor, you are absolutely right," she smiled. Actually, she had thought of not returning after lunch just to forget the whole damn mess, but she also wanted to get paid.

"Yes, I think it's best," he shifted in his seat. "I'll send you whatever I owe you, OK?" Without looking up, he waved her out of the room. As she rose from the chair, she watched his snout rest on the papers before him. That was some schnoz, she thought.

Suitably dismissed, she grabbed her coat and limped out the door. She flagged down a cab and fell into the backseat, heaving a sigh of relief.

Suzy paid the cabbie and walked down the street. November had started to get quite cold. She was shivering. It was now around the low 30s, and she most certainly was not used to cold weather. She hugged the thin cashmere coat that Emily gave her before she left Florida, but it was not warm enough. Dear sweet Emily, how much she missed her, she could hear that soft raspy voice as she walked along the street. Looking up she noticed a sign – 50% OFF – in large, bold, red print. The store was packed. Walking in, she pushed through the crowd to look for a coat. A woman was holding up a black fur coat, rusty from age. Probably 50 years old, it looked like a dead rat, Suzy thought, wondering who might have been the owner of this coat at one time. Going through the racks, she spotted an absolutely beautiful fur coat. The chocolate-colored satin lining was in excellent condition, and the monogram L intertwined with R over to the right side in a lighter shade of brown. Whoever owned this previously took very good care of it. It was immaculate.

Maybe this is fox, she thought. It had a fluffy reddish and darker brown tinge to the fur, too thick for mink; she wasn't sure what it was.

"Put that on!" said the woman beside her who was watching her, as Suzy slipped it on. "Oh, that is beeaautiful on you!" she exclaimed, as Suzy twirled in front of the mirror. "That is so you! Ohh, yes! It's 50% off today!" She grabbed the sales ticket gleefully. "So you have a beautiful coat for $100.

This is your lucky day!" They both smiled broadly at each other, and Suzy thanked her while she walked over to the cashier. Stepping out into the cold day, she pulled the coat closer; now she was nice and warm, she smiled to herself. At least the day had not been a total waste after all! At the corner of her eye, a male passerby did a double-take as she walked by. She caught his eye and smiled. Aahh, life is good!

CHAPTER THIRTY-TWO

Suzy stirred the pot. Dinner was almost ready. She placed the glasses with water on the table then took the roast out of the oven, covering it over with tin foil to keep it warm for Paul. He was due soon, probably fighting the traffic, she thought.

He was enjoying his new position at the Health Department. He was surprised by the number of variations of violations there were, which was totally different from the usual filthy and unsanitary conditions that the inspectors had found in these restaurants. And God knows Manhattan has millions of restaurants. So he certainly had job security for quite some time. Not only that, there also was a side she never saw in him before. He had begun to find these women who came into his court a little tantalizing – Suzy found this all laughable, a very different dimension to his personality.

The door flew open. Paul walked into the bedroom and threw his coat, hat, and briefcase on the chair by the bed.

"Hi, how was it today?" she inquired, studying his face. That usually was a good indication.

"Very busy day! But I got through it." He plopped himself down at the table, reached for the water glass and drank. "Oh, that feels better."

She sat across from him, eyeing him. "So...? Que pasa? Go ahead..."

"Well, this was something today!" he giggled shyly. "This very shapely blond with hair all wavy and down to here," pointing down his back, "came to court in a black leather mini skirt, right up to here" still giggling softly, blushing, he pointed to his mid thigh, "black spike heeled high boots to here," as he pointed to mid thigh, "and a lace blouse, you know, with a pin up here, here at the throat. She had a tiny waist - and buxom! Oh my, was she buxom!" His eyes rolled upwards as he continued. "So she has this very husky, deep, sexy Russian accent." He gurgled away. "And then she started explaining why she and her husband did not take care of correcting of the violations at their restaurant. God, I thought I was going to fall off the bench." He collapsed into laughter. "I, er, hardly understood a word that she said!" he confessed. "But I had to fine her and her husband, so I got them out fast. I had too many cases on the books to get through."

"So did the husband come with her?"

"Oh yes, a big guy, looked like wrestler, built like an ox, a big block for a head; his neck was as wide as his shoulders! God!" He shuddered at the thought of tangling with him on a quiet road in the middle of nowhere. He could lift him up in one hand, no problem. "The beauty and the beast!"

"Really?" Suzy said coolly, her head cocked to one side. "So you had fun today!" *Funny how men get carried away so easily,* she thought. She walked into the kitchen. "Well, I have your favorite chicken dish with roasted potatoes and fresh corn and spinach; hope you like it."

CHAPTER THIRTY-THREE

Sunday morning was cold and chilly. Paul and Suzy leisurely got dressed. Sam was coming to pick them up at 12:30. The plan was to go to the Village for lunch. Suzy liked Sam; he was a kind person. He was always obliging, she noted. Carita was some lucky maid. But did she really realize how lucky, was the point. Suzy studied her as they stood in line waiting for a table while Sam parked the car.

Carita had a new hairdo, which was much more becoming, and was wearing more stylish clothes. She seemed happier, and why shouldn't she be? Sam was a good man, he was very good to her, and he adored her. She had the world by the b's – well, at least one pair!

Sam had recently heard of this restaurant and was curious to try it out. Carita smiled as Suzy and Paul sat across from her. She was also happy that she now was able to speak in sentences, instead of understanding a word here and there. She glanced over to the entrance of the restaurant and spotted Sam.

"Sam!" she beckoned him over to them.

He took off his jacket, muttering, "Damn, parking is such a bitch. I had to park four blocks away!" as he sat down.

Paul was in his usual form. "So Carita," he moved forward, looking questioningly, "how's the English coming along?"

"Yes, eet ees good," she spoke slowly. "I am going to class two times a week now." She smiled broadly, her eyes sparkling. "I like very moch, si!"

"I'm very proud of her!" Sam put his arm around Carita and gave her a hug "Hey, in the next year, she'll understand everything!"

Suzy smiled. Or perhaps Sam preferred that she didn't. Paul and Suzy discussed this point several times in the past. Paul had always suspected that. Even though the two were close all these years, there were maybe reasons that Sam preferred Carita not to become too fluent in English. Maybe his being divorced twice was a very strong factor. Sam loved women, but unfortunately, he became bored with them and moved on to the next one time and again. But maybe now, age was beginning to slow him down.

"So how's your family?" Paul looked over to Sam as he munched on the rolls.

"My father's doing fine; we're going to Florida to see him in a couple of weeks. My sister's staying with him. She's got this new business she started and that is doing well. So everything's good!"

The waiter took the order and left.

"So Carita, where is your family?" Suzy asked as she buttered her roll.

"Oh, she has a large family in Guatemala," Sam spoke up. "She has five sisters over here, and I think she has three brothers back home, don't you, honey?" He then went on to translate into Spanish for her. She nodded.

"Well, no," she began, correcting him, "I have two brothers now because one of them, he die!"

Suzy looked up, concerned. "Really, what happened?"

"He die." She shrugged, explaining, "My one brother, the young one, he die two years ago. My other brother, my older brother, he big man in Guatemala; he have beeg house, and he leeve very well. He have a wife and how you say, three," she thought for a moment, "err, cheeldren!" She was pleased that she remembered the word.

Looking concerned, Suzy asked her, "So what happened to your younger brother? How old was he?"

"He was 33 or 34 years old," she began slowly, looking straight at Suzy, "but you know, he dreenk, he dreenk too moch," she emphasized the "moch" while rolling her eyes heavenwards. "And he fight with his wife, always he fight with her. She no like him to dreenk, no good, he give her black eye, many times, you know. He no remember the next day. So she make him some herb drink we have in the mountain in Guatemala. And he dreenk it - and he die!" She shrugged her shoulders, her face expressionless.

"Wait … what? Just a minute." Suzy cocked her head to one side. "Let me understand this. You say your brother drank this drink that your sister-in-law made, and then he died!" She gasped in shock.

Carita looked at her stone-faced. "Si, si!" she nodded, and then an impish thought crossed her mind. She eyed Suzy and Paul, giggling. "Why, you want me get recipe?"

Suzy roared and turned to Paul "Did you hear what Carita said?"

He looked up from his pasta. "No, what?" He wolfed down another mouthful.

"You mean you weren't paying attention? This is one of the funniest stories I've ever heard!"

He looked up between mouthfuls. "What did she say?"

"She said her brother had a drinking problem, and he used to beat up his wife. Anyway, the wife gets these herbs from the mountains, boils them, and gives it to the brother to drink! He drinks it - and he croaks! What a great country! You don't like your old man, so you poison him! Perfectly legal!" she howled with laughter. "These aren't mushrooms, are they?"

Paul looked at Carita. "Is that true, Carita?"

"Si, si!" she nodded.

And both of the women roared.

Paul looked over at Sam. "I can see why that would appeal to Lucrezia Borgia over here!" He pointed his fork in Suzy's direction.

"Carita, you are too funny!" Suzy grinned. "Oh, by the way, when can you ship some up? I'll be worth millions in no time. Imagine all those people getting divorced!" Her eyes lit up at the thought. "You could get rid of your husband, and save the courts a lot of time and yourself a lot of headaches. The possibilities are endless!"

"So what kind of 'erbs were they?" Paul was now curious.

"'Erbs? Why is it Americans say 'erbs? Isn't the word with an aich? The dictionary says H-E-R-B-S! It's herbs! The aich is not silent!"

Sam was chomping on his veal. "Yeah, why?" he wondered.

"I mean, do you say 'erbert 'oover instead of Herbert Hoover?" she wondered, stressing the aiches.

"And the exact same thing—well, don't they both mean the same?" she asked

Paul listened and laughed, "Yes, I never thought of it that way. You're right."

Paul was very quick to point out the absurdities of the English language. One day, for instance, he was blowing off steam that one of the attorneys that he was speaking with used the phrase "I see what you're saying," which a lot of people use. He balked at the ridiculous statement. To him, "I understand what you're saying" was appropriate. Paul was very precise, very old-fashioned.

When he mentioned this to Suzy, she smiled. "See what you're saying," she said the words slowly, paused, and continued. "Hmm, did you ask him if he saw it in black and white, or did he see it in color?"

"And the other one that I find strange - it's a true fact. A fact is the truth!"

He sat back in his chair and laughed.

"Yes, people do it all the time!"

"And the other, ax him instead of ASK him - how many people who should know better, with college degrees even, say this? It's appalling!" Paul used to cringe when he heard this.

"Yeah," Suzy agreed, "can you imagine walking around with a meat cleaver in your hand - I axed him! That's all I did, I axed him." She had a very visual mind.

"Well now, how about all those people who cannot say asteRISK! They say asteRICK! There's another."

Carita looked from one to the other; she was getting a lesson in English and becoming more and more confused. "Thees Eenglish, very deeffeecult, si," she agreed shaking her head.

CHAPTER THIRTY-FOUR

P aul and Arnie swept into the living room after throwing their coats on the bench and then threw themselves down on the sofa. It would never occur to them to hang the coats, Suzy thought. They had a long box that they dumped on the floor. Arnie, upon seeing Suzy, once again smiled broadly and patted her on the head, his favorite way of greeting her.

She smiled and made room on the couch for him next to her. She had been reading a magazine and jumped up when they arrived.

"So how was the auction?" Suzy curled up on the sofa and put the magazine on the coffee table.

Arnie and Paul had gone downtown to the Sotheby's auction.

Paul did not look too happy for some reason. He was absolutely livid.

"Oh, there were some interesting paintings that I had my eye on. There was quite a crowd," Arnie said.

"So Paul, you don't look too happy—something happened?" she inquired. "Shall I make you a drink—tea, coffee, anyone?" Paul looked into the distance, disgruntled, pouting like a spoiled brat.

"So what happened, Paul?" she repeated. "What's in the box? Is it yours?" Paul was shifting around in his seat.

"I can't believe that friggin' bastard! I was looking around, I spotted the Mayor, and as I was scratching my head for a split second I heard," he looked pale as a ghost, "going, going, gone, the gentleman in the brown suit over there. And I wound up with these friggin' swords!" He threw his hands up in the air, his eyebrows shot up into his forehead, and he gave the box a swift kick then grabbed his foot while hopping around on the other adding insult to injury. "God, oh God, Ouch, dammit, that hurt." Dandruff – it's a bitch.

"Cost me a fortune! Can you believe it? I went in for a painting and I wound up with these friggin' swords. I don't even want the damn things! What the hell am I going to do with them?" he muttered.

Suzy chimed in, "Challenge everyone you meet to a duel in Central Park at dawn?"

Paul looked disgusted at Suzy. He wanted to bang Arnie and Suzy's head, he was so irritated. Then he turned on Arnie, spluttering, "Why the hell did you take me there? I'm out five grand! For these – I can't even look at them!" Paul shot wordless daggers at Arnie, then started in, "This is the last time I go anywhere with you, d'you hear me?" He was now pacing up and down, he was so upset.

"But they come from a castle in Germany; they're from the Hapsburg family, I think! At least two hundred years old! Isn't that what the fella said? You got a good deal!" But Arnie could not calm Paul down. His anger was now at the boiling point.

Arnie shifted around in his seat; he didn't know what to say. He glanced out the window to the apartment across the street.

Suzy followed his eyes. "What's wrong, Arnie?" she asked.

"That woman over there – is she for real or what?" He stood up, walking toward the window. "Is she naked?" he wondered out loud.

"Yeah, you got me! I see her every day; she never moves out of that bed. All day and night, she just lies there! Bright lights on, like a shop window!" Suzy laughed.

"Well, I guess it's time to go to bed." She looked over at Paul, still steaming, as Arnie was putting on his coat and hat by the door. Suzy showed him to the door. He smiled down adoringly at her and once again patted her lightly on the head. "Good to see you, Suzy. Goodnight," he said softly, with adoring eyes.

"You too Arnie, so nice to see you too!" She smiled up at him.

Oh well, just another day in paradise, she smiled to herself.

CHAPTER THIRTY-FIVE

P aul and Suzy were sitting in the living room. "Well, I asked this girl at work if she would copy a letter that I'm putting together for John. She said she would do it on her lunch break. I wanted the back done so I would be able to lay it like this…" He pointed to the floor as he imagined what it would look like. She watched. The way he was doing it was all wrong.

"No," she said firmly. "It's got to be done this way," she said, smirking at his stupidity. She had realized Paul was a man who was very astute in the learned word; he could read and ingest intricate jargon at a glance, and yet it always amazed her that for simple, uncomplicated everyday mundane things, he had no common sense at all. First and foremost, he had no patience to figure it out. Anything that had to be fixed around the house always got one minute of his attention. Read instructions? Not bloody likely.

When the vacuum cleaner wouldn't work, he had the plug in one hand, fiddled around with the machine, and plugged it in, praying that it would work. If it didn't start, he'd throw his hands up and call for the maintenance man. "Remember," Suzy would say, "God helps those who help themselves."

He shot dagger looks at her. She was making a fool out of him, and he resented it. He glared, and between clenched teeth, growled, "No! It has to be done this way - OK! OK! It's my project," as he jumped off the couch and stood in front of her, pointing. "And that's final!"

"If you do it that way, it won't come out right!" she argued.

His hair stood on end; his hands were on his hips. "I've had enough of you! I am sick and tired of your snotty remarks and undermining me! I want you to leave, and if you could leave now, I'd appreciate it," he shouted, his blue eyes bulging out of their sockets.

"But I have no place to go!" She looked bewildered

"I don't care!" he roared. It was the dead of winter, her apartment was rented out for the season in Florida, and she really didn't have any place to go. God, what the hell was she going to do now?

She was so nervous, she started shaking. She needed a cigarette to calm her nerves, but she wasn't allowed to smoke in his place. She flopped down in the chair in the kitchen and cupped her hands to her cheeks, looking downward. There was no way to get away from him in the tiny apartment and it was very late. If it were earlier, she would run off to O'Hara's and kill time there until he calmed down.

He had gone into the bedroom.

"And call the airlines now! I want you to call them this minute!" he screamed at her from the doorway of the kitchen.

She looked at him. She was nervous as hell. He had the wrath of a hurricane whipping through, crushing, and leaving the area flattened in his wake. There was no way to talk sense into him right now. He was beyond that. There was nothing Suzy could do tonight. Her mind couldn't think fast enough at this point. She was fuzzy. She couldn't run out; it was almost midnight and it was freezing out there. Jesus, what the hell could she do? Her mind raced; how could she get away from him? Paul was like a grizzly bear charging to attack her, tear her up into fifty million pieces with his gargantuan claws and eat her entrails with a side of honey!

"And don't forget, sister, don't ever call me again, do you hear me!" he screamed at her, pointing his finger menacingly. "I want you out - OUT! And now!!"

Suzy was shaking like a leaf; she had to do something. She knew Paul wouldn't stop! She decided to take a shower, let the water keep running to drown him out, and maybe he'd calm down by the time she was ready for bed. She ran to the bathroom and turned on the shower. Tearing off her clothes, she jumped in. The warm water felt good on her body. Maybe it would wash him out of her hair – no, wait, this was not *South Pacific* – out of her mind, or better yet – out of her life!

"Hey, YOU! Don't forget to make sure you take all your clothes. I don't want anything left behind. I will not send anything to you. I'll throw it in the garbage, do you hear, sister?" He banged on the door. "Hey! You in there, *DID YOU HEAR ME?*" he yelled.

Suzy turned the water on full blast in hopes of drowning out Paul's voice but she could still hear him. And why the fuck did he keep calling her, sister? She never answered him; she was deathly afraid to. This was a wild man, a friggin' charging rhino, and he was going to charge right through that door and get her!

Suzy heard Paul again. "And tell your friends what happened!! Tell them the *TRUTH!* Make sure you tell them the *TRUTH!*" he roared.

God, what the hell did that mean? Tell them he's a misogynistic, Type A personality that cannot take advice from a woman? That scouring pad hair wearing, sword kicking, vitamin taking, sexless wonder of his Lordship straight out of the Old Bailey can kiss my ass. Suzy fell back against the shower wall. She didn't want to turn off the water. She didn't want to hear what he had to say. If she could, she would go home right now. Sit in the airport until there was a flight to Miami, no matter how long it took. She would be like Tom Hanks in *The Terminal* if that's what it took.

Suzy had been in the shower long enough for the hot water to run out. The walls and ceiling were dripping water, as a thick fog of steam billowed under the door into the hallway and through the window. Lobster red skin, shriveled up like a raisin, she leaned dejectedly against the wall, her matted hair falling into her eyes. How much longer could she stay in there? She still hadn't said one word to him; she didn't dare to say one word or even ask why he kept calling her "sister". Paul wasn't even Mormon, and Suzy was no nun. She shook her head, dazed. She had to get out. It was a Turkish bath in there and Suzy was having difficulty breathing. Trembling, she slowly got out and reached for the towels. Damn it, the towels were soaked! What could she do? She was afraid to open the bathroom door and get a fresh one from the hall closet. Nervously she wrung out one of the wet ones as best as she could and used her robe to dry herself a bit more. The robe was also sopping wet.

"Are you in there? I need to use the bathroom." Ah yes, the quiet was simply a short reprieve from this temper tantrum. "This is MY home, and don't you forget it, sister!" he bellowed.

Her heart was beating faster and faster. *Aw, damn . I have to go out there,* she thought. *Oh wait, I have to take something!* Suzy's teeth were chattering, and she fumbled in her bag to find the Xanax she had in there. She was so wired and she needed to sleep.

Trying to read the label, she couldn't quite make out what it said. She didn't have her glasses; they were in the living room by the coffee table. Not really thinking she'd need to read while taking a shower, Suzy did not bring them with her, and she was too scared to go get them for fear of the Dragon out there.

"Hey, I said - I need to use the bathroom -NOW!" shouted the Voice of Doom in the hallway.

Still trying to find the Xanax inside her cosmetic bag, Suzy grabbed a bottle and squinted, sure she read something fuzzily with an "x" on the end of the prescription name.

This must be the Xanax! I'd better take at least two to knock me out, she thought. Popping the bottle open and scooping water from the faucet into her hand, she hurriedly swallowed three pills, praying that they would work instantly to make this nightmare go away.

"Are you in there?" Paul bellowed, banging on the door.

She jumped, startled, "Yes, I- I'm coming out right now," she stuttered. Clutching her clothes to her chest, she quickly ran out into the living room and hurriedly pulled down the cushions to make her bed.

She heard his footsteps as he came tearing out of the bathroom toward her. Her mind was racing. "God Almighty, when is he going to shut the hell up? Isn't this enough? Damn."

Still pointing his finger at her, he said, "And make sure you leave in the morning!" She had her back to him trying to be invisible. "Hey! I'm talking to *YOU!* Are you paying attention?"

She slowly turned around, and quietly said, "Yes, I hear you," and with that, he turned to go back to the bedroom. *Hell, I'm ready to jump out the goddamn window right now! Anything to get away from this fucking ogre!* she thought.

Pulling the blanket around her and snuggling deep into her pillow, she just wanted to go to sleep and wake up in her apartment in Florida. "Please God, that's all I want," she prayed. Her mind was racing. Her nerves were screaming from each cell of her entire body. Suzy heard a screaming sound in her ears, a high-pitched screaming sound. It wouldn't stop, and for a second she wondered if the sound was coming from her. She put her hands over her ears to block the sound. Well, it wasn't her.

"Stop! Stop! Haven't I been through enough torture?" she begged the sound to go away. She looked at the kitchen clock. It was about 1:45. Suzy was wide-awake. Her eyes were open, the adrenalin was pumping throughout her body as if she had just run the New York marathon, and her heart was beating so hard in her chest wall it felt as if it was going to explode any second.

When are those damn pills going to kick in? she wondered.

Suzy could hear the drone of the radio in the distance. Seemed Paul could stay up listening to his talk shows no matter the occasion. *That frigging bastard can just go on as if nothing happened. Damn friggin' Men—they're all the same!* Suzy needed to sleep; she was so beat, and yet she could not relax! She lay down trying to get comfortable. It was not easy sleeping on the sofa springs. She moved around to avoid the one spring sticking in her back when, suddenly, *BOOM!* Sitting bolt upright, she felt her bladder blow up like a balloon with such a force! The pressure was excruciating, she cried out in pain. "Oh no! Dear God! What the hell is going on?" Running quickly to the bathroom, she flopped down quickly on the seat, just as the dam burst. She dared not turn on the light because she didn't want to chance waking Paul, although peeing like a race horse could also wake him, especially with those ears of his... Sighing with relief when she was done, even though she was shaky and weak, slowly Suzy got up and walked back to the sofa. As she sat down on the sofa, again, she sat up straight, clutching her stomach again. "Oh-oh!" and once again, her bladder filled up to the bursting point!

Oh no! She clutched her stomach and sprinted again to the bathroom. Another flood! And yet once again, she got up slowly, and went back to the living room. She had barely sat down when she had to go again! What the hell? Is this what happens when you overdose on Xanax? It wrings you out like a sponge? By morning she'd be nothing but a dried up husk of a person, blown away in the first good wind. Suzy quickly ran to the bathroom, and again, and again, and again! Exhausted, she wearily stood up from the seat. Then, again, she heard roaring from the bedroom. She stopped in her tracks as if a tomahawk had just pierced her back.

Oh my God, noooo!!!! The lion in the lair was roaring again! For the umpteenth time! *Oh, no - oh, God, no, I can't take him again!* She covered her ears with her hands. She thought he was done for the night. Now he was starting all over again, just like her bladder.

"Hey!" Paul yelled. "You think you're going to keep me up all night with that goddam banging in and out, huh? Is that your plan? I forbid you to go near that bathroom again, or I'll lock the door, do you hear me?"

Suzy stood in the hallway, stunned! She had to go; she was in a dreadful state. She felt the urge again; what could she do now? Perspiring, she clutched her stomach; her insides were aching and strained, so weak and drained, as if all life had been sucked out of her. Crawling on her knees, she went into the kitchen and took a plastic bowl and quickly plopped on that. At this point, she didn't care anymore. By now the dam had lessened somewhat. She lay back on the sofa, exhausted, and fell asleep.

The daylight finally woke her up. She heard Paul in the bathroom and didn't know if she should pretend to be asleep or wait to see how he was going to act. She covered her face so that he couldn't see her.

He came into the kitchen and stood in the doorway of the living room, peering over to her on the couch.

"Suzy . . . can we talk? It's almost noon!" His voice was soft and concerned, but hesitant.

His voice was softer and gentle, not quite the normal tone, yet she was reluctant to talk to him. She was afraid to poke the bear and cause the rampage to begin again. She needed to go to the bathroom. In a quiet voice she said, "I need to go to the bathroom; is that all right?" As she got up, she started to sob, louder and louder, flinging herself onto the toilet as she slammed the door. Sobbing hysterically, she laid her head on her folded arms on the sink as she sat on the toilet.

She heard him lightly tap on the door. "Suzy, come on, please," he begged, "please, can we talk this out?" She sobbed more, reaching out for a handful of tissues, blowing her nose loudly.

"I can't talk now, I'm too upset! Please, just leave me alone," she begged, sobbing hysterically again, burying her weary head in her arms on the counter top.

After a while, she finally calmed down, blew her nose, sniffled, and lifted her head up, exhausted.

She was hesitant to face him, feeling so weary and weak. Her mind was wondering what she should do, but all of her senses were dulled and confused. At the corner of her eye, she noticed the pill bottle on the sink that she had left from the previous night. Slowly picking it up, she peered through half closed eyes and studied the label for a moment. She still couldn't make out the name.

"Damn, where the hell are my glasses?" She fumbled in her pocket. She put them on. Now she could read the label clearly. Sitting bolt upright, staring in disbelief, she groaned.

"Oh noooo!" She slumped against the side of the counter. "I took Lasix - not Xanax! Oh my God, no wonder I was up all night!" It was then Suzy vowed never to take another pill without first putting on her glasses. It could be hazardous to her health.

When Paul and Suzy had their fights, she did not want to go to the apartment for fear of him lashing out at her. .

Another day led Suzy to spend another evening at O'Hara's Irish bar, now that she was a regular there. She was keeping out of Paul's hair—well, what was left of it. After consuming tons of vitamins all these years, he should have had a forest for hair by now. At the least, he should look like one of those chia plants that grew like wildfire. And with all that zinc, yohimbe, maca to name a few, his wang should have stood at attention every hour on the hour, like a cuckoo clock popping out. But no such luck. She leafed through another bestseller that she found in the thrift store across the road, a dollar find. Not bad for an hour or two of easy reading. She had gone out for months and not met anybody particularly interesting. So where were they?? Finding Mr. Right was such a tiring job.

Oh sure, she had a met a pervert or two. Really good looking perverts, surprisingly good looking, but perverts all the same. Sidling up next to her was Pervert #1. Tall, dark, and yes, handsome. Extremely handsome, Black Irish looks, with the deepest, bluest eyes—God, were they fascinating. He was a trader on Wall Street. Somehow the conversation turned around to high heels. He said he loved women in high-heeled shoes, especially with silk stockings. He noticed she had high heels - and stockings on. That was why he sat next to her, he explained... *Oh, silly me, and here I thought it was my sexy smile, intellect, and perky, voluptuous bosom.* While she was talking to him, he suddenly swooped down and quickly stuck his finger into the arch of her shoe. He greedily rubbed the instep of her foot with his fingers, brought his hand up to his nose and took a long whiff, closing his eyes, enraptured - as if he smelled some exotic perfume. "Wow!" he whispered. "That was wonderful!" His fingers lingered under his nose, licking them. "Mmmm, and I love sucking toes; how about we meet Saturday?" She looked at him in disbelief, gave him a quick kick to the shin, and ran out into the street!

Then there was the other one. He seemed such a gentleman, and trusting him, she innocently gave him her phone number. He was a debonair banker, with a keen eye for the ladies, amusing and charming. He called one evening out of the blue. But once on the phone, all that vanished into thin air. Instead, the Devil Incarnate emerged. The hairs suddenly sprouted from the palms of his hands, fangs protruded from his lips, while growing a pair of horns out of the top of his head. He told her graphically what he was doing to her and what he wanted her to do to him. His voice alternated between groaning and whispering. "You like what I'm doing to you, baby?"

he hoarsely groaned. "God, that feels sooo gooood! Baby…" A lot of rustling, panting. "Yes, baby, yes!" he groaned over and over. "Your hands make me so hard; you like my cock, don't you? Tell me how good it feels. Come on, honey," he begged. "Come on, you love it; I know you do," moaning, groaning, panting, "aww, you suck me good."

Sparks flew out of the phone as she slammed it down in the cradle, throwing it across the room onto the couch. Shocked, her mind was going into overdrive. Damn! And he looked like such a nice fellow! She grimaced, shuddering, Oh, that disgusting turd! She was fuming. Another disgusting disappointment. Coming back to reality, she thanked God Paul was out at the time, or else she would have had a stroke! And he'd better lose her number!

Suddenly the key turned in the lock as Paul strode in. *Well, wouldn't you know it!* she thought.

"Any calls?" he inquired.

"Oh!" He took her by surprise. "Err, uh, oh yes. But it was only the Firemen's fund. They wanted a contribution. I said I was the maid, so they hung up," She had to think of something!

He looked at her quizzically, noticing the phone was flung on the couch. "So why is the phone on the couch?"

"Oh, it was too hot to handle. You know what they say; firemen are always in heat." She got up to put it back on the wall and began to hum as she walked past him to the bathroom. She felt his gaze on the back of her head as he turned around and walked into the bedroom, shutting the door behind him.

Then there was another one. Pervert #3. She had decided to go to another watering hole close by, just for a change of scene. He came in behind her, noticing her fur coat. She knew he was watching her from his side of the bar. Finally he walked over.

"Hi! May I buy you a drink?" Smiling, he lightly tapped her on the shoulder.

And again, he seemed like a very nice fellow. The kind you could take home to Mother and she'd throw her arms around him immediately. But he had other plans. He kept eyeing her fur coat, stroking it sensuously as he spoke. "So, er, how about a nightcap at my place?" he suggested, a glint in his eyes. "I love that coat you have on." He stroked the sleeve, almost drooling. "How about coming back to my place and walk around naked, just wearing your coat and high heels, hon?" He wiped the saliva from the corner of his mouth.

"Oh! I'm sorry but it's very late!" She ran out of the place. Jeez! Didn't anybody do it the old fashioned way anymore?

She glanced at her watch. It was almost ten o'clock. Time now to face the Weasel up in his Inner Sanctum. She sighed as she looked up, noticed the light in the bedroom and grimly walked to the building entrance as if to face a firing squad. One never knew what to expect.

Turning the key ever so gently in the lock, she opened the door and saw the shadow of the night light on the bathroom wall and listened for the buzzing sounds of the AM stations as she hurriedly undressed in the dark and quietly took the pillows off the couch and popped into the bed. The steel bar of the couch, as usual, stuck in her spine, even after she had tried covering it over with an extra blanket folded in four, and tossing around did not give her any relief. She felt like the main character in *The Princess and the Pea*. God, how she wished her prince would find her. She lay still. The zooming traffic below was a comforting backdrop. There was no sound from the bedroom except the next caller on the talk show. Thank God, she had made it through another day. She sighed and fell into an uneasy sleep.

* * *

"Is Suzy there?" A familiar voice, Karen, from Florida, would call.

"No, she's out," Paul would say.

"Are you expecting her back soon?"

"Tell you the truth, I don't know. She's probably out boozing again. Who knows what time she'll be back?"

"Please tell her I called. Tell her it's Karen." But Suzy never got any of the messages.

On another particular evening, she decided to hang out across the street, as Paul was irritating her once again. Mornings and lectures were not her cup of tea. She was getting to the boiling point. It was cold and drizzling outside, but cozy and welcoming here, at least. O'Hara's was her second home by now. She had just sat down, opening up her book.

Shortly after, she noticed this tall fellow came in and sat a few seats over from her, beckoning to the bartender. "A Scotch on the rocks—oh, and a menu please!" he added. He perused the menu, while he sipped on his drink. The waiter approached and took the order to the kitchen. He glanced her way several times; she casually looked up and caught his eye. He smiled. "Hi, how are you?"

She smiled, "Fine, and you?"

And he introduced himself. "Hi, I'm Mike."

"Oh, Suzy, how do you do?"

And so the ice was broken. He was very well spoken, such a nice, respectful guy. His manners were impeccable, his clothes custom tailored. Immaculate. He was divorced, for about five years now. He bought her a drink and she smiled at him as they clinked glasses and cheered each other. She noticed he had big hands and big feet. About 6'1", light cologne, and clean-shaven, pleasant features. He seemed to have everything going for him. Wow, she could hardly believe her luck after all. They bumped into each other three or four times at O'Hara's. Evidently he liked her company; they found they had many things in common. She thought of him during the day;

it kind of helped her days to be more bearable. The Weasel was having his usual tantrums, and her patience was sorely being tested. *Is it April yet?* she prayed constantly. Her spine was having one hell of a nightly thrashing.

After about two weeks, he finally asked her out. They decided to meet Sunday late afternoon. "How about going to Central Park? Tavern on the Green?" he suggested.

That sounds like fun! I've been there before. Yes, that would be nice, she thought.

Through early dinner, she was finding him so attractive; whether it was his charming voice or his mannerisms, she felt very comfortable with him. She liked that he was so pleasant to the waiter; little things like that impressed her of a man's character. He was easy to talk to and interesting. He spoke about his family, how his father owned a company and built it up from scratch and it was now on the Stock Exchange.

"And I've been with Chase for about twenty years now, right off 80th. I like it very much; it's a great company."

He asked if she would like to come up to his place. It was on the West Side, close by.

"Sure," she smiled. "But I can't be long. I have to be at work early. Mondays! I hate Mondays!"

He switched the light on as they entered the apartment. "Let me help you with your coat."

She smiled at him. He was so considerate. She walked over to the window. "Oh my, how lovely!" She was enthralled. The view of Central Park, all the high rises, the skyscrapers in the skyline were breathtaking! All those twinkling lights! Her eyes sparkled. Somehow she knew he would have a beautiful apartment. He had very modern furniture, very tasteful paintings on the walls. Not one thing out of place, no newspapers cluttering up the coffee table. Very neat, just like he was. He turned on the stereo. *He* likes Barry White—*hmmm, didn't expect that,* she thought. *Love's Theme, his first big hit...*

"What may I offer you, Suzy?" he asked, smiling. "I have wine, I have brandy, vodka— would you like a Martini?"

"Oh, do you have any wine? Maybe a Chardonnay—is that OK, please?" She sat on the couch, watching him. His brown hair was softly wavy, turning salt and peppery; his features were in proportion, with wide brown eyes and mouth. *Very kissable,* she thought.

He sat next to her. "Here, I hope you like it." He handed her the heavy glass.

My, looks like Waterford, she thought. Its deep-cut, intricate crystal pattern shone like a diamond when the light caught it.

He moved closer and put his huge, soft hand in hers. "I'm so happy you are here," he shyly said. All of a sudden he became very boyish.

"Aaaww, me too!" she smiled back as he moved in to kiss her. Very softly, very gently, oh so, so tenderly. *So sweet,* she thought. He was growing on her. She was beginning to like him a lot.

When, suddenly, in a snap, he turned into a tiger. He kissed her passionately while his hands, those huge paws, grabbed her breasts and unbuttoned her blouse, grabbing her, pushing her bra up to fondle her breasts and nipples.

Wow! What happened to shy? she thought.

Now he scooped her up in his arms while kissing her passionately and threw her on his huge king-sized bed. Shoes flying in every direction, shirt and pants in mid air, he pulled off her skirt, now working on the stockings and panties, like a man possessed. He threw himself on her, his fingers feeling her while kissing her deeply, panting. "Wow, I can't get enough of you! You drive me insane!" he hoarsely whispered, when he came up for air. Once again his paws grabbed her nipples, sucking them hard. She climaxed three times. She reached for him. She felt for him, between the kisses; she wanted to please him. Then, reality set in fast. Mr. Big Hands and Big Feet turned out to be Mr. Little Boy. Erect, his penis was no more than a little boy. No more than one of her fingers. Not even an extension cord from Home Depot could help. This was smaller than a pea-shooter. Suddenly, from nowhere, she heard a vibrating sound as he deftly inserted. "It's good, honey; I just want you to feel good." My, he was so considerate.

She dressed quietly in the bathroom and left him snoozing in the bedroom. She tiptoed out into the living room and grabbed her coat, quietly closing the door behind her. Her heart was heavy. It would have been so easy to fall in love with him; he had so many good, decent qualities that she admired. He was kind, loving, and very considerate; he was the type that would have put her on a pedestal. She knew that. As she wearily got into the cab, she looked ahead, dejected, dazed, sighing. Sadly, this could have been Mr. Right. Her eyes welled up; silent tears flowed down her cheeks as she fumbled for a tissue in her bag and blew her nose loudly. The cabbie glanced to check on her; she turned quickly to hide her face.

She felt so bad for him. What a sweet, sweet man—he had everything going for him. But she did not know how to leave him. He really didn't deserve this, which now made her feel doubly bad. Crawling into bed, she thought of his sweet face. Tears ran down her face as she sobbed into her pillow, stifling the sound since Big Ears was in the next room. Life can be so very unfair. So cruel.

CHAPTER THIRTY-SIX

It was another dreary winter day. Oh, how Suzy longed to be back in Florida! "The temperature is 44 degrees and we will be expecting showers until about six this evening," the weatherman announced. "And now back to Jack Jackson of the Jackson Show." She sipped her second cup of coffee while she read the paper. It was absolutely pouring outside. Suzy looked out the window and across the street. The semi-corpse was flopped out on the bed, bright lights filling the room, watching TV, as usual. She shook her head. Paul had left for the office about twenty minutes earlier. Suzy got dressed and decided to get some groceries. As she put on her coat and galoshes, she walked to the door.

Suddenly the phone rang. She ran over to pick it up.

"Suzy! I have this fabulous, fabulous company on Park Avenue - they need somebody right away," the young man at the agency said excitedly, "Are you free today?"

"Free today? Sure!" she said enthusiastically. *I've only been free for four months!* she thought.

"They are one of the most well known companies in New York. I think you'll be perfect for the position. Call Janie at 456-7891. She's great, you'll love her, and she's expecting your call. Oh, and good luck!" he said as he hung up.

Suzy decided to take a cab. The elevator silently whooshed her up to the 44th floor. Stepping gingerly into the corridor, she saw Manhattan Enterprises ahead, knocked on the door, and it flew open as if someone had been waiting there, just hoping someone would knock.

"Hello! I've been expecting you!" Janie was a bright, cheerful administrator for the company. She was tall, thin, and very pretty and of course, wore black. All women in New York wore black! Black, brown or navy but mostly black, so she wasn't really sure why the stores showed all the colors of the rainbow.

"So, Suzy, tell me a little about yourself." Janie looked up from her desk, smiling. "I see from your resume that you come from Florida? This must be a big change for you," she said as she looked at the application form.

"Oh no, I lived in Manhattan before, but that was a while ago. I love New York; it has so much to offer!" she lied. Truly, at this point she was not too impressed. The months with Paul had certainly been a hard, long drag. Some days were fine, but on the whole it could be quite lonely.

"Well," Janie went on brightly, and told her of the position and what it entailed. Basically it was just a receptionist desk job and checking the surveillance camera to let in the staff. "And of course, as part of Manhattan Enterprises, you are entitled to health insurance as of today, as well!" Gosh, no 90-day probation? Forty hours and health insurance...from day one?? Now that was unusual.

That's all that this job was? She looked into Janie's eyes as she spoke. Janie gaily told Suzy about all the perks of working for this exciting and prestigious company here in the heart of Manhattan, on Park Avenue, no less, near the Waldorf Astoria and Grand Central Station.

"The agency said you could start now – today?" Suzy smiled eagerly, nodding vigorously. And with that Janie picked up all the papers, gave

Suzy back her driver's license and Social Security card, and smiled broadly. "Welcome aboard! All right, I'll take you down the hallway; follow me!" Suzy trotted behind Janie like a little puppy. She was floating on a cloud, as if on her way to Utopia, grinning from ear to ear.

After all this time, it was a pleasure to be dealing with normal people. This time when she answered the phone, she didn't have to deal with a crackpot wanting to know who called and why didn't I put the call through to them! Suzy wanted to scream from the rooftops, "Do you hear me, Dr. Upton? Forty hours and benefits, too, from day one!"

Suzy was giddy thinking back to the interview she had when she first came to New York at that world-famous institution, which now seemed a lifetime ago. Of course she knew she was capable of a lot more jobwise, but it covered her bills and was certainly not stressful and not only that, the people there were so nice. Going to work was such a pleasure; it felt like she was on vacation! All the stresses and disappointments of the last three months just melted away. Even the family that owned this conglomerate were so nice and down to earth, and so generous to their staff. It was hard to believe that they did own a sizable portion of New York, plus properties all over the U.S., and yet were so modest and unassuming. Many times she would open up the newspaper and see their name at some special function or gala in the Society section. They were great philanthropists for Carnegie Hall and many other institutions, and later were involved with the rehabilitation of the military.

At Christmas time, the front of the building, which was an entire city block, was piled high with all kinds of incredible toys and bicycles, which were donated to several charities. It was all quite thrilling. Suzy had never been on the 43rd floor of any building before, and to see the whole of Manhattan, Brooklyn, and the Bronx was exciting. Finally, things were looking up!

CHAPTER THIRTY-SEVEN

S uzy flung off her coat and ran into the kitchen. She knew Paul would be home soon, so she started peeling the potatoes under the tap, threw them into a pot on the stove. She looked in the fridge and found some carrots and French beans. She had bought a barbecued whole chicken—it was still hot—from the deli downstairs, and some coleslaw. She then hurriedly set the table.

Suzy heard the key turn in the lock as Paul tore in, dropped the briefcase on the floor and threw his hat and coat on the bed. The men in New York wore hats; it gave them a certain panache, she noticed. Made them more handsome, she thought. Like pilots for the airlines—they all seem much better looking in uniform.

"Hi!" She looked over at him quickly. "Dinner will be ready in about 10 minutes; want a drink or something?" she offered.

Paul waved at her. "No, it's OK, I'll wait!" he said as he headed toward the couch. Suzy wiped her hands clean and followed him in.

"Now this was something today!" he started, as he spread out on the couch, head back.

She sat on the couch opposite Paul. "So what was on the agenda today?" she giggled.

He shook his head, "Jeez, well, apparently these two old doddering spinsters have fifty cats in the house! Fifty! The neighbors complained to the city about the stench from their house, it was so bad. And then when the city went in, they found cat urine, feces, and food that stank so bad they had to run outside to keep from throwing up. There were litter boxes everywhere that were stinking, and litter had been kicked all over the floor!" He grimaced. "There were cats running all over the place! Everywhere! Filthy, dirty! Cat hair all over the floor, all over the furniture, torn drapes, the couches were all ripped up from the cats clawing them to shreds! And then these two old ladies became hysterical because they had to get rid of the cats! It was like something out of a Fellini movie; the whole thing was bizarre!" His big blue eyes widened. "I had to make a decision here, natu-rally!" His voice trailed off; being the defender of the law, bang went the gavel and the two old biddies were hauled out by the bailiff.

CHAPTER THIRTY-EIGHT

Happy New Year! It was January first and that much closer to April, when Suzy would have her place in Florida back. She hung the new calendar on the kitchen wall, and with a black marker, crossed off the days each day when she got home from work. Paul used to watch in silence, as if he really, in a strange way – a very strange way – did not want her to leave. Suzy took care of the apartment with no thanks from Paul. She cooked and cleaned; she did the laundry every week and ironed all of his clothes. No wonder he didn't want her to leave. As much as he was not capable of a relationship, the domesticity was endearing to him. But the underlying volcano that could erupt at a moment's notice had a tendency to erase any good feelings.

Things were not running smoothly like they were in the beginning. It was a case of waiting it out until April, when the snowbirds would once again head north. Things were rocky in the Paul Kane aka Weasel household, but both Paul and Suzy tried to endure the time as best they could. He knew she was extremely unhappy. When he was his normal self, the one she knew when she dated him back in Miami, he really wasn't such a terrible person.

He could be very bright, considerate, witty, funny, generous and pleasant, a real pleasure to be with.

But now, living together here in the Big Apple, every so often, one word out of place that she innocently uttered and he could be meaner than a dentist's drill and just as shrill. The wires in his brain just went screwy!

Possibly - and for sure, most probably - that was the reason why he had always been a bachelor. Maybe he had some kind of bipolar thing going on, but Suzy was no shrink and she knew Paul was not going to take anything but those damn vitamins. She couldn't for the life of her figure out any sort of rhyme or reason to his behavior, except for talking during dinner. What words or sentences brought on the episodes? Afterwards, Paul would feel guilty, just like any other abuser, and want to treat Suzy to something, maybe buy her a present or take her to a restaurant that she liked, to make it up to her. But she wasn't falling for his schtick. Too little too late, buddy.

"You know," he looked concerned as he went on, "I know it's hard for you being in a strange town with no friends, hey, New York is tough! You know, I try to help you as best as I can. I don't make any demands on you…"

WTF was he talking about? Of course he put demands on her: no chit-chat during dinner, making her sleep on the couch, and just being an all-around pain in the ass to live with.

"And believe me, lots of men would, but that's not what I want, OK? All I ask is that we try to work this thing out the best for you, and for me. Is that OK with you?"

He sat across from her in the kitchen, his voice soft and consoling. She was not an unreasonable person, he was trying to be decent, and she was trying to make the best of a bad situation until she could get back home. There was no point in making things worse; it was just a question of time now when she would head South and be gone.

CHAPTER THIRTY-NINE

A nd then this weird thing happened. One day Paul said, "Why don't we go to a singles' party? There's one this Saturday down on 25th Street. Would you like to go? Who knows, you might meet Mr. Right!" he said jokingly.

Now this was a 360. Suzy wasn't sure if he wanted to meet somebody new or if he wanted her to meet somebody new, or maybe both.

She looked at the floor, not sure how to respond. *Maybe he wants me out of his hair, or the scouring pad as the case may be; is that his angle now?* She was getting to the point where she didn't care anymore. Sleeping on the couch with that iron bar in the middle of her back was so damned uncomfortable she felt like she'd aged 10 years in the months she'd been here. She woke every morning to back pain but never mentioned it to Paul. Why? Was he going to give up his bed for her? Hell, no! She just suffered in silence and waited. April would be here before she knew it.

"Hey, why not?" She shrugged her shoulders. In a way she felt he was testing her to see how much crap she would take before she walked out. *Oh hell no, you little Weasel. You're not getting off that easy!* Judging by her past luck with men, Suzy did not feel there was a possibility of meeting anyone of any consequence. But hey, it was a few hours out of the apartment. And who knew? She might possibly meet somebody to bullshit with for a couple hours.

The cabbie turned off 23rd and slowed down in front of the club. Paul and Suzy stepped out into the street. The chilly night air went right through her as they hurriedly walked in, and Paul paid the cover charge.

A tall redhead at the desk asked, "Sir, would you like to be a member? It's only fifty dollars."

He looked over to Suzy as he ushered her in. "Maybe next time!"

They walked over to the bar. "What'll you have?"

"A Chardonnay, please." The bartender handed her a glass.

Both Suzy and Paul looked around. "Not too busy yet." He stood next to her checking out the room.

"OK, I'll see you later." He tipped his glass toward her and disappeared into the crowd. What a jerk.

Suzy wearily got up on a barstool. "Oh, so is this how it's going to be, is it?"

She looked over to the far side of the room. Paul had met a little brunette. She was a bit homely, but they were laughing and smiling while they talked. Things must be going well for him, Suzy thought. Secretly she wanted to run over to the girl and warn her. "Run away right now. Don't look back and don't slow down until you're in Staten Island." Screw it! Let her find out the hard way just like Suzy did.

She looked around the dimly lit room, checking out the men sitting at the bar. Most of them were staring into space like survivors of a horrific disaster, probably marriage, wondering at what point their lives had gone so wrong. Their shadowy, vacant faces every now and again would take a sip of their drink, realizing no amount of alcohol could wash away the detritus of their shitty lives.

Wow, what a motley bunch! Suzy thought, what an enormous collection of deadbeats. She took another sip, looked around again. Frigging zombies. This place needs to liven up!

There were a few women with their girlfriends chatting away, all expecting Mr. Right to waltz in, sweep them off their feet, and sail off into the sunset. Suzy watched more men and women come in. It was around 11:30 by now. The place was getting crowded. She sighed, feeling defeated. There were tall men, short men, men with bald heads and wisps of hair growing from their chins, and men with a full head of hair and a beard to match. Some were wearing casual clothes while others dressed in a jacket and tie. Some wore glasses. They all had one thing in common. None of them appealed to her. Some looked over to her, but she looked the other way. *This is just like shopping,* she thought to herself. *When I have money I can't find a thing and when I'm broke everything looks good! It's the same way with men. All the ones you don't like, seem to make a beeline for you.* She checked the time; it was 12:15.

Well, enough excitement for one night! she thought sarcastically, jumping off the chair. She put on her coat, didn't bother to look for Paul, and walked out into the cold night air. She stood at the curb, waved, and shouted, "Taxi!"

CHAPTER FORTY

Another Friday night rolled around and Suzy, as usual, had no plans. Paul left earlier. He had a date with a friend for dinner. Suzy surmised it was the woman from the singles' party. She didn't plan to stay home. She wasn't going to be in the city much longer, anyway, so she might as well enjoy all that New York had to offer while she could. Suzy turned on the stereo; the music was hot.

She put on her three-quarter length black wool dress with the long V-neckline. It looked good with boots. Then she put on her gold necklace and gold earrings; she loved gold. She thought that silver didn't have the warmth that gold did. Suzy was feeling good that night as she got dressed and sprayed herself with her favorite perfume.

She listened to John Mellencamp's *Wild night is Callin'* with the drumbeat and the rippling bass guitar...

"As you brush your shoes, stand before your mirror,
And you comb you hair, grab your coat and hat
And you walk the streets
Trying to remember...

…was whirring in her head as she combed her hair in the mirror, smoothing it down in the back, peeking to check her lipstick, and pulling on her black leather boots. *I just love wearing boots; boots are so sexy,* she thought. As she pushed the elevator button, she felt a surge of excitement build up inside her.

"*And everything looks so complete.*

When you're walking down on the street,

And the wind catches your feet,

Sets you flyin', cryin' …

"*Ooooo weee … Wild night is callin',*" the tambourines and bass guitar beating away.

"*Come on out and dance.*

Come on out and make romance…"

The words went around and around like an old 45 record, in her head. Suzy threw on her coat, took a deep breath, and headed out on the town. She felt really good. It was one of those nights when you just knew, that somehow, it was going to be exciting.

There was a crisp chill in the air that added to the excitement as she headed over to the Cigar Bar on Lexington. It was right down the street from the apartment. She had passed it many times but never went in. She climbed down the stairs and walked through to the bar in the back. The lights were seductively low, the shadows of the clientele adding an air of mystery and intrigue, while the wailing saxophone in the background played jazz, hot and wild. The bartender polished some glasses, turned around, and smiled when he saw her.

"Good evening, what can I get for you?"

"Good evening. A Chardonnay, please."

Looking around, she saw there were some people seated at tables, and a few at the bar. It was still early, about nine-fifteen. She looked down at her drink as if she might find the secret to the Universe at the bottom when, out of the corner of her eye, she noticed a young man standing beside her. He was tall and slim, with soft features and soft, wavy brown hair parted in the middle.

He glanced at her. "Good evening, how are you?" he said crisply as his eyes followed the bartender. He had a pleasant masculine voice.

Suzy casually glanced up at him. "Hi, I'm fine, thanks. How are you?" This time she more clearly noticed his small features, with pouty, full lips. She did a double take. *That mouth! My God, just like Elvis Presley! Elvis is alive,* she thought, turning around quickly, looking nonchalantly into the distance, taking a sip from her glass.

"I'll have a martini," he waved to the bartender, "straight up."

"Ooh, that's a powerful drink!" She looked up at him. *This one's all man, I see.*

"Yes, I suppose it is!" he answered. "Would it be all right if I smoked a cigar?" he asked.

"Well, this is the Cigar Bar, so sure, go ahead." She smiled broadly.

Mr. Pouty Lips sure was polite; obviously he had some breeding. Mommy and Daddy had sent him to the right schools, she concluded. What is the expression? Manners maketh the man. He had it in spades. Suzy noticed his suit as he spoke. It was conservatively gray with a herringbone weave pattern, an understated tie to match, and a white shirt. He was boyish, confident, considerate. But at the same time, there was a hint of arrogance. She liked the combination.

"I'm Jonathan, and you are?" he inquired and took a sip, looking into her eyes. He stood with his back leaning on the bar, his long legs crossed, checking his top pocket. His eyes swept over the room.

"Suzy. It's a pleasure to meet you, Jonathan!" she breathlessly answered, taking a sip of her drink.

"Would you like a cigar?" he asked as he snipped off the end and began to light it, and turned to her. "I like to see women smoke cigars. I think it's sexy."

"You do, do you? Not my style, but thanks," she laughed. She wondered what else he liked to see women do…Hmmm, this could be fun after all.

"I'll give you a hundred dollars if you would!" he insisted.

"I wouldn't smoke one if you gave me five thousand." She laughed again. "I don't like cigars for women. It's OK for a man. But I don't find it attractive."

He turned around, noticing a young blonde over in the corner smoking a cigar. He looked over his shoulder. "See… she likes them." His eyes rested on Suzy's smiling lips. He was certainly taking notes. Didn't peer pressure end after high school? Suzy asked herself.

"That's fine for her, I suppose, but not for me," she laughed. She was in a playful mood.

Two ladies were now seated across from them. They watched as the bartender placed their drinks in front of them. The ceiling lighting shone right down on their glasses. The drinks were sparking blue, like the ocean in a martini glass. Suzy stared, totally fascinated. She had never seen a drink this color before; she couldn't take her eyes off it. The drink reminded her of Florida, of the sun on the ocean, sparkling, twinkling—and here it was in a glass in Manhattan! It was if they were drinking the Atlantic Ocean. She visualized A1A on Fort Lauderdale beach, with the palm trees swaying and a soft warm breeze, the white soft sand with the deep blue-gray ocean meeting the blue, blue sky in the distance. All of a sudden she felt homesick. Maybe this was a sign.

Intrigued, she said to him, "What is that? It's beautiful!" Her eyes widened.

He followed her eyes over to the two drinks on the counter. "What?... Oh, those?" He called to the bartender, "What is that?" She noticed he had an authoritative tone in his voice. She loved it!

"They're martinis with a splash of Curacao for color."

"They're so beautiful!" she gushed. Her eyes were drawn to them.

He looked down at her and looked across at the bartender. "Get her one," he ordered.

"Get her one!" The words rang in her head. She loved the direct approach that he had. He was beginning to appear very attractive to her.

Gee, it wasn't that she asked for one - and he certainly didn't ask her if she would like one, she thought; he just ORDERED it for her! She looked at him without saying a word.

Here was a real man for a change, she thought. Oh my God, she was in seventh heaven. For a split second, she had fallen in love! This was her kind of man: a confident, take charge, take the bull by the horns, say what you mean, and mean what you say type of man. She knew he was no wimp.

She watched his pouty lips as he puffed on the cigar, his eyes intense, absorbed. Damn, too bad he was so young, but she forgave him for that. She noticed his brown eyes, and that pouty mouth drove her wild. An electrical jolt overcame her; sparks were flying like laser beams. Ping! Ping! She acted cool as a cucumber, flicking her hair from her eyes. He glanced intently at her, took a puff, and slowly blew the smoke into the air above her. Suzy watched the pouty lips in action while she played with her necklace. He was making her a tad nervous, hot and bothered. His eyes lingered on her neck and moved back to her lips.

The bartender brought the drink and placed it on the counter. She looked at it, fascinated, as it sparkled and twinkled in the light. It was almost too beautiful to drink. Suzy picked it up gently and brought it to her lips and sipped.

"Whoa!" It took her breath away. Her eyes began to water as the liquid coursed down her throat. Smoke came out of her ears and nose, while she coughed trying to catch her breath!

"Very good, thank you!" She spluttered. *God, that was potent!* she thought.

He ignored her. "I'll have another," he said as he eyed the bartender.

"So, do you work in the city?" Every man Suzy met was either a stock-broker or a banker.

"Yes, I work in the city, Wall Street. Been with Lehman, oh, I don't know, maybe five years now. My family is from San Francisco. New York's all right, I suppose, but I guess I'll be here for awhile and then go back," he explained, turning. "How about you?"

"Yes, over on Park Avenue. I work for a conglomerate. They're very nice people to work for," she offered. "It's a real pleasure to get up and go to work. I'm very fortunate."

He puffed on his cigar. "And do you live in the city?" he asked. She nodded.

The bartender placed the drink carefully in front of Jonathan, who lifted it up to toast. "Cheers!"

"Cheers. So where do you live? In Manhattan?" she asked.

"No, I have a house outside the city."

Probably Westchester, she thought.

He puffed away, blowing the smoke above his head. He was looking at her intently, studying her features; his eyes slowly swept over her hair, her necklace, looking down at her manicured nails holding the glass. He obviously liked feminine women; he must have liked her perfume too: Chanel, her favorite. He watched her mouth as she spoke, lingering, then up to her eyes, and back. There was no denying it; sparks were flying at each other. After all, he could have moved in a flash on to Cigar girl, puffing away in the corner, if he wanted to. Cigar girl was more his age. And she liked cigars.

He was the type that would, in a heartbeat. Instead, he was entranced by Suzy. An older woman seemed a good challenge to him, and he was the type of man who needed that.

He was talking, looking into her eyes. Words that may have had meaning, of San Francisco, of New York, words in that deep masculine voice. Words that were a total blur to her. He could have spoken to her in Swahili, and she would have said, "Yes." She stared at him, and those lips, and nodded, totally caught up in the moment but nonchalantly looking into the distance and glancing back at him.

"So how long does it take you to get home?" she inquired, tilting her head ever so slightly toward him. Like she really cared.

"Oh, about forty minutes. I take the train." He leaned against the bar. "Not too bad."

"Gee, a good looking man like you, alone on a Friday night? What's up with that?" she coaxed. She knew he had to have a wife or girlfriend, something told her. He was way too hot to be alone.

"So where's your girlfriend?" she said.

He shifted around, seemed a little uneasy for a minute, looked ahead, then over to her, took another puff, and rolled the ash off into the ashtray.

"She's out of town," he said quietly. "She had to go visit her family. " He looked at her.

"So have you two been dating a long time?" She sipped her drink.

"Yes, we've been together for a while," he added.

"So are you getting married?" She knew this guy was too good to be true. She slowly took another sip of the sparkling blue drink; she felt she was drinking the ocean.

"Uh, I don't know." He looked uneasy for a moment, staring at the bar ahead. "She won't have me! I want to, but she doesn't! She says she's not ready, whatever that means. I don't know." He shrugged.

I don't know, when a woman says she is not ready after living with a man for a while, it tells me she is not totally into him. Lucky bitch, she thought jealously. *Some women have all the damn luck.* Now this scenario was starting to make sense. They spoke for a while. He seemed restless, but certainly attentive as she spoke. Jonathan was polite, yet his arrogance seeped through every now and then. He amused Suzy. She noticed he never once smiled. That was okay; he didn't need to.

Suzy could feel the drink coursing through her veins; her whole body felt like it was on fire. Was it the alcohol or Jonathan? She could only sip a little at a time. Wow, martinis were powerful stuff.

He looked around. "So is there another place where they have music?" he asked.

"Yes, sure, there's the Sign of the Dove over on 65th if you like. It's very nice. I think you'll like it! They have excellent bands there especially on Friday nights," she offered.

He looked at her, looked over at the bartender, then raised his hand. The bartender nodded and brought over the check. Looking quickly at it, Jonathan felt in his pocket, counted out the cash and left it on the counter, turned to her. "Let's go!" She followed him out. It was chilly and she noticed he didn't have a coat.

"My God, it's freezing! Where's your coat?" It was near freezing, about 35 degrees.

"I left it at work. It's not that bad as long as you're moving around." He waved down a taxi with a yellow light on the roof.

"Come on out and dance;
Come on out and make romance...
Oooowee...Wild Night is callin'"

CHAPTER FORTY-ONE

Ttttt hey jumped in, huddled close to keep warm, and in practically two seconds they were in front of Sign of the Dove.

The place was jammed, wall-to-wall people. The band was hot that night, and couples were dancing cheek to cheek. Suzy and Jonathan pushed and shoved their way through people to get to the bar.

He looked at her. "A Chardonnay?" He didn't miss a thing, did he? He turned around, with two drinks in his hands, and gave her, hers. They clinked glasses and sipped slowly as they looked into each other's eyes; they were speaking volumes.

The music was good, and the atmosphere was humming with excitement. He looked over to the dance floor and then down to her. They were crushed together as more people surged forward. She held her drink carefully, so as not to spill it on him. He took the drink from her, and placed it on the bar. Grabbing her hand, he said, "Let's dance!" and moved toward the dance floor. He never asked her anything, she noticed; he just led her. And like a lamb, she followed him. He pulled her closer to him as they slow danced. She felt his body against hers. She was attracted to tall, slim men. As they moved slowly to the rhythm of the music, she felt his thigh against her leg. He had a tight strong body, she noticed. Her breasts rested on his chest while his hand was around her shoulders, slowly, ever so slowly, caressing her back. It was driving her wild. He certainly knew how to press all the right buttons for her. She laid her head on his shoulder, her arms curled around his neck, then looked into his eyes. They moved slowly, rhythmically, to the music, feeling their bodies intertwined. His eyes bore into hers. There was no mystery in his eyes; he knew what he wanted, and Suzy knew what she wanted, too. God, it had been so long! She looked at the pouty mouth. Hungrily they kissed. Oh God, it felt good; she wanted more of him. Jonathan was irresistible. He held her tight for a moment, and once again looked into her eyes.

"Can we go somewhere?" he asked quietly. She nodded. As he led her by the hand, they weaved through the crowds and into a cab. The ride was a blur to her. All she remembered was stepping out in front of five star hotel. *A man with good taste,* she thought, *right up my alley. It's about damn time!* So far, he had not disappointed her. She remembered the hotel, with its marble flooring, and soft lighting in the lobby. She waited on the other side of the lobby while he checked in. Somehow, she didn't feel cheap doing this with him. She didn't even think about it, really. It was so weird, but everything he did was magic. Whatever he was unknowingly doing, Suzy found him to be very powerfully attractive. No other man had ever been able to do it. It was intoxicating, alluring, as if he put a spell on her. It was dizzyingly seductive, and it felt good. He was beginning to be the answer to the Universe, after all. The man that you always dreamed that he would be. And there he was, as he stood in front of her, extending his hand. Slowly she got up, silently took his hand and once again, meekly followed him into the elevator.

Jonathan was young, hypnotic, tantalizing, irresistible, and he made her heart race. *That intangible magnetic powerful force between a man and a woman. Chemistry, in all its glory.*

The room was in beige—beige walls, beige carpeting, and beige bedspread, monochromatically luxurious. It was simply elegant, with a breathtaking view of the city. She took off her coat and sat on the bed. He knelt down in front of her, unzipping her boots, all the while looking deep into her eyes, not a word being exchanged. Suzy leaned forward and unbuttoned Jonathan's shirt, lightly kissing his lips and cheeks, while removing his shirt. She lightly caressed his chest, and then undid his belt and zipper. Man, she was coordinated this evening. Martinis can do that, apparently. He was excited. She caressed him gently as she kissed and licked his neck with soft, sweet kisses. He smelled good and tasted good, totally irresistible. The taserlike sparks were flying off both of them.

He gently helped her out of her dress and laid it to the side. He deftly took off her bra, exposing her large breasts, tenderly cupping them in his hands and whispering, "They're beautiful, just beautiful." He groaned with pleasure. Oh God, this man was wild, and she loved it. Silently, she watched him; her nipples were erect, red and hard. He sucked them gently, flicking his tongue around them. It sent shivers up her spine. She ran her fingers through his soft, wavy hair, brushing it back with her fingers.

"I'll be right back," she whispered. Suzy tore off the rest of her clothes and jumped into the shower. She looked around the bathroom with its marbled floors and walls, and the lush, thick towels hanging on the rack. The lighting was soft. Everything was just perfect! This man knew how to do it right. Her kind of man; for a moment she was envious of his girlfriend. On the other hand, if it wasn't for the girlfriend, Suzy wouldn't be here tonight. She dried herself and wrapped the towel around her. The hotel even provided toothbrushes for the guests, she noticed. What service! Jonathan was lying on the bed; he had taken the cover off and thrown it onto the chair.

Suzy lay down beside him and kissed him, lightly licking his lips. He gently stroked her arm, then jumped up.

"I'll be right back." He closed the door to the bathroom behind him. She heard him turn on the shower.

Suzy nuzzled under the covers, noticing the mattress was luxurious, thickly padded, and cushiony. *Heavenly!* she thought. It was like lying on a cloud compared to the torture of sleeping on Paul's crappy foldout couch.

She felt his damp, hard body close to hers. "Hi." He kissed her tenderly. He held her tight; wrapping their legs around each other, they moved closer together. She felt his hard, muscular chest on her breasts; she rubbed herself lightly against him. He hungrily kissed her, exploring her mouth with his tongue, again and again, now moving down to kiss her breasts. She groaned, taking deep breaths.

He leaned over to the nightstand. "Just a sec" he whispered. His mouth and those sweet lips on hers were pure ecstasy. She lived and died in his mouth, moaning, "Yes, oh yes." His stubble was hurting her chin, but she couldn't stop now. She felt him, hard, against her stomach, that rock-hard mound excited her. As he entered her, she writhed to take more of him, groaning with sheer ecstasy. She wanted all of him. With each stroke, he took her to a place that had long been dormant, but was now alive. They were like two tigers, panting, biting, kissing, voraciously devouring each other. "Oh, oh," she moaned breathlessly, her lips on fire, feeling lightheaded. Her body moved toward him, faster and faster, writhing, until a volcano erupted within her, taking her to heights she had never known before, as if she was floating higher and higher, up in the Milky Way with thousands of twinkling stars around her. They both fell back, exhausted.

She licked his neck, kissing his face, with its film of sweat; her fingers played with his hair.

"God, that was good. Wow!" he whispered as he kissed her tenderly.

"Mmmm, you're the best." She smiled sleepily at him. What a sweet lover he was. As they lay in the dark, she caressed him gently, kissing his chest. His skin was soft. Stroking him lightly, her fingertips traveled up and down his firm beautiful body. She kissed his thighs, slowly kissed the palms of his hands, her tongue making circles, kissing and sucking his fingers, one by one.

"Mmmmm, that is so good, mmm," he groaned, whispering, "I love it—don't —mmmm."

Slowly, he became more excited. Her kisses thrilled him and once again, he mounted her. It was just as good as the first time; they moved together as if united as one. She would gladly be his love slave; all her senses were on fire. He knew all the buttons to push. Boy, what a change, she thought. She held him close; she never wanted to let him go. She looked down at his lips, lightly fingering them, tracing them. Those soft, pouty, full lips—her Elvis lips. He tenderly kissed her finger. Those lips drove her wild.

"I'm glad you're here," he whispered.

"Me, too!" This was her night with him. Who knew about tomorrow? All she knew was now. This moment. There was no tomorrow. They held each other. Kissing her softly, he held her hand, brought it up to his mouth, gently kissing it, turned on his side, and drifted off to sleep, happily relaxed and exhausted.

She sleepily woke up as his hand was caressing her thighs, then touching her gently, once again arousing her, deep inside her; it felt so good. "Don't stop, oh please," she whispered huskily, as he gently lifted her breast to his mouth. Groaning, she moved closer to him, breathing more rapidly. "Don't stop!" She convulsed in pure pleasure. Once again, as stars shot out into the universe, she closed her eyes tight, holding on to the moment. "Oh, oh my, you are wonderful, just wonderful." She sleepily licked her lips. Moving down, she kissed his thighs. "Here, let me make you feel good," she whispered. She took him into her mouth, took his fingers on either side, her tongue exploring all of him. The more she kissed him, licking him in quick strokes, the more it excited her. This man was driving her insane.

"Fuck my mouth." She wanted more and more of him, as he breathlessly moved rhythmically. "Yes, yes, baby." She took all of him as he slumped back on the pillow in total exhaustion.

"Wow! Incredible!" he smiled sleepily and laughed softly. "Who would have thought? Wow!" As he kissed her and nuzzled her neck, she lay in the dark. He sighed, relaxed and happily spent, fell asleep, softly snoring in her ear.

This is the closest thing to heaven, she thought to herself. *How I wish I could have this every night ... and this mattress too!*

She woke up suddenly; dawn was breaking. Oh, God, it was late! She was afraid of the wrath that she was to face. She heard him softly snoring beside her.

She looked down at him. *He looks like a sweet, adorable baby,* she thought, bending closer and stroking his cheek tenderly. She had to go. She daren't wake him, though. She quickly went to the bathroom, closed the door gently, and quietly got dressed. She was putting on her coat as she entered the bedroom, when he drowsily lifted his head.

"Hi—what time is it?" he whispered, slumping back onto the pillow. He couldn't stay awake. He lay there for a minute.

"It's almost five thirty! I have to go!" she whispered as she zipped up her boots.

"Hold on a sec." He slowly got up and fumbled in his trouser pocket. "Here, will that cover the cab? Oh, wait a minute, here's my card, OK? Give me a call. You were great ... call me, OK?" he whispered, half asleep.

"Oh, all right, thanks, you too! You were wonderful!" she said hurriedly. They hugged and she grabbed her bag and, like Cinderella, ran off into the early morning silence.

Paul heard the key turn in the door. With those ears, he could hear a cat piss forty miles away; he heard everything. No matter how carefully she tried to be quiet, he could hear her. It unnerved her at times.

Suzy quickly slipped out of her dress, put on her nightgown, and lay down on the sofa—the goddamn sofa with the friggin' bar that stuck in her back. She truly despised it now! She put her head on the pillow, and went to sleep. She woke to hear Paul rattling his bottles of "'erbs" in the kitchen. His daily truckload.

She closed her eyes and thought about Jonathan. She remembered his touch, how his skin felt on hers, and that sexy pouty mouth. Ahhh, that mouth, those pouty Elvis lips! Again and again, she wanted to live and die in his mouth. From now on, she would always remember him each time she saw a picture of Elvis. He would haunt her in the sweetest way forever. Dear, sweet Jonathan, from San Francisco, via New York, standing next to her at the Cigar Bar, that arrogant, preppy tone of his hiding his boyishness, which amused her that much more. He was just perfect.

Sighing, she closed her eyes. Her lips felt sore, dry and cracked, swollen from their wild night. She licked them softly. She loved the afterglow of lovemaking. Her chin hurt from the shave burn; she probably had a big, round, red circle, but she didn't care, it was worth it. It was all worth it.

She wished Jonathan were there beside her now; okay, maybe not RIGHT now, what with the metal bar realigning her spine like some torturous chiropractic school dropout.

Lifting the blanket over her face and smiling secretly to herself, slowly grinning from ear to ear, Suzy felt like the cat that swallowed the canary. Closing her eyes, she imagined herself as a fat, fluffy white cat leisurely sashaying down an alley, with traces of feathers on her whiskers and a big, contented smile on her lips, swaying her hips slowly from side to side, a big fluffy tail slowly whipping back and forth rhythmically. And this pussycat was definitely purring. She smiled. She always had a sense of the ridiculous—one of her better traits, she believed. She felt like laughing out loud but then, he, the Generale over there, swilling down all those potent 'erbs, would suspect something if she did. He would want an explanation, but she wasn't in the mood for that. She was concentrating on her night, reliving it over and over again in her mind.

"Good afternoon. It's twelve o'clock." Paul's tone was quiet, but also curious.

The magical spell she was under went "poof" into thin air, like a dream you weren't ready to give up. Reality set in fast. Damn!

Paul waited for Suzy to get up before he ever so slowly tried to pry any information out of her. He quietly read the paper as she prepared her coffee. Yes, she bought a coffee pot and enjoyed her coffee, no thanks to Dictator Kane aka the weasel. There are certain of life's pleasures and to her, coffee in the morning was one of them. Case closed.

"Gee, I thought you might have been kidnapped!" He looked up for a split second. "I didn't know if I should call the police or what! I waited till about one o'clock for you! Then I went to sleep." She knew his tactics all too well.

"Really?" She acted nonchalant. "I met Marilyn from work last night, and we all wound up at her friend's house, and before we knew it, it was around five, so I left!" She sipped her coffee. She really needed it. The coffee was doing more for her than ten pounds of those vitamins would ever do for Paul.

"Oh, where was the house?" he said quietly. Typical friggin' lawyer—the facts ma'am, just the facts.

"It was near Marilyn's apartment downtown, off 35th." What did she care? She was leaving soon.

He looked up, flicking the paper. "Sooo, you had a good time?" He looked quizzically at her face.

"Yes, I guess." She acted disinterested, shrugging her shoulders. "It was all right..." Getting up, she said, "I'd better get dressed" and wearily stood up and shuffled off to the bathroom.

She heard him close the front door as she stepped out of the bath-room. She walked into the closet to get her dress and hung up her robe. She remembered Pouty Lips' card that she had hurriedly put in her coat pocket when she left the hotel. Reaching into her left pocket and then checking the right, she found a crumpled card. It read 'Mr. Chen's Chinese Laundry on Seventy Second Street.' "Oh, no! Damn it!" She looked horrified. It must have fallen out in the cab when she took out the twenty to pay the cabbie. "I hope I see Jonathan at the Cigar Bar; he's the best thing that has happened to me in years!"

CHAPTER FORTY-TWO

On Thursday, Suzy heard Paul in the bathroom as he prepared for work. She quietly rose and went to the kitchen and made herself a cup of coffee. She opened the front door to pick up the *New York Times*. The elevator was directly across from the apartment. A neighbor was standing in the hallway waiting patiently for the elevator and turned around and smiled as they wished each other "Good morning." Suzy left the newspaper on the seat of Paul's chair. She put out eggs and citrus for him and made the tea. She had just sat down when he rushed in and flopped down, tapping his eggs, taking a mouthful and swilling down the hot tea.

She looked out the window; it was a gray day. She hated gray days. They reminded her of her days in England. Growing up, she always hated the bleak, ugly, depressing rainy days of her youth. And what do you know! Once again, there was the neighbor, the semi-corpse, across in the street in the penthouse, flopped on the bed, watching TV, as usual. You'd think if she were dead her body would have started to decompose by now. But no, she just lay there watching television. Never getting up, never having a tray of food and eating, never walking around, never going to work, at least as far as anyone could tell. The plot thickened. It was all a big mystery.

Suzy took a sip of her coffee. One of her few delights in life was a good steaming cup of coffee in the morning. Paul looked quickly down at her cup with a face of disgust. Holy shit, it was judgment day again.

"Uh-uh! I see!" he scowled, as he opened the newspaper. "Some people never learn!" he went on, his features hardened. The bullet-like blue eyes penetrated into her skull, but she ignored him. Mornings were not her favorite time of day, especially when Paul was around. He never figured out that she was not a morning person. He was an extremely intelligent man otherwise, but totally clueless when it came to women. And these types of remarks were adding fuel to the fire that was burning inside her, ready to erupt.

Uh-oh! He's got his period. Early this month, huh? she thought sarcastically. She was fuming.

She patiently sat back and stared stonily out the window again. Paul flew up out of the chair, threw open the cupboard, and took several handfuls of vitamins—his daily fix, swilled down with glasses of prune juice. Taking so many, every morning, without choking to death was really astonishing; it always amazed Suzy.

He threw on his coat and gathered his paper and briefcase.

"How many times do I have to tell you?" he shouted, the Brillo' pad on his head bouncing around. "Coffee is no good for you, yet you insist on drinking that goddamn poison! That's poison! Poison!" he repeated. "You never listen! It's like putting TNT into your stomach! When are you going to learn?" His voice rose in disgust and anger.

"I would guess when I'm dead," Suzy responded. Paul's words were like a battering ram, creating a huge hole in Suzy's skull—bam! Bam! Bam!

"No, oh no," he went on, "you keep drinking that goddamn stuff and you'll get an ulcer first!" He began to laugh that dry, phony laugh of his. "Heh, heh, heh. Ha! You don't make any friggin' sense at all." He spun around and slammed the door behind him.

Suzy stood in front of the sink, her hands clenched on either side of the counter. She was breathing hard; her heart was beating twenty to the dozen. She looked down, picked up the glass that Paul had left in the sink, and with all the strength of a pitcher, threw it against the door. *BOOM!* Shards of glass shattered and scattered all over the door and floor.

"*SHUT UP!*" she screamed at the top of her voice. With that, she heard the whooshing sound of the elevator door open in the corridor across the hallway. "Bastard! Can't have any damn pleasure without him ruining it?"

* * *

The phone rang, by Paul's bedside. "Hi, is Suzy there?" It was Karen again.

"Err, no, she's out as usual, probably in some bar," the Weasel answered.

"Please tell her I called. Thank you." Karen hung up. She had called seven or eight times and yet never was able to speak to Suzy. She was getting concerned for her friend. But Paul was in charge of the use of the phone, and messages, it seemed. He never gave her the messages.

By now whenever he saw Suzy walk in, the bartender placed a Chardonnay in front of her. Tonight he cheerily said, "Good evening, how are you?" smiling at her.

She smiled as she hopped up on the chair and placed her book in front of her. "Oh wow, am I really that predictable?" She had become a regular at O'Hara's by now. Being in a bar was truly not what she was used to, but where was she to go? It can be very lonely in a big city when you don't know anybody, especially New York. Millions of people around, yet at the same time, nobody. The nearest movie house was about eight blocks away, and she didn't want to walk home at 10:30 at night and live on popcorn alone. Staying out of Paul's hair was all she wanted to do, and getting inebriated was part of it.

Paul was irritating her once again. She was getting to a boiling point; didn't he learn with the shattered glass a little while ago? It was cold and drizzling outside, but cozy and welcoming here, at least. She had just sat down, opening up her book. After all, she was here to kill a few hours, hopefully in peace. She could see, out of the corner of her eye, a figure in a dark overcoat sliding quietly beside her. He ordered a martini. Though she was reading, she could feel him surreptitiously glancing in her direction. You know the type, pretending to be disinterested but really *VERY* interested. She ignored him, of course, turning the page very slowly, and without glancing up, sipped on her wine and placed it in front of her. She read the same line twice, but he wasn't to know that. He looked quickly out the window, then looked around the restaurant, then back to check out the passersby. Glancing over at her, he cleared his throat slightly and leaned toward her. "That must be a good book you have."

Slowly, she turned toward him. He had a dazzling smile; his teeth were blindingly whiter than the ski slopes of Telluride on a sunny December morning. *What a perfect ad for a dentist!* she thought. She noticed his eyes. They were green but encircled with a hint of blue-gray. Just fascinating. His eyes wandered quickly from her mouth and eyes and back. Her blonde wavy hair fell softly on her cheek. She grinned inwardly. She couldn't believe her luck. He seemed a little shy though.

"Yeah, I've been meaning to read Grisham for quite some time now," she replied casually. And so the ice was broken.

They planned to meet for lunch at the Tavern on the Green in Central Park on Saturday and wander through to the zoo afterward. She kept pinching herself at her good luck. He was a banker from New Haven, of Italian heritage. He lived on the West side near Columbia, and yes, he had been married and had a thirteen-year-old son who lived with Mommy out on Long Island. David was just gorgeous and a dream come true. He was funny and bright and had a terrific laugh. His deep masculine voice sent chills up her spine. At the bus stop, he kissed her gently as he held her hand, and then asked if they could perhaps meet to go to a movie the following week... God, was he sweet...

Suzy had to run some errands that afternoon and then met him at 4:30 pm. She saw him coming down the street as the bus neared her stop, waving and smiling. Her heart skipped a beat.

"Hi!" he smiled broadly as he took her hand and walked briskly toward the movie house as it was chilly. The Weather Man predicted rain later.

"So what did you think of the movie?" he asked as they pushed their way into the street.

She laughed gaily. "I loved it! This is the first Woody Allen I truly enjoyed. Mira Sorvino was so perfect. I loved the pig clock! You have to be quick to pick up the lines. I think the audience was asleep; they hardly laughed at all!"

"Yes, I thought the girl in the movie was so good, she really was. So how about Chinese?" he suggested. "There's a great place just down on 82nd. I love the Szechwan!" And they talked and talked. He was so interesting—almost the perfect man, she thought. He held her hand as they left the restaurant. "So, would you like to come up for a drink?" he suggested. "I only live five minutes away". She looked up at him and nodded. Actually, by now she was hoping he'd suggest it. His eyes carried her into a state of perpetual heat. And with that, "Taxi!" he shouted and stuck his hand out.

As the door opened, she noticed the beautiful hardwood floors covered with huge Chinese rugs. He took her coat and ushered her into the living room. Looking around, she noticed how tastefully it was done. *Must have had a decorator,* she thought.

"Would you like a drink or perhaps a liqueur?" he suggested. "I have Scotch, gin, vodka, wine, oh, let's see" as he stooped over in the cabinet "I have Frangelico, Bailey's, brandy, or maybe Kahlua?"

She nestled on the couch. "Oh, Frangelico would be fine, thanks."

"Coming right up!" He went into the kitchen for ice.

Looking around the room, she jumped up. "What a view!" she exclaimed, marveling at the Manhattan skyline. It was certainly was a sight to behold. It took her breath away.

"Yes, I never get tired of living here; that's why I bought the place. Penny wanted this but I felt it was better for our son and her if they lived near her family, plus the schools, you know," he replied as he handed her the drink. So considerate of his family, what a nice fellow. Cool jazz was now softly playing in the background. She looked around at him as he pulled her down slowly on to the couch and kissed her ever so gently. His touch was magic.

"Why don't we try the Jacuzzi together, honey?" he whispered hoarsely in her ear, as he disentangled himself from her and in a flash, disappeared into the next room.

Lying back on the couch, she heard the sound of water and the air filled with exotic perfume. Sipping the Frangelico, she closed her eyes. *This is heaven,* she thought with a smile. Hearing footsteps, she looked up to see him wearing a robe. A robe... and a big grin, flashing those pearly whites. And she was ready to go to the Pearly gates with him.

Taking her hand, he walked her toward the bathroom. Flickering candle flames danced up and down the walls, while steam billowed out into the hallway. This was so romantic. He guided her to the bedroom; he had already pulled the cover off, Gee, how thoughtful... Kissing her gently, he began to slowly unzip her dress with one hand while extending the other around her, as it fell to the floor. As she slipped out of her heels, he gently helped her out of her panties and bra and laid her on the bed. He was on top of her, his robe fell away, and she could feel him hard against her stomach. He suddenly spun her around and massaged oil from a bottle that was already opened by the bedside onto her buttocks, massaging, and now caressing them, then kneading them deeper and deeper.

"God, you are so beautiful! Here, let's go to the tub," he whispered, panting heavily and quicker. A wild look came into his eyes as he swept her into the bath.

"Oh yes, oh yes," he panted as he frantically explored forbidden orifices of her body. "Turn over!" he begged as they splashed around and he deftly maneuvered her onto her side, as his fingers gently caressed her. "Wow! Baby, what are you doing to me!" He lifted her, wrapped her in the thick towel and carried her over to the bed, gently laying her down.

"Lie on your stomach," he hoarsely whispered, "I want to see all of you!" Spreading her legs apart and kneeling above her, he began to kiss her buttocks, kneading and softly spanking them, and alternately licking and kissing them as if she was a giant marshmallow, groaning all the while. "Baby, oh baby, ooh baby, ooh Baby, ooh baby, ooh God!" He suddenly writhed rhythmically. "OOH, yes, yesss!" He jumped up and ran to the bathroom and she heard the flushing of the toilet.

Frantically she looked around, bewildered. "What the hell was that????"

She lay still for a moment. David loped over to the side of the bed and put his arms around her, nuzzling his face into her hair. "Suzy, *WOOOOOWWWWWWW!*" He grinned from ear to ear, sighing blissfully. "You are the *BEST! WOWWWWW!*"

She looked up expectantly; he was shaking his head, slowly chuckling with such pure joy as he rolled over on the bed.

"*WOOOOOWWWWWW!*" he gasped, grabbing her hand and kissing it gently. "Yeah baby, *wooowww,*" he swooned.

Gazing stonily at him for a second, she slowly rose, pulled the towel over her, and with one hand grabbed up her strewn clothes and dashed toward the bathroom. She could see him in the mirror of the reflection of the city lights, grinning, satisfied and spent. Turning around, she glanced in the mirror; her ass was red and so sore. Burning, in fact. She was fuming, fit to be tied. That fucking bastard.

Noticing his clothes in a heap on the floor, she knelt down and felt for his wallet. Five crisp $100 dollar bills. *If you're going to treat me like a whore, then pay me like a whore,* she thought. She dressed hurriedly, strode into the living room, and threw on her coat as he ambled into the living room.

"Baby, you were great!" He held her arm. "When can we get together again? You really were great. Can I call you next week?" he begged. His silly grin almost made her puke.

"Oh, anytime honey! So were you!" she sneered. Her eyes were as cold as ice. "You have no idea! It certainly was a night to remember!" She laughed emptily.

* * *

The phone rang; it was the podiatrist's office calling. "Just confirming your appointment for Monday at 5:30, Miss Grant."

"Yes, I'll be there. Thank you."

She had been having problems with her feet. Since moving to New York, all the walking had caused her to develop bunions. She was hoping to have the surgery as soon as possible.

CHAPTER FORTY-THREE

T he Sign of the Dove bar was crowded. The band was already playing, and the joint was jumping. Suzy pushed her way to the far side.
Trying to order a drink was quite an ordeal, similar to making it through
an obstacle course, but hey, that's Friday night in Manhattan. A lady stood
by the bar and saw Suzy push her way through.

"You can stand here, if you like," she offered. There was a little space
next to her.

"Whew, thanks!" said Suzy and beckoned to the bartender. "A
Chardonnay, please!"

She looked around, and immediately in front of her to the left was a
huge torso leaning over the bar, angled in such a way that it was taking up
the most room possible. The torso had a head and the mouth was talking
to two women on the farthest end of the bar. Suzy was so tightly squeezed
in that she could hardly breathe. The place was so packed. She carefully
took a sip.

Suzy looked at the woman beside her, shaking her head and grimacing,
"Y'know, he's taking all the damn room!" With that Suzy tapped him on
the back. "Excuse me, would you move over?"

Torso was in the middle of his conversation and turned to look over his shoulder. "Excuse me?"

Suzy moved in closer. "I said, would you move over please, there's no room!" She smiled brightly. And with that she watched him slowly straighten up. The long torso became taller and taller, like watching the Empire State Building rise in front of her very eyes! A hundred floors towering over her!

"Jesus, Mount Everest!" Her eyes popped.

He had a shock of black wavy hair, with snow-white skin. His big, brown eyes were hooded by thick, black beautiful, expressive eyebrows; he had a voluptuous mouth. He wore a dark suit with a white shirt, and a bright yellow tie with an interesting print. Immaculate, metro-sexual style, like he just stepped out of the pages of GQ magazine.

Mmm, he looks interesting, she thought. She noticed he was looking at her. She smiled.

He bent down to talk to her. "I'm sorry, but the woman next to you—I was standing here and she wanted to talk to me, but I wasn't interested. So I turned around and started to talk to these two, and it's so noisy in here that I had to lean over to hear them."

She noticed his cologne as he talked into her ear. It was very masculine and heady.

"Oh, that's all right," she smiled. "It's a nice place; have you been here before?" she asked.

"Yes, I have been here a couple times." she noticed he had a bit of an accent, but she couldn't quite place it. It was a deep voice, very masculine. "How about you?"

She sipped on her wine. "Well yes, I've been here a couple of times. I like it. I love the music, the band is excellent!"

"Well, I really don't go out a lot. I'm busy working usually."

"Working where?"

"Oh, off 57th. I have a clothing store, and that keeps me busy."

"Yes, retail is as bad as having a restaurant; you have no time for yourself!"

He noticed she had finished her drink. "Would you like another?" Suzy saw he had perfect white teeth, and the longest, thickest eyelashes.

"Oh! Thank you, yes, that'll be fine."

He beckoned the bartender. "Same again," he said as he paid the bartender.

"Cheers!" She noticed he was drinking beer. "Hey, what's your name?"

"Johnny."

"So Johnny, how many of these have you had?" she asked.

"Oh, about four maybe!" He laughed. "Why?"

"Oh, just wondered how many I needed to drink to catch up! So, where are you from? I know you're from Greece or some place in the Middle East. I can figure out that much from your accent but can't place it exactly."

Johnny nodded. "I'm from Italy originally. My father was French and he met my mother in Lebanon while he was living there. After they got married they moved to Italy. My father owned several businesses in both countries; he was in the jewelry business."

"Oh, you're a long way from home!"

He had a soft laugh for such a big fellow, she noticed. "And where are you from?"

"Well, actually I was born in England, and then I came here. But I really live in Florida now."

"England? We lived in England for six months. It rained and rained every day; the sun never came out!" Johnny laughed as he remembered. "We, my wife and I. My wife was older than me. She picked me up at the Hilton in Paris. I was twenty-four and she was thirty-four!" he laughed. "I like older women. I don't feel comfortable with younger women. They're brainless and so boring!" Seriously, how could you not like this guy? What a charmer!

"What about their gorgeous bodies?" Suzy asked as they both watched a beautiful twenty-five-year-old walk by with a figure that had the men drooling. He glanced at her, but turned to Suzy.

"Yes, that's true, but I still prefer an older woman. I don't know; I always have."

He looked into her eyes, smiling, as they talked and talked. It was as if they had known each other for years. Conversation flowed easily, and they laughed at each other's absurd observations.

Johnny offered her another drink, but she opted for a ginger ale instead. She noticed he drank about four more beers and yet it didn't affect him at all. Meanwhile, she was feeling a little woozy. She could never consume much. Suzy had a low tolerance for alcohol.

"God, how can you drink so much?" She looked amazed.

He laughed, "I guess because I'm tall. I fill up one leg and then the other!" They both laughed at the absurdity. She wasn't feeling so good right now. Suzy heard that damn screaming sound in her head. She didn't want him to notice, but she was feeling a little rocky.

"Last call!" the bartender shouted. Lights were turned up. "Last call!"

She turned around. "What? What time is it?"

Johnny looked at his watch. "Let's see, it's almost three."

"Whaaat!!" She totally forgot the time. "Oh my God!" She put her hand over her mouth, thinking of Paul and the disparaging looks she'd have to face. "Oh no, it can't be!" She tried her best to focus. She didn't want to embarrass herself in front of him.

"Yes, it's late, or very early, depending on how you look at it." Johnny looked down at her, and smiled. "Would you like breakfast? There's a place just down the block."

She'd better eat something. Suzy felt that gnawing in the pit of her stomach; she was hungry. "Yes, that would be great!" Why worry about Paul? She was already late.

CHAPTER FORTY-FOUR

I t was freezing; the sidewalks were icy. She shivered, and he gently offered his hand to her. "Let me take your hand; it's very slippery." And the two of them carefully walked down the block to the restaurant.

The waitress poured coffee for them; it was steaming and strong. Suzy poured the cream, stirred it, and lifted the cup with two hands, steadily bringing it to her lips, trying desperately not to spill it for fear she might embarrass herself in front of him.

"Mmm, delicious!" she said as she took a sip, then slowly, put the cup back very carefully on the saucer.

The eggs were on their way and Suzy was starving. And more than a little buzzed. She tried to focus on different things around the room, but everything looked fuzzy to her. She looked down, staring at the floor; then concentrating, she looked over to Johnny, with eyes glazed, and a deadpan expression. Somehow, he didn't look quite right, either. He was fuzzy-looking, too.

A deep voice was asking her if she was all right. She nodded. She wasn't sure who spoke to her though. She decided that maybe if she concentrated on his left ear, perhaps he would think that she was focusing on his face when he spoke... She tried it for a few seconds, but that was not working too well. Suzy then looked at Johnny's right ear. Now she saw three heads! She jumped back in her seat. *Dear God!* she thought, shuddering.

A deep male voice was saying something to her from all three heads but it sounded like it was in really slow motion. Somewhere up there, up above her head. She was afraid to look up.

Blinking, Suzy decided to look instead at the floor. She hoped he hadn't noticed her staring at him. The waitress brought the eggs. Thank God, she could at least see them okay, and they tasted good, too. The coffee was helping. As she finished the last mouthful, she looked up at him, smiled, and patted her lips with her napkin. "Boy, I needed that, thanks!" She hoped she didn't look too pathetic.

Johnny paid the check. As they stood outside the restaurant, he looked at her. "Would you like to come to my place? I have to work in the morning, so I'll be leaving about 8:30, but you could get a few hours' sleep at least," he offered. His deep masculine voice seemed so sincere.

Suzy thought of that goddamn sofa incessantly jabbing her in the back, and spending the night with Johnny seemed like a good idea. Actually, it seemed like an excellent idea. She was exhausted. "Oh, I have to leave early, too." Hmmm... She thought about it for a moment. "All right." He flagged down a cab.

The swarthy-looking doorman checked her over when they walked in, and watched them get into the elevator. Doormen are so damn nosy ... each and every one of them! Yeah, it's what it looks like, buddy! His beady little eyes followed them to the elevator. The apartment was small; it was in one of the older buildings downtown.

"I have a spare toothbrush if you'd like. And there's a fresh towel over there on the sink," he offered.

"Thank you!" Suzy said, properly impressed.

She went into the bathroom and took a quick shower. She was exhausted, and her eyes burned from the smoke at the bar; it was on her clothes and hair. She felt dirty from all the smoke. She wrapped the towel around her. The lamp at the far end of the couch was softly lit.

He was sprawled on the bed, propped up against the headboard. He turned to see her, and with his outstretched hand, he pulled the sheet back for her. "Here," he said softly. She lay down beside him.

Putting his arm around her, Johnny kissed her gently. He was like a big, sweet teddy bear, oh so, so gentle. He treated her with the care and attention that one would treat a priceless piece of porcelain. She felt very comfortable and good with him. He gently kissed her eyes, her neck, her chest and slid his hand down to her thighs, stroking, and gently kissing her. Long, sensuous kisses. He kissed her mound, her thighs and back up to the top of her legs, spreading her legs slightly, darting his tongue in and out.

She moved closer and began kissing Johnny's face, his neck, moving slowly down his chest. She was caressing his thigh, and tenderly kissing his lower stomach.

Her hand bumped up against something. She looked down and stopped mid track. "Oh my. Oh my God!" She had never seen anything like THIS before. She was now wide-awake and completely sober. "Oh my God!" she screamed.

He looked up. "What, what's the matter, sweetie?" he whispered.

For a second she felt like Little Red Riding Hood. "Oh my, what a big cock you have," she said, while he just smiled. Seriously, it was huge, like an anaconda. Suzy's mouth could never take this. She'd get lockjaw—or worse, choke to death!

Suddenly she had a vision …

"Well now, sir, how did this happen?" the policeman stood, pen in hand, eyeing Johnny.

"She was asphyxiated, officer, but not by me. I mean not really." His face showed equal parts innocence and despair.

"Oh, how is that, sir?" The policeman's penetrating eyes stared at him as the officer moved closer, writing notes. "Tell me about it then."

Johnny looked like he might actually cry. "It was my penis, officer! I'm sorry. It went down her throat and then wrapped itself around her neck three times! I couldn't help it. It's like the thing has a mind of its own."

Before the policeman could finish writing the ticket, Suzy's vision vanished into thin air and she was back to reality.

Johnny caressed her shoulders gently, coaxing her like a boxing coach between rounds. "Come on, sweetie, it's waiting especially for you." She was sweating like a boxer, too.

CHAPTER FORTY-FIVE

I t had snowed during the early hours of Saturday morning. Suzy and Johnny ran into the street, waved down a taxi, and jumped in the back. As the cab flew up Second Avenue, he softly kissed her cheek. "I like you very much," he whispered, kissing her again tenderly. "Can I see you tonight? I'll be home about eight, is that OK? I'll order dinner in." What a charmer; he was irresistible.

She felt so tired, she nodded wearily and said, "Sure, that sounds fine." How could he look so good with only an hour's sleep? she thought.

He fumbled in his pocket for his card and handed it to her. "Here sweetie, call me if anything comes up. Okay?"

He jumped out at the corner, waved, and blew her a kiss as she headed uptown. Lying back in the seat, she closed her eyes. When she slowly opened them, the cabbie's penetrating gaze of disgust was eyeing her in the mirror. Suzy could read his eyes: "You little slut." How could you not? Staring back coldly for a moment, Suzy answered with her own: "Keep your eyes on the road, you perv. Your job isn't to judge me." She was too tired to care what he thought. As he slowed down in front of the building, she flung the money into his hand and hurried into the lobby. She could still feel his cold stare as he sped off. At least she had the satisfaction of knowing that in New York it would be highly unlikely that she would ever get in his cab again. That nasty creep, she thought.

It was still dark in the apartment, although the gray light of morning had started to seep through the window in the living room. Paul was asleep in his room. Suzy undressed hurriedly so as not to wake him. He had left her bedding on the couch for her. It was a nuisance to make and un-make the bed every day, but that was how it was. She went into the kitchen for a glass of water. She looked at the calendar on the wall, picked up the thick black marker and crossed off another day with a big X. Yippee! Only fifty-four more days left to April 1—April Fool's Day—how appropriate. Quietly, turning off the light and tiptoeing to the bed, she wearily lay back. Feeling the iron bar in her back, Suzy shifted around a little to get comfortable, but still it stuck in her back. Finally she fell into a restless sleep in which she dreamed about boa constrictors trying to slither their way into her throat. Nothing Freudian about that.

Paul was getting dressed, banging into the bathroom door. The noise woke her, then she realized he probably wanted to wake her. It was after three in the afternoon. She wondered where he was going; he was so secretive these days. He made plans and then as an afterthought might mention it to her, as he was walking out the door to join whomever. Suzy couldn't complain though, since she'd been seeing guys on the sly. The cat and the mouse were watching each other. While they appeared to be unconcerned about each other's actions, they were caught up in this charade. Cats and women are so much alike. They both enjoy playing with their prey before they kill it. Cats throw a mouse up in the air, play with it a little, the mouse lies still. The cat sits there, licks her paws, and looks in the opposite direction, seemingly disinterested. The mouse stirs slightly, eyeing the cat. Thinking the cat is not paying attention, the mouse suddenly moves. The cat, with one fell swoop of her paw, whacks the mouse into a tailspin, flying through the air and splattering on all fours to the ground with a dazed, glazed look in its eyes.. Women at their best!

CHAPTER FORTY-SIX

T he doorman stood in the doorway with his hands behind him, legs slightly apart. The braiding on the amulets and cuffs and the cap gave him an air of importance, undeservedly so. After all, doormen weren't military personnel on guard duty at the White House or in a foreign country. He did not carry a weapon, yet here he was trying to give the impression that he was so important, authoritative, when he was no more than a glorified bouncer.

"Yes, ma'am. Which apartment?" He looked at her searchingly. This doorman was young with thinning hair. He did not miss a thing either. Did these doormen always seem to have a lurking sleazy gleam in their eye, or was it her imagination?

"Mr. Varzanne, Apartment 1505." She felt his eyes on her back as she swept past him toward the elevator.

"And your name, Miss?" he inquired loudly.

"Johnson, Miss Johnson!" she called back as she hobbled by. She certainly was not going to give her real name.

The door was ajar. She knocked. "Hi." The lights were dim, and the wine glasses were on the coffee table. Johnny hugged her. He had just taken a shower and his cologne was intriguing. He seemed boyish and a little shy as he led her to the couch.

"I bought you some wine; I hope you like it. I stopped by the corner store when I came home. It should be chilled by now," he said as he went to the kitchen. She heard him opening it.

"What kind is it?" She smiled. She wore her slacks tonight and a thick sweater. She was relaxed even though she hadn't had much sleep.

"It's Chilean, here take a sip." He poured some in the glasses.

She tried it. "Mmm, yes, it's very good—not too fruity and not too dry! Just how I like it! Actually, they have some excellent wine from Chile. Mmmm, this is good." She took another sip.

"So, how do you feel?" He sidled up next to her on the couch, reaching for her hand. He looked refreshed, as if he had slept all day instead of working ten hours.

"Oh, fine. Certainly a lot better than when you saw me this morning!" she laughed. "God, I was dead, oh my God!" She looked heavenwards as she laughed again. "How about you?"

"Oh, I was fine until about eleven o'clock. Then I went downstairs for about fifteen minutes and stretched out on the chair, then I got a second wind. Saturdays are very busy." He thought for a moment. "Oh, damn!" he snapped his fingers. "Damn! I had a present for you, but I left it in the store." He looked into the distance, "I'll try to get it for you next time." He shook his head, angry at himself for forgetting.

She looked at him wide-eyed. "Me? A present for me?" she repeated, impressed. "Really?"

"Yes. I hope it fits." He looked at her eyes. "I have an idea of your size, but I still need you to try it on."

She stared at him. "That's very sweet of you!" He was a kind person, and Suzy liked generous men. Who doesn't, right? At least he wasn't a taker like so many men.

"So," he carried on, "how was your roommate?" He was curious. She had explained to him the arrangement she had with Paul.

"Oh, fine, I suppose."

He looked at her. "Did he say anything when you came in?" He took a drag from his cigarette.

"No, he stayed in his room, reading the paper and talking on the phone." She shrugged.

He shook his head, unable to make sense of this arrangement. Oddly enough, neither could she. It was just a matter of time before she was leaving. Paul had made arrangements to be with other friends and company without her, so what was she supposed to do?

Changing the subject, she asked, "So tell me about your family back in France. Do they ever visit you?"

"No, I speak to them on the phone a lot. My mother, of course, misses me. But my brother and sister are both married and have families. They both have businesses, too, so they can't leave—you know how that goes!" He lay on the couch, leaning his head on her chest.

She was slightly surprised, and yet she liked it. She cradled him in her arms. She could feel his breath on her breasts as he spoke. He obviously felt content to be with her.

He looked up at her and spoke softly. "You know, it's funny, but I feel very comfortable with you. Do you feel the same?" he wanted to know.

Looking down at him, she smiled. "I do." Here she, was all of 5'2", and there was this huge man of 6'3", with the long legs and torso, trying to wrap himself around her, a big, soft teddy bear. It was kind of amusing, and very sweet.

"Would you like something to eat? I'm starving! There's a restaurant down the street." Johnny sprang from the couch and handed her a menu. "See what you want." He reached for the phone and dialed.

"Yes, good evening! I'd like the shrimp."

"Oh, honey," she tapped him on the shoulder. "Make that two please" she smiled. "Sounds delicious!"

That night, the lovemaking was slower, more sensual. He tenderly kissed her all over—her neck, her ears, her back, her thighs, her legs, and once again he slowly kissed her legs, lifted each leg up to his lips and traveled down to her ankles.

Dawn was peeping through the window when they finally fell into a deep slumber. They drowsily woke, and he kissed her back softly. "Good morning," he whispered, cupping her right breast in his hand as he gently stroked it. She groaned and moved closer to him. She could feel him hard against her back. Turning, slowly, as he moved rhythmically inside her, she writhed with each thrust.

"Yes, yes," she begged. She licked her lips; they felt full and tingling. "Yes, yes," she whispered as he thrust deeper, faster when suddenly she screamed and convulsed. He breathed hard against her back, and fell back, panting, his eyes closed.

He brushed the hair from his eyes, smiled sleepily, and rubbed her arm gently. "You're too much, whew!" He looked over to her. "But I like it!" he laughed. After a moment or two, he looked over to the clock on the nightstand. "Oh my God, I'd better get up! I'm supposed to open up for the girls!" And with that, Johnny sprang out of bed and Suzy heard the water running in the shower. She lay back, drowsy and relaxed, with her eyes closed.

She heard him standing by her side of the bed. "Special delivery! Special delivery!" he softly said. Turning slowly toward him, peeking through half closed eyes, she saw him. There he stood, naked, with her panties and bra in each hand, and her stockings draped over his erect penis.

"I don't believe it!" she giggled softly, her eyes widening.

Laughing with her, he said, "I did say special delivery —especially for you! See what you've made me? A delivery man."

"And no brown uniform?" she inquired.

"I said special delivery," he grinned.

She took the lingerie from him.

"Well, don't I get a tip at least?" he looked down at Suzy.

"I think that's my line," she replied. Suzy looked up at Johnny, grinning, and slowly moved to him, licking him with quick darting strokes.

He stood there, eyes closed, groaning, and moved closer. "Oh my, oh, oooooh, yes, yes…" Huskily his voice trailed away as he rocked slowly toward her.

"Is that enough of a tip, sir?" she asked in her little virgin voice, looking innocently into his eyes and bursting into laughter as she fell back onto the bed.

CHAPTER FORTY-SEVEN

Paul had left by the time Suzy got home. *Thank God,* she thought. She looked around the apartment and decided to do some laundry. As she folded and put away the last towel, the phone rang.

"Hi! How are you? I finally got you! I have tried calling you for ages." It was the thick, creamy voice of her friend, Karen. How she wished they were back in Florida together. Suzy was really homesick and Karen was such a dear friend.

"Oh, hi Karen!" she excitedly answered. "How are you? Gee, it's so good to hear your voice! Why, when did you call? Paul never mentioned that you called. I wondered how you were. Many times, I thought of you. Your ears must have been ringing every week! Paul doesn't want me to use the phone, you know. He's being a complete son of a bitch. But it's so good to hear your voice. I'm so happy. Anything new?"

Karen did not have any luck with men. Why should her luck be any different today? This hot, volcanic mountain of womanhood, gone to waste— Jessica Rabbit, with that mane of red hair, big doe eyes and luscious lips, slinking around the room, was still looking for her Roger.

"No," she sighed wearily. "Same shit … different day. You know how it is… You seem pretty chirpy though." Cupping her hands, Karen whispered into the phone, "So, where's the Weasel?"

The deep tone of her voice reminded Suzy of Orson Welles' flashbacks in *Citizen Kane,* echoing "Rosebud" with the same mysterious, penetrating intensity.

"Oh, he's out somewhere. I have no idea. Gone out with one of those princesses he meets at the singles' thing, I think," she brightly answered, feeling free of fear of Paul being anywhere near the apartment and overhearing her.

"Are things still pretty sticky?"

"Hell yes! Crazy glue sticky. But I just try and stay out of his hair." Suzy couldn't contain herself one more minute. "Guess what! Karen," she said excitedly, "I met someone the other night and he is gorgeous! Gorgeous! Nice to have a hot man on a cold night for a change!"

Suzy could almost hear Karen's ears perk up on the other end. "Yeah, really?" There was static on the line, and Karen could barely hear her. "You met somebody?" she repeated.

"Yeah! And he's gorgeous! And," she cleared her throat, "and he's young, Karen! God, I can't believe it!" Suzy couldn't control her excitement for Mr. GQ Magazine, with his high-end Armani tailored suits, customized shirts and designer ties, with that shock of black hair and thick eyebrows and those long eyelashes and big expressive eyes that any woman would envy.

Karen was excited for her. "Yeah! I am cougar, hear me roar. Oh, this damn phone! How young?"

"Oh, about thirty or so, but he's about a foot taller than I am! And big!" She could barely hear with the crackling sound on the line. "Karen," she said slowly, in a stunted tone, "you have no idea how BIG he is!"

"Big?" she repeated.

"Yeah… When I say big, I mean like Mr. Big, but this guy is more like Mr. HUGE! God, it's like, I mean, looking at the Alaskan pipeline and wondering where it ends!"

Karen was quiet for a moment. "How big is he?" Karen repeated slowly, intrigued. She was pretty lusty herself, that Grace Kelly type of cool but with throbbing, intense overtones one didn't suspect.

"I said, he's as big as the Alaskan Pipeline! When I first saw it, I thought it was going to wrap around me like a boa constrictor and squeeze the life out of me!" Getting no response, Suzy looked quickly at the mouthpiece of the phone. "Hello, is this thing on?" What was the matter with Karen? She was acting so dense today. She normally was not that way. On the contrary, she was far from dense.

"How big is he?" Karen repeated, dazed, still in awe, intrigued. "Wow!"

"Like the Alaskan pipeline! From New York to, err, Anchorage—wherever the hell it goes!" she yelled.

"Whaaat! What was that about Alaska? No."

"Yeeeessss!!"

Karen paused for a moment. "The Alaskan pipeline does not go to New York!"

"Oh? No? Well, anyway, this one does!. This is the New York extension!" She burst into gales of laughter.

"Nooo!!!"

"And he's gorgeous. He has a store near the Russian Tea Room off 57th. I've seen him two nights in a row. God," she yawned, "I am so exhausted." She flopped down on the chair in the kitchen.

"I'll bet you are. He-he-he," she agreed, with a dirty laugh and a hint of sarcasm in her voice.

"Yeah. God, oooh," Suzy groaned, "I think I need a pair of crutches I'm so sore!" She wearily added. "When I first looked at it, I screamed. I never saw anything like this before! Never!"

Karen's voice changed. "Not screaming anymore, I'll bet!" She burst into laughter. "So, uh," she went on, "what are you going to do with Ole Blue Eyes?"

Reality was setting in fast. Suzy really didn't want to go there. "Oh, I, um, don't know," Suzy started. "Who knows about anything?" She didn't want to face that particular problem today.

"So, how are you going to explain yourself?" Karen was so smart and analytical. She thought things through first whereas Suzy was less about having a plan and more about being adventurous, impulsive, and wild. "Weeell," Karen drawled, "you'd better think of something. The Weasel is not going to put up with this; you know that, don't you?" she warned.

"Not today, honey. I'll deal with it another day." Suzy had a habit of burying her head in the sand.

It was midweek and slow at the store. Johnny called her at work, and they chatted for a while.

"Do you like Rod Stewart?" Suzy asked.

"Rod Stewart? I don't know, why?"

"Well, he's going to be at Madison Square Garden in a couple of weeks! I've seen him in Miami. I love him!" she gushed.

"Would you like to go? I've never been to a rock show, but if you want, we can go." Boy, she loved that Johnny was always willing to go and do things, not a stick-in the-mud type.

"You've never been to a rock show? You're kidding! God, I'm so excited! But I don't want to get the tickets over the phone. You need to go over to the box office and pick out the seats. I went to a Beach Boys' concert, and wound up in the nosebleed section. I went to see that Andrew Lloyd Webber show—you know, the one with the girl from Saigon or someplace—and I was so high up, all I saw was the tops of the actor's heads, and they weren't cheap tickets either! I was so mad I swore I would never use them again."

"The box office it is then," promised Johnny.

CHAPTER FORTY-EIGHT

"O h, I brought you these from the store. I wasn't sure of your size, but try them on and if they don't fit I'll have them altered."

Johnny handed her a shopping bag with the name of his store. She looked inside, and there was a package wrapped with a gold seal that also had the name of the store. She opened it and there were two silk blouses. They were exquisite. Her eyes lit up.

"Oh! Oh my! They are so beautiful." She jumped up off the sofa and ran to the bathroom mirror and tried them on. The colors of gold and green looked good with her skin. She ran over and kissed him. "Thank you, sweetie, that was so kind of you! It's a little big here," she pointed to the sleeves. "They need to be taken up a bit. That's no big deal. Thanks so much for thinking of me!"

He smiled. "I wanted to surprise you. I'm glad you like them. I have these made especially in Milan, and everything in my store is from Italy. All my clothes come from the factory; all the fabrics and styles are Italian." He grabbed one of the blouses. "See this stitching? They don't do it this way in the United States. Here, feel the quality." Suzy felt the fabric. It felt heavenly. "You just can't get it here. We have two seasons, and we order our collections, one in the spring and one in the fall," he went on. "My customers come to me all the time and I choose the whole ensemble for them. They rely on my judgment." Johnny took a drag from his cigarette. "It's hard work, but I enjoy what I do."

Turning to Suzy, Johnny put his arm around her shoulder, kissed her, and quietly said, "I'm glad you're here. I liked you ever since I started talking to you," and then looking deep into her eyes, he said very seriously, "And I'm really glad you picked me up!" He threw back his head and howled with laughter.

"You picked me up, you mean!" she laughed.

"Yes, that's true." He paused for a moment, cocking his head. "Really, are you sure?"

He felt for her hand and squeezed it, "No, I'm teasing." He looked into her eyes and touched her cheek. "Are you hungry? I can order and it will be here in a little while." Johnny got up and brought her a menu. "Pick whatever you like!" He leaned over for the phone.

CHAPTER FORTY-NINE

S uzy's foot surgery was planned for the following Friday. Paul was acting weird. *So what else is new?* she thought. He seemed extraordinarily busy these days. Suddenly he had friends coming out of the woodwork. Paul had told Suzy not to answer the phone when he was out. This was an order, too. Straight from the Weasel's mouth. Obviously his social life was in high gear, and he was trying not to have sex with more women than just Suzy. His stony silence was almost intolerable at times, but the alternative was worse. However, when Paul found out Suzy was going to have surgery, the news brought out a warmth and genuine compassion in him, despite everything that had transpired.

Paul took her to the doctor's office promptly at 10:15 as instructed by the doctor's office staff, left her so he could run a few errands and arranged to pick her up by noon. The operation was simple enough, as operations go. She hobbled to the door, and Paul jumped up to give her a hand. It had snowed while she had surgery, and there was slush all over the pavement and they gingerly held on to each other as they got in the cab. He managed to get her back to the apartment. She lay on the sofa with her foot elevated on a couple of pillows. He brought her a sandwich and made her some tea.

She needed ice compresses. The compresses melted in no time, it seemed. She slept for a while, but awoke just as he was leaving. He was all dressed up, with his hat and coat on, and key in hand.

She sat up on one arm, turning in his direction. "Uh, where are you going?" she asked quizzically.

He looked at her. "Uh, I've got somewhere to go."

"Whaat? Somewhere to go? Tonight?" She couldn't believe him! "Do you see my foot? I can't *WALK*!" she yelled. "What am I supposed to do for dinner? Oh, and how do I get to the bathroom? Oh, excuse me, but would you hand me those friggin' wings by the door so I can fly around the apartment," she said sarcastically. "I hope one day, when you need help, nobody will be there for you. God, you are unbelievable!" Suzy snapped, looking heavenwards, and slumped back on to the pillow.

Looking sheepish, Paul sputtered, "Well, I had made these arrangements." He walked over to her. "Here's a twenty; call the Chinese place down the street. They deliver. I shouldn't be too long, okay?" He was feeling guilty, but not guilty enough to change his plans, she noticed. Damn selfish bastard—she was fit to be tied..

"But I can't get to the phone. Can't you understand that?" Raising her voice, she pointed repeatedly to her foot. "I can't get up and walk to the phone!" She sat bolt upright. "What am I supposed to do?" Her eyes were blazing. *Fucking men, can't rely on them for anything!* She shook her head in disgust. The one time you needed a man's help, he pretended to have a friggin' date. Suzy did not believe it for a second.

"I'll be back early," he promised limply.

"Well, don't bother to come back on my behalf, please!" she sneered. Son of a bitch. She was fuming under her breath.

He closed the door hurriedly, turning the key in the lock. Now she needed to go to the bathroom, damn it!

Sitting up on the sofa, Suzy eyed the bathroom door. From where she was sitting, it might as well be in Australia. How the hell was she going to get over there? She thought about crawling on the floor, but the floor was a little too dirty. She eyed the door again. She didn't have a cane since nobody at the doctor's office had mentioned anything about needing one! A slight oversight! She looked over to the kitchen table. Oh yes, that's it. Of course!

What was that expression? *Necessity is the mother of invention,* she thought. She carefully hopped over to the wing chair by the couch, then swung her leg over as she groped for the table, slowly grabbing the window sill, resting for a moment, and then hopping over to the dining room chair, plopping down for a second and then getting up. Using the back of the chair to hold her weight, she pushed it, scraping the wooden floor, hopping slowly to the bathroom. She awkwardly threw herself on the toilet seat, being careful not to hit her foot. She smiled to herself, feeling proud that she was independent. Fuck you, Paul!

On Saturday, Suzy rested all day, watched TV, read the paper, and put ice on her foot. It was not throbbing as much, but it was still painful despite the pain medication that the doctor prescribed. Wagner was playing on the radio in Paul's room. He brought her the cold packs from the fridge and made her a sandwich. He called all his new friends, which was his ritual now on weekends. He had more news to bestow on their big ears, she surmised, with the recent chain of events. Like the poor husband of the cheating wife, he had all of their sympathy piled a mile high.

Of course, he was the victim and Suzy was the Scarlet woman. Not that he would ever tell them of his neurotic behavior that drove her to this in the first place. She hadn't planned to meet these men; it just happened. She had gone out for months and not met anybody particularly interesting until recently.

Oh sure, she had a met a pervert or two. Really good looking perverts, surprisingly good looking, but perverts all the same.

CHAPTER FIFTY

"So how's it going? Where's the Weasel?" whispered Karen into the phone. *Dear Karen, without her, where would I be?* Suzy thought. Having no friends in New York City made it a very lonely town, and it was such a treat to have a friendly voice to talk to. Both of them had lived through life's upheavals and shared each other's romances over the years. Trying to find Mr. Right was such a project. A never-ending battle, it seemed. It's amazing how fast Mr. Right can become Mr. Wrong.

Suzy cupped the phone, speaking low because she didn't want him to hear her in case he was in the hallway. Then again, there was really nothing she could do about it if he did hear. Suzy was looking forward to leaving for sunny Florida soon.

"He's gone to get groceries; he'll be back soon. Damn my foot! It's all bandaged up. I had the surgery last week and I'm not sure what to do about it. It's freezing here, snow up to my ass!" she wailed.

"About what?" she asked.

"The concert! It's Monday night at Madison Square Garden! The Rod Stewart concert!"

"Suzy, are you insane?" Karen's voice hit a shrill note. "You cannot go with that foot!"

"He has the tickets, we have to go!" she wailed.

"Not with that foot. You can't even walk! It's a rock concert. People will be trampling all over you. Are you totally out of your mind?" she went on. "What's he going to do? Carry you, for God's sake?"

"I know, I just don't know how to tell him," she grimaced. "Jesus, the tickets are seventy-five dollars each, Karen!"

"You'll just have to tell him. What's he going to do, sling you over his shoulder caveman-style and take you? He might be able to find someone else to go with him if you tell him early enough. Remember, the place is going to be jam-packed and someone will bang into your foot. You can't walk. There is no way you can go. Just NO way!" She hung up.

Suzy looked down at her leg. "Damn it." She didn't realize she wouldn't be able to walk.

Paul came back, put the groceries away, and sequestered himself in his room again. A Brahms violin concerto filled the air. Suzy was casually reading a magazine. It was about 8:30ish when she heard the phone ring and Paul answered it in his room. He was the Keeper of the Phone, like the Constable of the Tower of London. He was the only one allowed to answer his phone—ONLY him. Orders from the Court must be strictly enforced. One may be allowed to answer the phone in his absence according to New York Statute 509XYZ, but only with a permit signed and notarized by His Lordship.

Paul popped his head around the corner. Looking hard at her, he grimly said, "It's Tarzan – for you." His face was a mask of shock and disbelief.

"Really? Who? Her face scrunched up, not sure what he had said.. Tarzan?" She looked up at him, curiously. *Tarzan fought his way out of the jungles of Africa, swung on some vines across oceans, and miraculously made it to America where he's standing on a street corner in New York City wearing nothing but a loincloth and calling me from a phone box?? Of all people!*

"Who?" she repeated. "Tarzan? " said Suzy cheerily. Where the hell did he get the name Tarzan from? Suddenly she could hear Carol Burnett yodeling in the background.

Oh! Varzanne! Suzy looked a little embarrassed. "Oh? Thank you." She got up slowly, hopped on one foot, the other leg bent at the knee to keep her foot off the ground, and managed to push the chair to the other side of the room where the phone was, near the kitchen.

"Hello? Oh, so nice of you to call. I'm all right, considering." She swung around to see Paul throw on his coat.

"Going for a walk!" he shouted and flew out the door, slamming it behind him.

Glancing at the door, she turned around. "Oh, Oscar the Grouch went out for a walk." She started to giggle.

"What's so funny?" Johnny was curious.

"He called you," she spluttered into the phone, "Tarzan! He thought your name was," more shrieks, "Tarzan!" She paused for a second. "Tarzan. Guess what? It suits you."

With a naughty gleam in her eye, she recalled her Alaskan pipeline joke she told Karen. *You Tarzan, wearing a loincloth and banging your chest like a tom-tom—or banging me, would be better.*

They chatted for quite some time. "Has he come back yet? He left at least half an hour ago. He must have gone through the tunnel and into New Jersey by now," Johnny giggled.

"Where the hell could he have gone? He's been gone forever," she wondered.

"He could be in Atlantic City at this rate."

In about another hour, Paul finally returned. Suzy was lying in bed feeling the metal bar like a stab in the back when Paul quietly walked in without turning on the light and went into his room.

Sunday was another gray day. Suzy had pain, so she took the painkillers. She was planning to go to work the next day. Paul helped her with the cold packs and offered to buy her a walker. He was kind toward her, and very solicitous, in spite of everything. He could be sweet at times, she thought. She was regretting the times that they had clashed. In a way, it had marred their friendship as she really enjoyed his company, but when these explosions occurred, she could not handle him and one word leading to another, led to World War Three!

Suzy lay on the couch, with pillows propping up her foot. Mozart was playing on the stereo and Suzy could hear Paul moving around in his room, probably getting ready to go out once again. Silently, she watched him put on his scarf, coat and hat. She shrugged, resigned to the fact that there was nothing she could do about anything anymore. It was lightly snowing, and she watched the snowflakes on the window then turned on the TV; 60 Minutes was coming on and then the nine o'clock movie. She was ready to be a couch potato for the evening.

The phone rang, but Suzy wasn't expecting a call since Paul was out. She slowly moved to the end of the couch to answer the phone. She was only allowed to pick it up when he was out. It was Paul. She heard a lot of noise in the background; he was in a bar or restaurant somewhere.

"Hi, Suzy? It's me, Paul. Can you hear me?" His voice sounded anxious.

"Yes." She was shocked to hear his voice. He had never called when he was out before. She peered over at the clock in the kitchen. It was only 10:30.

"About you going to work tomorrow—I really don't think you should go!" he said.

"Oh? But I have to," she implored.

"Really, I don't think you should go. You can't walk. It's insane. You will just have to call them and explain to them why you can't come in."

She listened but didn't know what to say. Paul could be unbelievably kind at times and this really threw her off her perch.

"I have been thinking about it! I, er, look, I'll pay you for the day that you lose, OK? But I don't want you to go in, OK? Maybe the next day, but not tomorrow, Suzy. Do you hear me?" His tone of concern really surprised her. Apart from living under the same roof, they did not have too much in common. He seemed to be very busy with his social life these days.

Stunned, she quietly said, "Yes Paul, I hear you. Thank you!"

"Ok, I'll see you later." He hung up.

Whaaa! What a turn of events! Was it Tarzan that made him think twice, or what?

She was totally confused now. Between Paul and Johnny, she couldn't think straight anymore. Now she felt guilty about the show tomorrow night. What the hell was she going to do?

She tossed and turned all night, torn with guilt. Either way, everybody would be mad at her, but he was right, she couldn't walk! Her mind was going in fifty different directions. How was she going to swing this?

Monday morning came. Paul hurriedly left for downtown as she lay there. She awoke around 9:30, looked up to the ceiling, and then down to her foot, which was throbbing. Hobbling over to the kitchen, she poured herself a cup of coffee and propped up her foot.

She listened to her favorite radio station and they were playing Rod Stewart's hits. All of a sudden, her ears pricked up. *Did I hear that right? What? Yes, thank God, oh thank God.* She silently screamed. *There is a God!* Rod Stewart had laryngitis and his show was cancelled for Monday evening and would be rescheduled for later in the spring. She collapsed on the bed, in a torrent of laughter and sweet relief.

CHAPTER FIFTY-ONE

"S o, sweetie, how are you doing? How's your foot?" It was Johnny calling from the store. Suzy had just hobbled into the apartment and Paul had been running errands all afternoon.

"Oh, hi. It's OK. I've been going to work with a walker all week, and now I'm using a cane. It's slow, but I'm healing, thanks."

"Well, how about you coming over on Wednesday night. Can you?"

"Well, I'll see. I'll give you a call," she hung up. Now she was wearing a godawful ugly flat shoe with Velcro° straps. It wasn't fashionable, but at least she was mobile now, albeit slow.

It was Wednesday, early evening, and Suzy was watching the 5:30 news when Paul came in and went straight to his bedroom. She had taken off her dress when she came home, and put on her nightdress, and flopped on the sofa bed. She felt that damned iron bar sticking in her back. It didn't matter how many times she folded the blanket; there was no relief from that damn bar. She heard him banging the closet door in his bedroom. *Getting ready to go out again? Where the hell was he going?* Suzy wondered. She heard him open the closet and put on his coat and hat. "See you later!" he called out as he locked the door behind him.

With eyes twinkling, an impish grin crossed her lips, curling into a big smile, she slowly turned around, grabbed her cane, and hopped over to the bathroom. She carefully took a shower with her foot covered in a plastic bag so as not to get wet. She flung open the closet and dressed quickly. Better wear slacks, she thought, and a sweater. She threw on her fur coat, and using her cane, hobbling as fast as she could, and hit the elevator button.

The doorman helped her into a cab, and off she went down to 34th and Second. The swarthy doorman with the braiding on his coat looked at her and her foot suspiciously, as if she were trying to smuggle something in.

"Yes, miss?" he inquired, his tedious, beady eyes giving her the once-over yet again.

"Mr. Varzanne, 1505." She glared at him.

Turning, he dialed the house phone and announced, "Ms. Johnson."

His sneaky eyes followed her to the elevator. *What an asshole,* she thought as she limped over to the elevator. *I'd like to stick this cane right up his ass!*

Johnny was putting the plates on the table as she hobbled in. He hugged her and helped her gently with the cane, pulling the chair out so that she could stretch her other leg. He was very sweet about it, and it didn't seem to faze him one bit. They chatted away as they sat down to eat. He had the lights down low, with a candle burning on the table. He was so romantic, she thought.

He reached over and picked up a shopping bag. "Oh, here are the blouses. I had them tailored for you, sweetie."

She kissed him and excitedly looked into the bag. "Oh! How sweet! That is so nice of you!" She threw her arms around him and kissed him again.

Johnny kidded her about the foot, and said it looked like she had stolen one of Frankenstein's. Suzy waved her cane at him, pretending to scold him, and they laughed about how ridiculous it looked. After dinner they moved to the bedroom because it was easier for her. He gently reached for her, kissed her neck, between her breasts, licking and kissing her stomach while his fingers explored her, moving slowly to her thighs, long, beautiful, delicious kisses until she could not resist him anymore. She arched her body in expectation, wanting him, moving her hips to take him.

She leaned over to him and said, "I'm impressed that you could do all that without hurting my foot."

Johnny lay there with his eyes closed and began to smile. "I could do that even if you were swinging from a chandelier and I was blindfolded."

She laughed, ruffled his hair. "I'd like to try that one day!" Suddenly she gasped, "Oh my, what time is it? I have to go; it's getting late."

He held her arm. "Must you go? Why don't you stay till the morning? Please stay," he begged.

"What time is it?"

He looked at his clock by the bed. "It's almost 10."

Struggling to get out the bed, she said, "What? Oh no! I'd rather stay but it's best if I go. I really don't want any problems with Paul. Thank you for a lovely evening, sweetie." She kissed him and hobbled out quickly with her cane to the elevator.

"I'll call you tomorrow. Oh wait, here are your blouses." He picked up the bag and ran over to the elevator. She thanked him again and blew him a kiss as she got into the elevator. The surly doorman waved down a cab for her and she was whisked away into the night.

As Suzy turned the key in the lock and opened the door to the apartment, it was pitch black inside. She was relieved to see that Paul had not returned yet. She quickly threw the bag with the blouses by the hallway table and hurriedly took off her coat, ran into the bathroom, washed her hair and took off her makeup. She blow dried her hair, and put on her nightdress, quickly hobbling as fast as she could with the cane over to the bed, turned off the light and slid under the covers. No sooner had she laid down and gotten as comfortable as possible, she heard Paul's key in the lock. *Talk about timing,* she grinned to herself. He walked quickly into the dark apartment, into his bedroom, switched on the light, and gently closed his bedroom door so as not to disturb her.

CHAPTER FIFTY-TWO

The next evening, Paul walked into the apartment. Suzy was flopped on the sofa once again. He stood in front of her, looking concerned, and said in a quiet voice, "So why don't I take you out tomorrow night? Take you out for dinner, huh? You've been cooped up here all week, and I'm sure it has been difficult for you."

He looked at her and seemed kind of guilty to see her like this every night while he was out on the town doing whatever he did, which was not having sex.

She looked up. She must have looked sad and forlorn to him, for some strange reason. Puzzled, she said, "Oh, that would be nice." She couldn't understand why he was behaving this way. Little did he know about her rendezvous the previous night, obviously.

Paul took her to a place called the Velvet Room. They had been there before. It was decorated like a Victorian era bordello, draped with lots of wine red velvet lush curtains, Victorian style chairs and sofas. How appropriate, she mused. She found the atmosphere intriguing. Suzy watched Paul as he was slowly eating, fork in hand, an expression of contentment on his face. Paul was being very nice to her this evening, solicitous to her every whim. Almost like he was sad that she was leaving soon, she thought. Then again, she didn't want to give him that much mental and emotional credit. He probably ran out of single women who didn't like sex.

"Sam called. He wants to get together on Sunday with our cousin, Mimi, for lunch. Is that OK with you?" he asked.

"Sure, that'll be fine," she said in a quiet voice, as she wiped her mouth with the napkin. He was being so nice to her all of a sudden she wasn't really sure how to respond. There had to be a catch and she was trying to figure out what it was. Always trying to outthink him.

Paul went to the dry cleaners on Saturday morning, so Suzy called Johnny at the store.

"I'm sorry, he went out," the sales lady said curtly.

"Oh? Tell him I called, please." She thought it was strange, but hey, he couldn't be there all the time. She wondered where he was.

Like every other night, Paul was getting dressed for an evening out. Again Suzy wondered where the hell he was going. She was watching TV when he called out, "See you later," as he ran off into the night. She checked the clock. She checked her foot; it was doing much better, even though she still had to wear the godawful Frankenstein shoe. She looked out the window and sure enough, the woman across the way was flopped on her bed watching TV. Maybe she was an agoraphobic. If it wasn't for the fact that she moved her arms around every so often, one might think she was a mannequin, lying lifeless on the bed all day and night.

Suzy also noticed the lights of the city, twinkling all around her. She didn't want to stay in again tonight. She was bored. She looked around the apartment for something to do. She had no one to talk to, and cabin fever was setting in. Franken-foot, cane, and unsexy hobble be damned; she was going out.

Suzy hobbled over to the bathroom and put on her makeup. She hummed to herself as she sprayed her favorite perfume all over. She looked in the mirror and blew herself a kiss (mwah). *You can do it, girl.* She donned her coat and reached for the cane. She was ready to get her drink on.

The bar was getting crowded, and Suzy inched her way carefully with her cane, hoping no one would stomp on her uncomfortable and butt-ugly Velcro˚ shoe, causing her to scream in pain and beat the shit out of the person with her cane. Not the kind of attention she wanted. Suzy found a tiny spot by the counter and propped herself alongside it. She ordered a cocktail, looked around the room, checking if there was anybody interesting. Two men sitting at a table by the window had eyed her when she walked in. *Mmm, could be,* she mused as she brought the glass up to her lips, and sipped, *could be.* She casually looked over to her left, to the other side of the bar and suddenly, she did a cartoon double-take, her eyes popped wide open. There was Johnny! That son of a bitch. Like the Empire State Building, you couldn't miss him even if you wanted to.

Johnny, who couldn't be bothered to call her back—and here he was, bent forward, chatting with the girl beside him, completely engrossed in conversation.

Suzy turned around quickly, acting like she never saw him. Her heart skipped a beat, but she wanted to act as cool as she could, act as if she had not seen him. Just under the surface, though, she was seething. Good thing I brought the cane, she thought.

The short fellow sitting by the window sidled up to her. He smiled and said, "Hi, how are you?" She looked at him. He was nice looking, with a beautiful mouthful of perfectly white teeth. For a moment, she blinked and had to shade her eyes from the teeth. It was like being snow blinded. The man was in his early fifties and his wavy salt and pepper hair was very attractive.

She detected an accent as he spoke. "So, where are you from?" she asked as she puffed away.

"I'm from Brazil," he said with a smile. She blinked again from the glare of the white teeth and briefly considered putting on her sunglasses.

"Really?" she smiled. "How nice!" She glanced over at Johnny as she blew out the smoke. This should do it. She sipped her drink. "And what brings you to New York?" she inquired.

And on he went, telling her his entire life story in excruciating detail, about his children, his girlfriend back home, about his divorce, about the economy, and on and on. Finally he stopped talking long enough to take a breath and looked down at his glass and hers. Then he looked up at her. "Would you like another?" he offered.

"Oh, sure, thank you—that's very nice of you!" she smiled.

He smiled. "So why don't we meet for lunch tomorrow? My friend has to leave now." He scrambled for a napkin and wrote down his name and hotel number for her.

"Sure, why not?" she said, with no intention of calling him. "That would be wonderful," she beamed.

"Call me around 10:30, OK?" He smiled that movie star smile at her one more time, waving, as he headed to the door.

She took a sip of her drink and placed it on the counter, when a tall Brooks Brothers type walked up and stood next to her. He looked interesting, she thought. He had that preppy look, with his hair slicked down and the tortoise shell-framed glasses. He ordered a cocktail, took out a cigar, and proceeded to snip off the end and light it.

He bent down to her. "I hope you don't mind?"

Too late now if I did! she thought. *Rude, much?*

They spoke for a while and just like the guy before, he told her his life story. *What the hell—do I look like a therapist? Shall I tell him I charge $200 an hour to shut him up?* Some people enjoy hearing themselves talk.

This guy was an attorney and practiced international law. He had a horse farm in upstate New York and lived down the street. Suzy watched his hands as he spoke and tried to look interested while she listened. She got the feeling he was married. It might have been how he said something or what he said that clued her in. She couldn't quite place it, but she had a sneaking suspicion.

"So, are you married?" she asked.

She was simply killing time until Johnny noticed the guy with her. After all, this man was tall and there was no way that Johnny would not see him, or her with him. Suzy looked up at Preppy as if he was the most exciting and interesting man she had ever met. He beamed at her, enjoying the ego boost, and ordered himself another drink. Never mind that her glass was empty; he never offered. Even if he did resemble Robert Redford, and Suzy was always madly in love with Robert Redford, she would have still turned him down. He already had three strikes against him: cheap, which was unforgiveable, inconsiderate, and a cheater! Not to mention a pompous ass, as well, in his case.

But he was serving his purpose. He was standing there with her. She glanced over at Johnny and their eyes met. She smiled radiantly. At first he looked surprised, then quickly gave her a crooked smile as he waved. She waved, looking surprised to see him for a moment, then grinned from ear to ear and turned her back quickly to talk with Preppy, who was completely oblivious to anything that was going on around him. He was too interested in his own boring story.

But Suzy gloated; she was the cat that caught the canary.

"So, are you married?" she asked again. She already knew the answer; she'd been playing with him all night. He wanted a piece of ass, and she made him think that he was going to get lucky. She smiled up at him as if he was her hero.

Preppy kept trying to duck the question. While Suzy could not have cared less, she had a sadistic streak watching him squirm.

"Well, um," he started and looked around, flushed. "Well, uh…"

Suzy helped him out. "Yes, you are," she said quietly. He knew she was onto him. "So where is she?" It was getting late, and the bar was thinning out. She saw Johnny sitting two barstools on the far side with an older woman. She had a sudden urge and wanted to go kick the legs out from under him. She noticed the older woman had her arm on his, both looking into space, not saying a word. Suzy looked away. She was feeling a little buzzed by now. Preppy watched her carefully with a gleam in his eye; he bent forward.

"You can come back to my place; it's only up the street," he urged. "My wife and kids are out of town. They're back in Denmark for a month." He was licking his chops at the prospect, gloating.

Smiling, she said, "Oh, I'd love to, but I have to go!" She fumbled in her purse, threw the money on the counter and jumped off the barstool. She looked over at Johnny; he sat motionless with the woman. Suzy grabbed her cane and hobbled out quickly.

Preppy ran after her, looking on in disbelief. Could she really walk away from a great prospect like him? "But I, er, where are you going?" he asked as Suzy flagged down a cab outside. She turned, jumped in the back seat, and as the cab pulled away, she saw him waving in the distance but she didn't bother to wave back. Good riddance.

She tried to get into the apartment building but it was locked, with a huge plank stuck between the two handles. What the hell was going on, and why the high tech solution? Suzy banged on the door, and finally the doorman sleepily staggered out of the little back room and let her in. He looked irritated, but said nothing. She was swaying, but still managed to stay upright as she hobbled to the elevator. She was fit to be tied.

How dare that son of a bitch ignore her? How could he do this to her?

CHAPTER FIFTY-THREE

U pon reaching the apartment she stuck the key into the lock. "Damn, it won't go in!" She peered at the key but couldn't see it properly. It was a little fuzzy, then fumbled again, . She stood outside and propped her cane against the door.

It fell to the floor, banging against the doorframe as it fell. "Oh Jesus!" she shuddered. "Paul will be screaming any minute now." Suzy bent down to pick up the cane, rocking a little again. Finally she stumbled in, took off her coat like she was wrestling with a bear, and hung it in the closet. She undressed hurriedly and put on her nightdress. The entire evening's events were swimming around in her mind. She was mad as hell; she was ballistic at this point—tendrils of blue smoke poured out of her nostrils. Staggering over to the phone, she dialed Johnny's number. She was going to leave him a message that he would never forget!

She listened to it ring, and her mind was thinking of what she was going to say, when suddenly Johnny answered.

It took the wind right out of her sails. "Hello?" the deep voice said quietly.

She looked at the mouthpiece. *How the hell could he have gotten home so soon?* she wondered.

"Hello!" she drunkenly bellowed.

"Yes?" His voice was very firm, cold, and impersonal. "And what do you want?"

"Oh, Johnny," she said in her snide voice, "so what were you doing with that wrinkled old hag you were holding hands with at the bar? Is that the best you can do?" She wanted to crucify him.

Annoyed, he shot back in a quiet and authoritative tone, "First of all, she happens to be a friend of the singer, and second, it's none of your business!"

"What do you mean, none of my business?" she shouted, when out of the corner of her eye, Suzy saw Paul standing in his underwear, balanced on his skinny white chicken legs, his hair standing on end, looking like a crazed Einstein or Don King, waving his arms around. He was grimacing, mouthing something at her, now with his hands on his hips, but she couldn't concentrate on two things at once and this phone call was of the utmost importance; the alcohol told her so. All she could see was Paul's mouth distorted in all directions and his skinny arms flying around, pointing at her repeatedly.

Oh God, she thought, *this is fucking bedlam!* She ignored Paul for now and focused on her discussion with Johnny.

"What do you mean?" She was mad as hell; flames were shooting out of her ears.

"And what about you with that man all night? I saw you!" His voice was getting increasingly angry.

"What's that got to do with you?" she screamed.

"Exactly. So what I do is none of your business!" he said coldly. "Fuck you!"

Suzy's jaw dropped. For once in her life she was at a loss for words. "Whaaat?" she gasped, horrified. Why, nobody, never ever, had ever spoken to her like this before in her life! She was starting to sober up more and more.

"You heard me. Fuck you!" the deep monotone voice repeated.

For a split second Suzy got the full view of Paul's face but right now it was a blur in the background. "Fuck you!"

No! Suzy thought. *He said fuck you? Oh! What a nerve!* Her eyes popped out of her head. The words were ringing in her ears. How dare he?

"The only way I will forgive you is if you come over. Right now!" he said threateningly.

What did he say? Come over here. Is that what he just said? She couldn't believe her ears. "What? What did you say?"

"I said the only way I will forgive you is if you come here right now!"

Suzy's head was swimming. *My God, it's almost four o'clock in the morning.* She paused for a moment.

"Are you coming?" he asked, cold and flat.

In a tiny, childlike voice she responded, "Do you have some milk?" Every night before bed she drank milk.

"No," the voice on the other end said, "But I'll get some by the time you get here!"

Meekly, she said, "OK, I'll be there in ten minutes!" and with that she spun around, threw on her slacks and sweater, grabbed her cane and hobbled out. She didn't even see Paul in the doorway of the bedroom. He was stunned, splattered up against the door like a Jackson Pollack, mouthing away. But Suzy didn't hear one word.

She hobbled to the elevator, pressed the button repeatedly, and waited. She waited and waited, then pressed it several more times. Still the elevator didn't come up. She noticed the lobby light was lit but the elevator was not moving and she couldn't possibly walk down seventeen floors. Oh no, she groaned at the thought of Paul. She had to go back to the apartment and call for the elevator to be sent up. She crept back in as quietly as she could and picked up the house phone. She heard the doorman's voice. "Hello!" she whispered, cupping the phone with her hands, so as not to wake Paul, "The elevator," she hoarsely whispered into the mouthpiece. "Hello! The elevator – it's not working!" she hissed into the phone. She was terrified to wake him up.

The doorman said, "Hello? Speak up please, I can't hear you."

Once again, she hissed into the phone, "The elevator - it's not working!"

"Which floor are you?"

Cupping her hands around the phone, she hissed, "Eighteen!"

"I'll send it up!"

She grabbed her cane and hobbled out to the elevator again. The doorman stood silently as he let her out while his stony expression told another story. *To hell with him, I'm leaving soon anyway,* she thought.

Suzy decided to walk to Lexington because the cabs would be going downtown from there. Dawn was breaking.

She felt a chill as she pulled her coat closer to her. It did not help having her damn foot in what looked like a clown's sandal and holding the cane as she gingerly hopped along. She was sobering up fast. *I must be insane!* she thought she waved down a cab. *I can't believe I'm doing this.*

The swarthy doorman at Johnny's building called upstairs and watched her hobble in the elevator with her cane. Intrigued, his eyes followed her as he held the elevator door open.

Johnny had left his door slightly ajar. The apartment was dark as she hobbled into the living room. Throwing off her coat, she walked into the bedroom and looked down at him. He was lying there, eyes closed, with his arms folded behind his neck, his full, sensuous lips pouting. She bent forward, slipped out of her pants, and straddled him, throwing the cane onto the bed. Okay, maybe slipped is too elegant a word. With that silly Franken-foot of hers she had to rip open the Velcro closures, then she could slip out of the pants with the good leg, but it was more of a hop and an "oomph" with the post-surgery leg. Getting the important question out of the way first, she whispered, "Do you have the milk?" as she kissed him.

"Yes, it's in the fridge," he said quietly.

They looked at each other, and without another word being spoken, kissed passionately. She sat up as he helped her off with her sweater. Her bare breasts looked like beautiful oversized creamy peaches, firm and full. He devoured them, and helped her on him, as if they had to hurry up before the new day was dawning. They made love, wild, abandoned, until exhausted and spent, they fell asleep in each other's arms. Somehow, Suzy forgot all about the milk.

CHAPTER FIFTY-FOUR

Suzy quickly turned the key into the lock of Paul's door. It was almost eleven o'clock. She had to hurry if she was going to make it on time. Suzy and Paul were scheduled to meet Mimi, Sam and Carita for lunch, and she didn't want to be late. The door to Paul's bedroom was shut tight, she noticed. Normally, it was open with the stereo playing classical music. But today, there was an eerie silence from within, as if she had stepped into a morgue. Something was not right... Though exhausted after getting only a few hours of sleep, Suzy felt good. Looking in the mirror, she noticed the large dark circles under her eyes. *God, I look like an owl!* she thought as she piled on more makeup to cover the circles. She was tired but somehow she seemed to have a reserve of adrenalin that morning.

Suddenly she looked up and saw Paul right in front of her. She had not heard him walk into the living room. How did he do that? He stonily looked at her. "You don't have to come, you know." His voice was colder than ice.

Oh, I see, she thought, *my name is You Know now.*

His tone was flat and cold. Paul had always been quite adept at turning things around so nothing was ever his fault. "I'm sure you're very tired," he added with a sarcastic edge. It seemed strange, but she could have sworn that there was a tinge—no, a snow shovel—filled with jealousy and maybe a little hurt, too.

"Oh," she said airily, "no, I wouldn't think of not going. I made the arrangements and I'm going!" She looked into his face.

"Well," he went on, "I don't think you should." His blue eyes were blazing.

What he really meant was that he didn't want to take her. She knew that, and she wasn't going to let him win.

"No!" she insisted, "I don't back out of my commitments." She went back to putting on her mascara. Besides, she had got up especially to go since that was the plan. She could have stayed at Johnny's place and slept all day; in fact, he wanted her to!

Paul stood in the kitchen door, not knowing what to do. He looked at her and realized she was determined to go, so he turned around, defeated, and like a puff of smoke, disappeared into his room. Probably pouting, she thought.

By the time they got to the Russian Tea Room, Mimi was waiting for them at a table by the window. The restaurant was just around the corner from her apartment. She waved, and they joined her.

"Paul, how are you? It's lovely to see you all!" He was her favorite cousin.

She hugged and kissed them as they sat around the table. The waiter took their orders and vanished into the kitchen. Mimi looked around the table and asked Carita how she was coming along with her English.

Looking happy, she smiled. "Mimi, I am reading and writing English moch better!" She was thrilled with her accomplishments.

Paul, the professor, asked, "So now you can understand most everything!" He looked happy for her. He looked over at Sam, who was looking at the pretty blonde walking by. His eyes rested on her breasts. Both Suzy and Paul caught him. Sam turned around quickly, and they laughed.

Mimi turned to Suzy. "My, Suzy, you look radiant!" she oozed. "What have you done to yourself? You look more beautiful than ever!" Turning to Paul, she said, "Doesn't she? She looks wonderful. You must be doing something right, Paul." She smiled, nodding at him.

Suzy heard Paul choke on his water.

Suzy, looking at Mimi with an expression of sheer wonderment said, "Oh really, Mimi? Why, that's very nice of you to say! You always look beautiful; you're the perennial beauty!" Turning to Paul with a concerned look in her eye, she asked, "Are you all right?"

Spluttering, he waved his hand. "Yes, I'm fine!" he muttered in a raspy voice as he fumbled for his handkerchief, tears running down his face, catching his breath.

Brunch at The Russian Tea Room was always such a pleasurable experience. The conversation turned to the family and they caught up on some current events, then Sam looked at his watch, pulled back his chair and suddenly announced, "Oh, we have to go! We have to go to her sister's birthday party at three, so we'll drop you two off, and then we'll get there just in time." He helped Carita up. "Come on honey, mi amor!"

Suzy watched as Sam walked with Carita, his arm around her shoulders as they walked toward the door of the restaurant. Paul was holding Mimi's arm as he slowly led her out of the restaurant. It all looked so blissfully wonderful.

After Sam dropped them off, Suzy went to the supermarket to get boxes for moving. She was leaving soon, so she started to pack. Paul had gone out, as usual. One of the unsolved mysteries of Manhattan—where the hell did Paul go every evening? Suzy wasn't sad to leave; it was time, that's all. She had crossed the days off the calendar with a thick, black highlighter since the first of January, like a jailbird waiting to be paroled. She was homesick; she missed her friends in Florida, not to mention the beautiful weather. The wind coming off the East River chilled her to the bone. It took several hours to thaw out each day, and her finger joints and knee joints throbbed with excruciating pain. The weather in New York was so changeable. Every day was such an ordeal wondering what she should wear in the morning. It either poured with rain, snowed, sleeted, or there was a heat wave. At least in Florida all one needed was a warm jacket in the winter, and an umbrella for the dog days of summer. It was that simple!

CHAPTER FIFTY-FIVE

I t was a bright sunny day, around 30 degrees that morning when she left
home. Shivering, she ran hurriedly to the subway. It was just a block away
from the apartment. The East River wind whipped through her, chilling
her to the bone. Pulling her hat over her ears, she thought, *Thank God, it
won't be long now. I can't wait for that sunny, hot humid Florida!* She enjoyed
walking home in the evenings; thirty blocks was a piece of cake. *I'll miss
that though,* just not the minus zero weather!

It was her last day working for this wonderful company. She really was
going to miss them. It certainly was a very pleasant experience in the morning, seeing her lovely, tall blonde boss come in, swathed in her black mink
coat and hat to match, with high-heeled shiny leather boots, looking like
an '80's movie star version of Gloria Swanson from *Sunset Boulevard* with
her cigarette in hand and her perfume wafting by, while her chauffeur in his
black suit and cap and white gloves, tagging behind her, was so glamorous.
The only thing that was missing was the cigarette holder poking in the air.
Suzy had to remind herself this was not a movie set.

"Good morning Ms. Kraminsky!" Suzy smiled broadly.

"Hi Suzy." That nicotine and whiskey-soaked sounding voice of hers always amused her as she waved "Hi" to her, making her way down the hallway to the inner sanctum where she ruled. As a young girl, she started working for this illustrious company and built up her department to such a success and now, twenty years later, was the queen of the company. She was head of the department with three men as her team, making money hand over fist for the company.

At the end of the hallway, her secretary had her desk by the window. When Suzy went to grab a coffee in the break room, which was located at the end of the hallway, Suzy glanced over to her desk and saw she was playing Solitaire on her screen. She walked by in silence, looked down at her watch. Only 11:30 A.M., and she's playing Solitaire already? Can't be that busy, then.

Suzy noticed many times that it was very quiet back there in the building and her boss's door was always closed. *I guess they're all in a meeting,* she thought. *Must be serious,* she surmised… Until one day, when one of the owners of the company came downstairs to see her. As he opened the door and stepped in, she could see the four of them huddled around her desk, cigarette dangling from her lips, and holding a bunch of cards in their hands. Was it rummy? Or bridge? Or Poker? Stacks of playing cards, ashtrays, and mugs of coffee were on her desk. "Way to go, Gina!" "Now that's how to do it!" Suzy cracked up, laughing softly all the way to her desk. Sometimes at the lunch hour, the men used to come and sit across from her desk, wanting to chat. Or in the afternoon, to break the monotony. Frank was from Manhattan; he was good looking, always dressed impeccably. They would talk about anything and everything. He got a big kick out of Suzy.

"You like ZZ Top?" he laughed. "You, Miss Prim and Proper over there? I would never have guessed that in a thousand years!" Suzy giggled. *Yes, Miss Prim and Proper!* she thought If only he knew…Which made it even funnier. Like they say, perception is everything.

"Yes, I love ZZ Top," she laughed. "'Cos ev'ry girl's crazy about a sharp dressed man..."

At precisely 4:45 P.M., the chauffeur came by, and out came Ms. Kraminsky once again, glamorous, glorious Ms. Kraminsky, the Queen of Park Avenue, who stopped by at Suzy's desk, gave her a hug and wished her well. The rest of the team, headed by Janie, the sweet Italian girl, also came by and gave her a farewell hug, then they were on their way to Grand Central station for the 5:30 to Long Island.

At 5:30 sharp, she put on her coat, hat and gloves then walked over to the window. Her last look at Manhattan from the 43rd floor. The world looked very differently from the 43rd floor. She took one last look at Brooklyn and the Brooklyn Bridge, with thousands of red lights worming their way slowly to their destinations. It had been a wonderful experience, they were by far, the best and most generous company she ever worked for. They even gave her a Christmas present even though she had only been with them a short while. Her eyes popped out of her head when she opened the gift and saw the famous Tiffany turquoise box inside, She almost fell off her chair. Tiffany! My God! How generous of them... How lucky could she get! She treasured that gift so much. She so wished she could stay and was very sad about leaving. But owing to circumstances beyond her control, really, there was no choice. Things in the Kane aka Weasel household were very hard to deal with... At this point, Fort Lauderdale beckoned her with open arms.

CHAPTER FIFTY-SIX

Friday night came around fast, Johnny promised he would meet her later that evening. "And anyway, wherever you go, I'll find you. Don't worry." Spoken like a true Scorpio. She got dressed and peered at the phone several times. No message.

She picked up the receiver and listened for a dial tone. The phone was all right, no problem there. He hadn't called. Men are so goddamn irritating. She had decided she would not wait any longer, "To hell with him!" Suzy stuck her nose in the air and headed for the cigar bar down on Lexington.

The bartender recognized her, and smiled. "Good evening! How are you this evening?" Funny, she was only there possibly a couple of times. They were always so cordial and pleasant.

"A Bellini, please." Suzy looked at her watch. It was almost 9:30; where the hell was he? She looked toward the door for him. No Johnny. Wouldn't that be something if Jonathan walked in, she thought...No, she couldn't get that lucky.. She sipped slowly, listening to the music in the background. The band would be starting in another half hour or so, and she wrestled with the idea of staying or going somewhere else. The man next to her was brooding, staring at his drink. He looked a little on the neurotic side. She didn't want to talk to him, that was for sure. If she wanted neurotic she could stay home with the Weasel. She wanted to laugh and have fun. After all she was leaving Sunday. Suzy finished her drink. "Check, please!" She had made up her mind.

The bar was smoky and crowded. She pushed and shoved her way to the bar and ordered a drink. She took a sip and noticed a good-looking fellow behind her. She saw him looking at her. He smiled at her. "Hi!"

She nodded. "Hi."

He looked interesting, but then she noticed a lady standing behind her next to this man. Suzy looked at him; the two seemed to know each other. She wondered if he was with the other woman. Suzy's eyes wandered over to the far side of the bar. Suddenly, she did a double-take.

Talking to a blonde, sure enough, there he was—Johnny! She definitely was not going to talk to him this time.

Suzy turned to the lady and smiled. She smiled back.

"It's always busy, isn't it? It's a madhouse!" The noise was quite unbearable.

She then spoke to the mustachioed man to the right of her. Must be friends with these other two, she thought. They must have all come here together.

"Hello, I'm Bob," Green eyes introduced himself, smiling down at Suzy.

"Hi, I'm Suzy." She grinned from ear to ear. He was gorgeous! She noticed a wild look in his eyes and heard the lady behind her talk to Bob. At this point, who should turn around and spot her? Why, Johnny, of all people!

He came over, and said, "Hi," just as the blonde was asking him something, and then a dark-haired girl joined them. They looked as if they were friends. Suzy acted nonchalant. Anyway, she was busy now with Green-Eyed Bob and looked off into the distance.

Johnny moved over to Suzy. "Listen, I have to go with them to meet somebody downtown. I'll be right back," he promised. She watched him leave with them.

"So, what brings you here?" Bob smiled.

"It's Friday night!" Suzy smiled broadly.

"So, you live around here?"

"Yes, just a few blocks."

"I live on the Upper East Side."

"So, er, where do you work?"

"Near the Waldorf, on Park."

"So what do you do, Bob?"

"Oh, I work in radio. I'm a producer."

"That must be fun!"

"Ever heard of the Jack Jackson show in the mornings?"

"Yes, hasn't everybody? It's the number one show. I listen to it every day. I love it!"

"Yeah, well, I produce that show."

"Really?" Suzy noticed the woman behind her watching quietly. She smiled at her. "Are you friends?" Suzy inquired.

She nodded. "I guess."

Curious about that answer, she said, "Why, what do you mean?"

She smiled and shrugged. "Oh, nothing, no, nothing really."

The mustachioed man spoke to her; they looked like they knew each other very well, somehow.

Bob was talking with a number of people. He was very popular, she thought. He looked around for her. "Suzy, can I call you?"

"Sure, yes, that would be fine!" He fumbled in his pocket and scribbled her number.

"Maybe we can meet tomorrow for lunch? Is that OK?"

She nodded. "Yes, I'd like that very much!"

She noticed the woman behind her smile. "Do you know him?"

She looked over at the mustachioed man, as if she was looking for his approval, it seemed. "Yeah," she smiled, "Bob's my husband."

"What? What's going on here?" Suzy was aghast.

The woman looked into the distance, then looked at her. "It's OK," she reassured Suzy. "We live separate lives," she went on to explain. "Bob's my husband, and this," she turned to the mustachioed man, "is my boyfriend!" He put his hand on her shoulder. Green-Eyed Bob was busy talking and didn't seem to be concerned.

"Wait a minute, you are married to Bob, and you're the boyfriend?" Suzy's eyes popped out of their sockets. She had never known anything like this before.

"Yeah," he smiled. They all seemed to be comfortable with that.

"Do you all live together, then?" She had visions of *Bob & Carol & Ted & Alice.*

The woman laughed, "No, we have a young son, so we try not to get him involved."

"A child?"

The mustachioed man just looked on. He stroked the woman's arm lovingly.

"We live in the same apartment, but we have other relationships." She looked into Suzy's eyes as she explained, with a half-smile.

"So why don't you get divorced?"

She shook her head. "No, it's not necessary." She turned to Mustachio. "We see each other when we can, and he dates other women, so we just go on like that, that's all." She made it sound so simple.

By now, Bob was standing behind her; the three decided to leave together.

"I'll call you in the morning, OK?" He waved to her as they trooped out.

"What the hell, what's wrong with lunch?" she mused. This could be interesting.

CHAPTER FIFTY-SEVEN

Suzy looked up and noticed a man with a kind of swarthy look smiling at her. He took a drag from his cigarette, looked at her from the corner of his eye, turned, and smiled and stood next to her. She noticed he was staring at her velvety white skin. His eyes gleamed in wonderment; he was in seventh heaven.

"So where are you from?" he asked.

"I'm English actually, but I've been here since the seventies. Where are you from?"

"Tunisia. My family moved here ten years ago. We have an electronics business here in Manhattan. My name's Khalid, what's yours?" He blew out the smoke and stubbed out his cigarette.

They chatted for a while, but when the band started to play it was difficult to hear each other over the noise. He looked around quickly, then glanced over at Suzy. "It's so noisy in here. Why don't we go somewhere else so we can talk?" he said in his thick accent.

It was getting late, but still too early to go home. What the hell, she was leaving in a couple of days.

"So come on," he insisted, "let's go somewhere else."

Suzy grabbed her cane and hobbled out into the street where Khalid was parked. He drove them to a little club right off 72nd. It was quiet. The singer was taking a break. They sat at the bar and he ordered Suzy a cocktail.

"Cheers!" She was feeling a little woozy by now; she hadn't had much to eat tonight.

He looked at her. "You are so beautiful. I would like to take you back to my country, to meet my grandmother." A tear glistened in his eye. "I miss her so much; she would love you!" His eyes drank in her pure lily-white skin, he rubbed his hand up and down her arm, he was breathing hard, and with a lecherous smile, suddenly lunged forward to kiss her hard on the lips. She broke away, and once again he lunged forward, again kissing her passionately. As she broke away, she heard a deep masculine voice in the background.

"Hello, Suzy."

She blinked, looking at the randy Tunisian, thinking, *That's funny, I could have sworn that I heard somebody call out my name!* She fumbled in her bag for another cigarette. Nobody here knew her; she shrugged her shoulders, must have been mistaken.

"Hello Suzy." She turned once again, blinking. She definitely swore she heard somebody call her name. *There it is again,* she thought. She definitely heard the same monotone, deep voice again. Slowly, she turned around to face the bar and did a double-take. Johnny was sitting there watching her from across the bar, his face solemn.

She looked up, and in a surprised voice said, "Oh!" She looked harder. *Oh Jesus!* she thought, trying to regain her composure, smiling. "Hi sweetie, do you have any cigarettes?" she cooed.

Johnny was sitting with the blonde. She looked nonplussed at Suzy. Slowly Johnny, aka the Empire State Building, rose and walked in her direction and without saying a word, emptied a couple of cigarettes on the counter near her, flashed her another disgusted look and went back to his seat.

"Who is he?" Khalid hissed, eyes flashing like bolts of thunder. "You know this man?" He was ready to jump him.

"Who? What?" She had forgotten all about Khalid for a split second. "What? Why would you say that?" she wondered out loud.

His eyes and teeth flashing, looking like a Rottweiler ready to attack, he blurted out loud, "You called him sweetie!"

"What! Of course not!" She didn't realize she said it. "I don't know him. I met him one time, that's all," she tried to pooh-pooh the whole idea, waving her hand as if annoyed. "He's nothing! He's nobody!" she insisted.

By now, she was feeling a little sick and the room started to revolve. Suzy put her hand to her mouth, rocking slowly back and forth in her seat, and groaned.

Khalid looked at her. "Are you all right?" He seemed concerned. "Shall I take you home?" She must have looked a little strange. He helped her out of the seat, guided her out of the restaurant, as she steadied herself with her cane, and into his car parked outside. She laid her head back on the headrest, groaning, closing her eyes.

Everything started spinning around her, "Oh no!" she groaned. "I'm going to throw up. Stop the car!" She fumbled for the door handle.

He stopped just in time. "Are you all right?" he asked.

She nodded, wiping her mouth. "Oh please," she begged, "get me home quick!"

As he turned the corner to the building, Suzy asked Khalid to park up the street, not in front of the building. Those damn nosey doormen! He helped her out.

"I'll take you upstairs," he offered as he gripped her arm.

Her eyes popped. Suddenly she saw her whole life flash before her very eyes! "Oh no! It's quite all right, I don't want to wake up my roommate; she's, uh, a very light sleeper!" she stammered. Fear gripped her throat, and she broke out into a cold sweat. Jesus, she could just picture the scene!

"Oh Paul, by the way, this is Khalid. He'd like to join us tonight. We're having a sleepover!" Then turning to Khalid, "Khalid, would you kindly remove the ax Paul just jammed into my skull? It's giving me a slight headache."

Suzy glanced quickly at Khalid. "No, no, no, no!" she said hurriedly. "That's very kind of you, but no. My roommate, she um, she … No. Don't worry about it. I'll be fine, thanks. Really, I will!" Jesus, she had to get rid of him! Quick!

"Are you sure? OK, I'll call you tomorrow, and we'll go out, okay?" he begged. She waved goodbye to him as she slowly walked down the street and into the building. The doorman watched her in amazement.

She walked by him, trying not to look drunk, walking straight ahead with her head up. Propped up by the cane, she swayed forward when she hit the button for the elevator, and then swayed back like a palm tree blowing in the wind, feeling the doorman's eyes on her, drilling a hole in her back.

Screw him, she thought, as the elevator doors opened and she hobbled in. When Suzy entered the apartment, she hurriedly took off her coat and hung it in the closet. Oh no! She ran, knelt in front of the toilet, and threw up again. She felt all of her insides trying to come through her throat. She retched and retched, and finally put on her nightdress, and crawled into the bed, shaking, and weak.

CHAPTER FIFTY-EIGHT

The sound of the phone woke her. Peeking out from under the blanket like a scared child, Suzy noticed it was a miserably gray day. She heard Paul's muffled voice, then his door opened and his footsteps came toward her on the couch. He looked at her disapprovingly. With that look, she knew. *Uh-oh, things are going to get worse,* she thought.

"It's Tarzan." His voice was harsh. She felt like hell, and there was that damned high-pitched screeching sound in her ears again; it sounded like a 747 coming in to land on her head. With one eye slightly slit open, she looked up slowly to check. She couldn't lift her head from the pillow it ached so badly. She couldn't talk; she was as sick as a dog.

She groaned. "I can't talk to anybody," she whispered, holding her forehead, hoping that Paul would take the hint to talk quietly. "I just can't."

"Well, this is the second time he's called!" he barked. He obviously did not get the hint.

His voice grated through her head, covered her ears. "Please! Ssssshhh," she groaned, "don't talk so loud! My head, oh…" she groaned.

She was thirsty as hell; she wanted to get up and make a cup of coffee, but her head was throbbing so hard, she didn't have the strength to get up. She feebly licked her lips. "Tell him I'll call him back," she begged in a baby voice.

She fitfully fell asleep. She awoke to hear Paul rattling his bushel of vitamin pills in the cupboard. He came in and looked at her. It was about two or three o'clock in the afternoon.

"How are you feeling?" he said flatly.

She looked up at him. She was slightly better. "Oh, OK," she said quietly, and wondered what else was coming her way. Somehow she knew there was more. There always was.

Suzy got up and made a cup of coffee. She sat down in the kitchen and sipped. *Oh, that was good, did I need that!* she thought. She tried to get her head together. The screeching sound had subsided somewhat, but she still felt drained, limp, and lifeless.

"You know," the Weasel came tearing into the kitchen. "I can't believe you!" he started.

Oh, here we go. Oh, no, I can't take anymore, she thought. *My head is ready to explode.* She took some Tylenol.

"You have no consideration for anybody! I can't believe you!" he repeated, his eyes widening, raising his voice angrily.

"You meet all these guys, give them this number, with no regard for me! You just take over, like this is your place!" His eyes and face of thunder. "I've been woken up all night by these different men you're picking up in all these bars. You're nothing but a drunk!" His eyes turned purple. His scour pad on his head was flapping in the breeze by now, ready to take off and fly around the room.

"A drunk?" Suzy said. "Hey, at least I'm tidy!" she said quietly. "And as tipsy as I was," she went on quietly, "you'll notice I put my clothes away. Not like some sober people who drop their clothes all over the floor! Why, who called?" she wondered. Frankly, she could not concentrate, or care at this point, her head throbbed like a battering ram..

"Well, some guy woke me up about five o'clock. I think he was shocked to hear a man's voice, but he asked for you. I said you were asleep, and he wanted to know how you were. That was one; then about nine, there was another!" He looked knowingly at her. "Jungle Jim." Paul couldn't bring himself to say the guy's name. "And then about ten, this other guy called. Then the other one called again. All these different guys! Unbelievable!" He looked shaken to the core; he was beside himself. "All different men!" he repeated, shaking his head. His hands flew up in the air, eyes widening.

She looked at him. "The fellow that called around ten—what did you tell him?"

"Yes, I said you were asleep. He was surprised to hear a man's voice, too!"

"What? Oh no! Did he say he was going to call back or did he leave a number?" She was upset.

"No, he just hung up." Paul looked at her and shrugged his shoulders.

"Well thanks, that was only the producer of the Jack Jackson Show," she said dryly. "He was calling to invite me to lunch, that's all," she said wistfully. "Now I'll never know, thanks to you."

His eyes lit up. "Really? He was from the Jack Jackson show?" Now he felt guilty. "Oh, I'm sorry, I didn't know." He seemed impressed but it didn't stop him berating her.

"Yes." She looked at him wearily. "Yes, you're right. You didn't know," she said flatly. She drank her coffee, looked out of the window, and closed her eyes. *Damn, he really screwed that up for me.* Her eyes strayed over to the other building and sure enough, there she was, the semi-corpse sprawled on the bed watching TV. Suzy shook her head in disbelief. Still it was rather comforting that you could count on mannequin lady to be there every time you looked over.

Paul had on his coat and hat. "And let me tell you one thing, sister." Walking over to her, pointing his finger in her face. "If that phone rings tonight and wakes me up, you will be out on the street. I don't care what time it is, but

I promise you, you will be out! I should have got rid of you before, but I'm a nice guy, and you are not going to take advantage one more minute, sister!"

Nice guy, my ass; you sleep on that fucking couch, then tell me you're a nice guy! Suzy thought. And why must he keep on with the "sister?" She saw the menacingly wagging finger in her face and it was all she could do not to grab it and snap it off, like a fresh French bean. She had to hold herself back.

The finger kept wagging and wagging. She looked at the finger and then his face, back to his finger and back to his face, his voice lashing out at her in fury, but she wasn't hearing the words. She was focused on the finger sticking out in her face like a carrot. She was so tempted to lunge forward and bite it off, then spit it out across the room. On and on he went, spewing out like a volcano erupting with a giant finger that would not stop wagging. Jesus, what his home life must have been like as a child! She shook her head slowly. The whole thing was nothing more than a blur in her head.

CHAPTER FIFTY-NINE

T hank God, it was all over. Suzy didn't have to count days anymore. Now she was counting down hours like Cape Canaveral counts off minutes. Three, two one, blast-off! She'd be on a plane in less than twelve hours. Blast-off, and out of here! As she thought about it, a rush of tranquility and peace came over her.

She watched Paul close the door. She looked at the suitcases, spread all over the living room.

Suddenly the door flew wide open. "And make sure, you take everything! Everything of yours, that is!" She looked at him in disbelief.

"Oh, and why would I ever want anything of yours?" This was the final insult. How dare he! "Hey, I may be a drunk, if that's what you want to call me. And frankly, I'm not a drunk, because I'm aware of everything that's going on, trust me. I may be buzzed, yes, but I am not a drunk!" Her voice was now three octaves higher, and getting louder still. "And secondly," she angrily went on, "don't you ever," bristling with fury, she stared at him menacingly, "ever accuse me of taking anything of yours. I have _never_ taken anything of yours. Why would I? I have a lot of beautiful things; I don't need anything of yours! Or anybody else's. How dare you!" Flames were coming out of her nose and ears at this point.

He grimaced with pain, covering his ears with his hands. "Don't raise your voice! Yes, you're right," he nodded repeatedly. "I have to say one thing for you, sister," he nodded again as he spoke. "I have to give you credit. You are honest! You may not be many other things, but that," he stressed the word, *"THAT,* you are!"

He paused for a second then glared at her. "You know, you're some damn tough cookie all right. You know that?" he roared.

"Yeah! Damn right I am!" she shouted, headache or not. "And don't you ever forget it, buster! Why, you think I'll let you get the best of me? What, like all those idiots you took out and they wound up in the loony ward?" She was livid. "You met your match this time!" Her eyes were blazing, flames came out of her eyes and nose. *These fucking men really think they can get the best of you, well, in your dreams, Buddy! I piss on better!*

Paul turned on his heels and rushed out the door. Flopping in the chair, she sighed, shaking her head slowly. *Yeah, maybe plastered, but not a fucking bastard, like you. I need this shit like a hole in the head,* she wearily thought.

Suzy looked at the clock. It was almost three o'clock. *Oh, and speaking of bastards, let's get the other son of a bitch on the line.* She dialed the store. "Yes, may I speak to Johnny?" she asked the young lady.

"Hold on, let me get him for you."

She heard a muffled voice. "Hello."

"Hello." She was cold and indifferent to him.

"Oh, it's you. Hold on one second, I want to pick it up downstairs."

"OK." She wondered why, but whatever.

She heard a click. "Hi? Are you there?" Johnny asked.

"I heard you called a couple of times today." Her tone was cold.

"Yes, I just wanted to ask you something," he said in that monotone, expressionless deep voice of his.

"What?" She didn't have a clue what it could be.

"So Suzy, I was just wondering. What were you doing kissing that black dwarf you were with? Aren't you lowering your standards? Where did you find him? Down an alley in a dumpster?" He was getting his digs in. With a shovel. Insulting bastard.

"You know, whatever I do," she hissed down the phone, "is none of your business. He was Tunisian, if you must know. And anyhow, what were you doing with that floozy you were with? Did you pick her up from the clearance bin at Sluts R Us?" She was fuming.

"No," he continued in his monotone, cool as a cucumber voice. "No, as a matter of fact, I've known her for a while. She's a Russian girl that dates a friend of mine, and they had a fight. She wanted to talk to me."

"I'll bet!"

"But you, how could you be with that ugly, creepy-looking guy? Ugh! I couldn't believe that was you with him!" He was in his glory, gloating.

"And how come you were at the Velvet room so late? Were you still negotiating a price?" she icily said.

"She happens to be a very nice girl, and that's all!"

She was in no mood for him, or anybody else for that matter. "I don't care what you do, so do what you want. I'm sick of you, too!" She slammed the phone down.

CHAPTER SIXTY

S uzy had to finish packing, and it was getting late. Paul was out again. She prayed that nobody called. She was exhausted and ready to get back home where she belonged. She set her alarm for 6 A. M., and the cab was due at 7:30. She looked out the window for the last time. The whole town was dark, as black as coal. Somehow, all the sparkling, twinkling lights of Manhattan had lost their glitter. All she could see were images of lifeless buildings against the backdrop of the dark sky, as if a switch had turned them all off. Suddenly, looking again, instead, she saw the sun rising up from the ocean in the distance, the swaying palm trees, and the beaches of Fort Lauderdale. She zipped up all her bags and stacked them by the door. She was ready for her exit from Manhattan and Paul Kane. More than ready. The Weasel and she were officially over—had been for some time … fade to black.

It was almost 10 o' clock. Suzy reached over and turned off the light.

"Thank God I'll be in my own bed tomorrow night—no more iron bar sticking in my back!" She lay back, exhausted, closed her eyes, and began dreaming of the waves crashing onto the sandy beaches of Fort Lauderdale, sitting under an umbrella, slathering on sun tan oil. She could even smell the ocean as she sipped on one of those blue, blue martinis, thanks to Pouty Lips. Aaahh, yes, Pouty Lips Elvis from San Francisco at the Cigar Bar on Lexington… she regretted that she would never, ever see him again. She would never forget him, even in her dotage. Those lips, drove her crazy, sweet memories. Yes, she admitted, he surely was Mr. Magic.

Then, in the fuzzy distance, she thought she heard the shrill ring of the telephone…

The End

ABOUT THE AUTHOR:

BORN IN ZAMBIA OF BRITISH PARENTS, THEN MOVED TO JOLLY OLD ENGLAND. SINCE THEN, I HAVE TRAVELLED HALFWAY AROUND THE WORLD BUT LOVE TO COME BACK HOME. ALWAYS ENJOYED READING AND WRITING, AND WON THE BEST ESSAY FOR MY SCHOOL FROM THE LIFEBOAT SERVICE. I ALWAYS WANTED TO WRITE AND MAKE THE WORLD SMILE AND LAUGH, AS A LEGACY. I HAVE ALSO WRITTEN A CHILDREN'S BOOK SERIES OF A LOVABLE CAT, WHICH WILL BE IN PRODUCTION SOON.

I AM AN AVID READER, AND ENJOY ART AND THEATER. I LOVE MOST ANIMALS, WHO GIVE ME GREAT JOY.

I CAN BE REACHED AT lfm41301@yahoo.com

ENDORSEMENT from AUSTIN MACAULEY PUBLISHERS:

I CAN CONFIDENTLY STATE THAT "WHERE'S THE WEASEL?" WAS FOUND TO BE A CAPTIVATING NOVEL THAT WILL INTEREST A WIDE VARIETY OF READERS. SUZY IS AN INTRIGUING YET RELATABLE PROTAGONIST, AND AS READERS FOLLOW HER JOURNEY THROUGH LIFE AND LOVE, THEY WILL QUICKLY FIND THEMSELVES WONDERING WHAT SUZY SEES IN PAUL..AS THE PLOT RACES FORWARD AND MORE AND MORE IS REVEALED TO THE READER, THEY ARE SURE TO BE GLUED TO THE PAGES TO SEE HOW IT WILL ALL END. YOUR NOVEL IS FILLED WITH HUMOR AND DRAMA AND IS SURE TO APPEAL TO A WIDE VARIETY OF READERS, BUT ESPECIALLY THOSE WHO RELATE MOST WITH SUZY AND HER POSITION IN LIFE, AS THEY WILL TRULY BE ABLE TO UNDERSTAND THE MANY STRUGGLES SHE FACES THROUGH THE NOVEL.

www.ingramcontent.com/pod-product-compliance
Lightning Source LLC
Chambersburg PA
CBHW052008020726
47501CB00004B/1058